THE SPECTATOR BIRD

WALLACE STEGNER

The Spectator Bird

A BISON BOOK

UNIVERSITY OF NEBRASKA PRESS
Lincoln and London

First Bison Book printing: 1979
Most recent printing indicated by the first digit below:
    2   3   4   5   6   7   8   9   10

Library of Congress Cataloging in Publication Data

Stegner, Wallace Earle, 1909–
   The spectator bird.

   "Bison book edition."
   Reprint of the ed. published by Doubleday, Garden City, N.Y.
   I. Title.
[PZ3.S818Sp   1979]   [PS3537.T316]   813'.5'2   78–26789
ISBN 0–8032–9107–8

Bison Book edition published by arrangement with Doubleday and
Company.

ONE

1

On a February morning, when a weather front is moving in off the Pacific but has not quite arrived, and the winds are changeable and gusty and clouds drive over and an occasional flurry of fine rain darkens the terrace bricks, this place conforms to none of the clichés about California with which they advertise the Sunshine Cities for the Sunset Years. No bland sky, no cool morning overcast, no placid afternoons fading into chilly evenings. This is North Sea weather. The sky boils with cloud, the sun glares out now and then like the opening eye of a doped patient, and the brief beam of intelligence it shoots forth lights on the hills and turns a distant subdivision into a view of Toledo.

Fat towhees sidle up to one another, pinheaded doves forage in the grass, the field next door is suddenly full of robins who arrive like blown leaves, picnic awhile, and depart all together as if summoned. From my study I can watch wrens and bush tits in the live oak outside. The wrens are nesting in a hole for the fifth straight year and are very busy: tilted tails going in, sharp heads with the white eyebrow stripe coming out. They are surly and aggressive, and I wonder idly why I, who seem to be as testy as the wrens, much prefer the sociable bush tits. Maybe because the bush tits are doing what I thought we would be doing out here, just messing around, paying no attention to time or duty, kicking up leaves and playing hide-and-seek up and down the oak trunks and generally enjoying themselves.

It is meditation of this kind that keeps me, at nearly seventy, so contented and wholesome.

Ruth, finding me irritable and depressed, has pushed and pestered until she has got me to promise I'll go to work on the papers again. Eight years ago I took them from the office like a departing bureaucrat trucking off the files, thinking that at the very least there were things in them that would get me a tax deduction if presented to some library. I thought I might even do one of those name-dropping *My Life among the Literary* books out of them. Ruth still thinks I might. I know better.

The writers I represented have left their monuments, consequential or otherwise. I might have done the same if I had not, at the bottom of the Depression, been forced to choose whether I would be a talent broker or a broke talent. I drifted into my profession as a fly lands on flypaper, and my monument is not in the libraries, or men's minds, or even in the paper-recycling plants, but in those files. They are the only thing that prove I ever existed. So far as I can see, it is bad enough sitting around watching yourself wear out, without putting your only immortal part prematurely into mothballs. I am not likely even to put the papers into order, though that is the excuse I make to Ruth for not starting to write. A sort of Heisenberg's Principle applies. Once they are in order, they are dead, and so am I.

So I watch the wrens and bush tits, and paste photographs into albums, and read over old letters, and throw some away and put some back, and compose speeches to Ruth to the effect that it is one thing to examine your life and quite another to write it. Writing your life implies that you think it worth writing. It implies an arrogance, or confidence, or compulsion to justify oneself, that I can't claim. Did Washington write his memoirs? Did Lincoln, Jefferson, Shakespeare, Socrates? No, but Nixon will, and Agnew is undoubtedly hunched over his right now.

As for Joe Allston, he has been a wisecracking fellow traveler in the lives of other people, and a tourist in his own. There has not been one significant event in his life that he planned. He has gone downstream like a stick, getting hung up in eddies and getting flushed out again, only half understanding what he floated past, and understanding less with every year. He knows nothing that posterity needs to be told about. What he really does in his study is pacify a wife who worries about him and who reads newspaper psychiatrists urging the retired to keep their minds active. Now I finally get around to writing something—not *My Life among the Literary*, nothing more pretentious than *My Days among the Weeks*.

Ruth herself, having got me, as she thinks, working, goes forth into the world and agitates herself over environmental deterioration, the paranoias and snobberies of our town council, the programs of the League of Women Voters, and the deficits of the Co-op. Once a week she goes down to the retirement home (convalescent hospital, death camp) and reads aloud to the shut-ins. A couple of times I have gone there to pick her up and have come out with the horrors. How she stands spending a whole morning among those dim, enfeebled, tottering dead, knowing that she and I are only a few years from being just like them, is beyond my understanding.

"They're sweet," she says. "They're lonely, and friendly, and game, and pathetic, and grateful. They have so little, some of them." I suppose they are, and do. As if to shame me, one of them even made me, in gratitude to Ruth, a psychedelic typewriter cover, green baize appliquéd with orange and magenta flowers, asserting something sassy into the teeth of time. They have asked me to come down and talk to them about books, but I have not gone. I have no more to say to them than if we were refugees from some war, streaming along a road under air attack, diving for the same ditches when we have to, and getting up to struggle on, each for himself.

What Ruth fears most in me is depression. Well, I wouldn't welcome it myself. So I will try her prescription (Write something. Write anything. Just put something down) for a week, the way a kid lost in the mountains might holler at a cliff just to hear a voice. I do not expect revelation to ensue, or a search party to emerge cheering from the bushes.

At eleven this morning, as usual, I walked down the hill for the mail. Up on top in the sun it was so warm that I went in shirt sleeves, and at once regretted it, for on the drive cut into the north-facing hill it was as clammy and fishy-smelling as a cold lake shore. The gully below the road muttered with the steep little stream still running from last week's rain. The steepness aggravated the pains in my big toe joints and knees. I found it hard to believe that no more than a year ago I used to plunge down that drive fast, letting gravity take me.

Halfway down, I stopped to watch a couple of does bedded in fresh grass across the gully. We are much too tamed in these hills for mountain lions, and too subdivided for hunters. Result: an ungulate problem worse than Yellowstone's. They come in, twenty at a time, to sleep in our shrubbery and eat our pyracantha berries, roses, tomatoes, crabapples, whatever is in season. I have old socks full of blood meal hanging from trees and shrubs I value, because deer are supposed to be offended by the smell. I have even contemplated getting a shipment of lion dung from that place in Los Angeles that sells it, and have only been deterred, or deturded, by the reflection that lion dung would probably offend me as much as it would offend an ungulate.

These two lay tame as cows under a big oak, their jaws rolling and stopping and rolling again as they watched me, their club ears forward, their tails twitching. Morning, neighbors. And stay the hell out of my garden if you don't want your hides full of bird shot.

At the bottom of the hill I came out of the tunnel of trees where the culvert leads the runoff under the road and between two big eucalyptus trees. At one stride I passed from chill to warmth. The sun flowed over me, the grass brightened, the goose pimples smoothed out on my arms, my low spirits briefly rose. California February, as new and green and sodden as a fern basket dipped in a pond. *Hoc erat in votis*, Horace said. This used to be among my prayers: a bit of land not too large, which would contain a garden and near the house an ever-flowing spring, and beyond that a wood lot.

Exactly. What we came for, what we have. I should be as placid in my mind as those two deer ruminating my shrubbery up on the hill. For a while I was, at times I still am. At the moment, in the generative sun, I felt practically no pain. O brave new world, that hath such Februaries in it.

Or Febuaries, as Cronkite and half his tribe would say.

I walked on past the Hammond cottage, which I will never get over thinking of as the Catlin place, though Marian died and John and Debby moved away four years ago. People we loved; there are too few of them. The very sight of their house darkened the day again for me.

Nobody home, as usual. Mrs. Hammond sells real estate, the girls are in school, and old Hammond is off in Baluchistan or somewhere training gendarmerie for the Iraqi government, exporting American know-how to help put down the Kurds—the *valiant* Kurds, as I remember them from "Sohrab and Rustum," the Kurds who are demandeen self-government, as I hear from Cronkite.

Damnation. Instantly irritable, I compose a letter to the press instructing news commentators that those who use the language publicly and professionally should be advised that there are two r's in February, that *ing* is not pronounced *een*, and that verbs enjoy other possibilities than the present participle. *The White House announceen today that it has called a meeteen of business leaders for early Febuary.* Just saying it to myself, like the old pantaloon I am getting to be, brought my blood pressure up to about 250/200, and when I found that the mailbox was empty, that the postman was late again, I announced a loud God damn to the startled creekside and sat down to wait on a pile of timbers that was once a bridge until I replaced it with a culvert. My internal grumblings went on, the way a high-compression engine running on low-octane gas will go on galloping and coughing and smoking after the ignition is shut off.

It's a bad sign, I know it. Ruth tells me at least once a day that old people, or people getting old, tend to disengage, back away, turn inward, listen only to themselves, and get self-righteous and censorious. And they *mustn't.* (*I* mustn't.) She hates to drive anywhere with me because I am inclined to cuss out drivers who don't please me. What *good* does it do? she cries. *They* can't hear you. All you do is upset *me.* It lets off steam, failing which I might explode, I tell her. What are you doing *now* but exploding? she asks.

Right, absolutely right. Faultfinding doesn't let off pressure, it only builds it up. It is only one of many processes, none of which I like and most of which I can't seem to help: the decreasing ability to stand heat or cold, something to do with the expansion and contraction of the capillaries. The slowing down of the mitotic rate in body cells, with resultant deterioration and lessening of function. The accumulation of plaque in the artery walls and of calcium spurs in the joints and of uric acid, sugar, and other undesirable chemicals in the blood and urine. Inescapable, irreversible, hateful.

Like last week, when the dentist told me that the molar he has been trying to save by root canal work will have to go. I can read the future in that direction without cards or tea leaves. First a bridge, if he can find anything to hitch it to. Then a partial plate. Finally a complete cleaning out of old snags in preparation for false teeth, on television called dentures. There will be a morning when I look in the mirror and see an old sunken-cheeked stranger with scared eyes and a mouth like a sea urchin's.

I can stand it, and I really ought to try not to let it and other things make me crabby. But I damn well don't look forward to it, and I don't like any of the signs that the cookie has already started to crumble. The other day at the museum the young thing at the gate took one look at me and said brightly, "Senior citizen, sir?" and passed me out half-price tickets. That shook even Ruth. The way I felt, half price was an overcharge.

I had been sitting on the old timbers for about ten minutes when Ben Alexander drove in from the county road in his convertible. His top was down, his hair was tangled, and he had Edith Patterson in the seat beside him, looking like a raccoon in her wraparound Hollywood shades. It was all so young and gay and California that I had to laugh. Ben is the very chief of the tribe that makes old age out to be a time of liberation. He is writing a book about it.

He stopped beside me and ran down the window and sat looking at me with his hands on the wheel. Until he finally retired a couple of years ago he used to be my doctor, and he can still make me feel as if I am sitting there on the table, ridiculous in my shorts, waiting for the rubber hammer under the kneecaps and the steel handle against the soles of the feet, and the finger up under the scrotum (cough), and the rubber glove up the ass trespassing on my most secret prostate. (How's the urine? Good stream? Have to get up in the night?) He is a man I admire and trust, one of the godlike ones who direct lives, their own and others'. Maybe that is what keeps me from ever quite relaxing around him, for I am one of those to whom life happens. Maybe I disbelieve his pollyanna doctrines about old age. Or maybe it is only the doctor-patient relationship that makes me slightly uneasy. It is hard to be relaxed around a man who at any moment might examine your prostate.

His gray medical eyes were noting the condition of my eyeballs, my paunch, the stiffness with which I stood up, for all I know the spots on my lungs and liver. "Resting, roosting, or nesting?" he said. Edith, with her curved, reflecting blackout windows turned toward me, made a little smile.

"Brooding," I said, and rose and dusted off my pants. "Molting. Hello, Edith. Don't you know a girl can be compromised, running around in a convertible with this old rooster?"

Which was plausible enough to be not so plainly spoken. Ben being Ben, you always wonder when you see a woman with him. His wife, who was wonderful and whom he adored, died several years ago. Ben is seventy-nine, he has sons over fifty and grandsons who have voted in the last two presidential elections, he wears a hearing aid when he wants to hear from the right side, a pacemaker is implanted under the skin of his chest, and his left hip joint is aluminum, newly installed. Nevertheless, with vitality like his, you never know.

As for Edith, she is always a little cool and aloof and amused. Not unattractive—she is as attractive a sixty-year-old as you ever saw. Her air of faintly mocking imperturbability has a remembrance of Dietrich sultriness about it, and though I never saw anything even slightly askew between her and Tom Patterson, an architect whose name is as well known in Karachi and Tel Aviv as in his home town, and who has had two operations for cancer of the tongue, that didn't prove anything either. One of the few wise sayings I am sometimes tempted to pass on to breathless posterity is that anything is possible at any time.

"They fight for the privilege," Ben said. "What *are* you doing, waiting for the mailman?"

"What else do you do for the damned mailman, except give him five dollars at Christmas?"

"Ruth home?"

"Yes."

"Edith wants to see her a minute. Edith, why don't you take the car and go on up? I'll sit down here and console Joe."

Edith, who had been looking off down the creek, turned her black windows again. The molded mouth and nose and cheeks below them were expressionless. She nodded, and as Ben got out, helping himself with a cane, she slid over, put the car in gear, quirked her mouth in the slightest of smiles, and drove on. Ben stood with his cane planted and both hands stacked on it and looked down on me from his stooped six feet five.

"I wanted to ask but didn't quite dare," I said. "How's Tom?"

"He's a dead man. I've just been down at the clinic with Edith while she heard it from Arthur."

"Oh, Christ. I *thought* she was being pretty silent."

"She's all right. You know what she wants to see Ruth about?"

"What?"

"To tell her she can't play the piano for the shut-ins for a while. Wants to arrange for someone else."

I thought about how much my mind would be on those shut-ins if I'd just got Edith's news. "That's touching," I said. "Does Tom know?"

"He's known for a week. I talked with him." The gray corkscrews of hair stood up on his head. The breath he breathed down on me was loud and sour. "We both thought it was better she should hear it from his doctor. Tom couldn't quite tell her. That's a very close marriage."

"I guess," I said. "They're always so composed about everything you get to thinking of them as unflappable."

A little gust of wind came up the valley, the roadside darkened under a swift cloud shadow. I rubbed my goose-pimpled arms. "Well, damn everything," I said. "Damn the clouds. Damn the dawdling mailman. Damn the collective carcinogens. How do doctors stand being always cheek by jowl with the grim reaper?"

"Death?" Ben said, surprised. "Death isn't that much of a problem. It's as natural as living, and just as easy, once you've accepted it. I've been dead twice myself. Both times when they hooked up my pacemaker I died on them, and they revived me."

"Well, at least your book on old age has a logical ending."

I must have sounded bitter, because he fixed his old medical eyes on me again. "I haven't seen you around much lately. What've you been doing?"

"Tending my garden."

"You ought to wear a sweater in this kind of weather. Been having any more pain?"

"Who told you I'd been having any pain?"

"Your doctor," Ben said. "To whom I referred you. I looked at your last tests. Jim thought he might have depressed you with that diagnosis of rheumatoid arthritis. Did he?"

"Depressed me? No. I didn't exactly cheer, but I wouldn't say I'm depressed."

"What's he giving you?"

"Allopurinol for the uric acid, indocin for the pain, synthroid for general metabolic reasons, oronase for the blood sugar, something else for the cholesterol, I forget its name. I just take the handful of pills Ruth hands me."

"I forget, have you got a heart history?"

"Myocarditis once, years ago. Or pericarditis, endocarditis, nobody ever quite labeled it. I got these chest pains, and the electrocardiograph went crazy, and I dropped about twenty pounds. They kept me in bed and it went away after a while."

It was just like his office. He made me feel defensive, standing there planted on his cane and scowling at me. He grunted and wheezed, and again I smelled his sour breath. It annoyed me to have this giant ruin acting as if he was immune and immortal, and probing around in my insides, when he was ten years closer to the edge than I was. Sure enough, he undertook to reassure me.

"That's one thing that suggests rheumatoid to Jim, that myocarditis," he said. "It's associated with rheumatoid the way rheumatic fever's related to coronary disease. But I don't necessarily believe he's right. Lemme see your hands." He examined the knuckles of the hand I held out, then ordered up and examined the other. He did not say what the inspection told him. "Even if he should be right," he said, "you're not to worry yourself into a wheel chair."

"I'm not worrying."

Wheezy and loud, his voice rode over mine. We stood in the green angle of the roadways, with the creek rustling in its deep channel, as if we were engaged in a quarrel that we didn't quite want to make plain. "Diseases don't live up to their full potential any oftener than people do," he said. "You've got at most one chance in five it will really cripple you. You get plenty of exercise?"

"We walk, I work in the yard."

"Good. You're in good shape. You'll make it into the eighties."

"Why, thanks, Doctor," I said. "I appreciate the offer."

That old reptilian eye again, a snort through the long nose. "You know what you've got? You've got a bad case of the sixties. The sixties are the age of anxiety. You feel yourself on the brink of old age, and you fret. Once you pass your seventieth birthday that all clears away. You're like a man with an old car and no place in particular to go. You drive it where you want to, and every day it keeps on running is a gift. If you avoid the killer diseases and keep the degenerative ones under control with a sensible diet and regular exercise and whatever chemotherapy you need to stay in balance, you can live nearly forever. Strictly speaking, there doesn't seem to be any such thing as old age. You can keep chicken tissues alive indefinitely in a nutrient broth."

"You know, it's a funny thing," I said, "I never had the slightest desire to live in a nutrient broth."

I exasperated him. "You're bored with your garden. If I'd been there when God set Adam and Eve in that perfect place I'd have given them about four months. They'd have lasted longer in Las Vegas. Who do you see? Who are your friends, besides the ones I know?"

"Have you been talking to Ruth?"

"No. Should I?"

"No. But she has this notion you do, that I need more people around. I never *have* needed many people around. I always had more than I wanted. A few friends are enough. There are lots of perfectly pleasant people whom I like, but if I don't see them I don't miss them. What kept me in New York was work, not people. When the work ended, most of the people ended, all but the handful that meant something. Maybe that's alarming, but that's the way I am."

"All right," Ben said. "Some are. You don't have to start going to Arthur Murray. But I'm not kidding, old age is too God damned often self-inflicted. You don't want to turn into a hermit saving string and bottle tops and running the neighbor kids out of your yard. Come out more. Come to lunch with me."

"Sure, any time."

"I'll call you. And for God's sake don't go thinking yourself into any God damned wheel chair!" He reversed his cane and thumped me for emphasis on the breastbone and almost knocked me down.

"What the hell *is* that, a shillelagh?"

"Haven't I shown you that?" He held it up. To the shaft, which looked like cherry wood, had been fastened this big bone, obviously the ball of the ball and socket joint of some large animal. The knob was the size of a handball, with a frill of bone around its base and a two-inch shank of bone projecting from that and bound to the wood with a wide silver band. As the finial of the polished, elegant stick of wood the handle was grotesque, the sort of thing any self-respecting dog would bury and never go back to.

"That's my hip joint," Ben said. "When I broke my hip, and they had me in the operating room, the last thing I said to the surgeon was, 'Doctor, save me that joint, I want it.' I'd walked on it for seventy-nine years and I damn well wanted to go *on* walking on it."

By then I was laughing and holding my nose and pushing away the cane that he held up in my face. The thing looked as if it might smell. "Couldn't you at least have left it out in the sun to bleach?" I said. "That's an awful brown untoothsome-looking bone."

"That's a *sound* bone. When I saw it I was proud, by God. Look at it. No spurs, no decalcification, no nothing. Except for that fall, it would have lasted me a lifetime."

The white convertible eased into sight around the corner of the hill by Hammonds'. "Here comes Edith," I said. "Do I act as if I know?"

He considered only a second. "I wouldn't. If it was me, I wouldn't hide it. But she's like you, she'd rather go off by herself and grit her teeth."

She pulled up, impassive behind the glasses, her flat cheeks looking deceptively young, her mouth fixed in the usual expression of remote and forgiving amusement. Ben opened the door, she slid over, he got in and threw the cane into the back seat. "Think about it," he said. "I'll call you for lunch one of these days." They lifted their hands and drove off, and I sat down again on the bridge timbers.

I don't respond gladly when other people show a willingness to direct my life, routines, or feelings. Ben has a way of making me feel about fifteen years old, an age that appeals to me even less than sixty-nine. He never doubted himself in his life. He is one of those people, insufferable when you think about them, who have always been able to do exactly what they set out to do. The son of a China missionary, he came to California without a dollar, determined to become a doctor. He became one, a very good one, some people think a great one. Even yet, when he has all but quit practicing, people come from a long way off to be treated by him. He has doctored everybody from Admiral Nimitz to Angela Davis, he has more celebrities in his files than I have, and on more intimate terms. I have only read their manuscripts and taken them to lunch and prepared their contracts and advanced them money and bailed them out of difficulties. He has examined their prostates, or the equivalent.

Wanting money, he made it, made two or three million dollars. And give him credit, he practices what he preaches. When he built his big house in six hundred acres of foothills he didn't retire, he pulled the world out to him. It is about as secluded as Vandenberg Air Force Base. Two or three nights a week his Chinese couple serve dinner to twenty or so people, the kind of people who have been everywhere and done everything. From his little vineyard Ben makes every year a thousand bottles of extraordinary Cabernet Sauvignon. He is a director in a half dozen Peninsula electronics firms, he has served on a half dozen presidential commissions, he owns vineyards in Sonoma and ranches in Mendocino County, and he collects things—friends, books, money, limericks, dirty stories—the way an air filter collects lint.

Also, I was thinking as I sat on my splintery 8×8 beam, he is one of the few men I know thoughtful enough to go down with Edith Patterson while she received her husband's death sentence, or take a few minutes to read the lab tests of Joe Allston, a crybaby former patient, and make a special trip out to calm his mind.

Grit my teeth, did I? The hell I did. I complained by withdrawal and irritability and silence. Ten minutes with Ben Alexander and I was resolving to quit being a sissy about growing old.

Eventually the mailman's red, white, and blue truck came in, and the mailman, as cheerful as if he had been on time, handed me out a little bundle. Most of the letters, as usual, were addressed to Boxholder or Resident. Those that were not seemed to be appeals. That is another symptom of retirementitis, the way the mail decreases in amount and significance. I put the bundle in my right-hand pocket and walked back up the lane, reading as I walked, and transferring the read items to the pocket on the other side.

2

Enter the unexpected—and I dislike the unexpected, as the man said, unless I have had a chance to prepare for it. The fourth item I took out of my pocket was a postcard, closely written, and forwarded from our New York address of nine years ago. At the bottom of the hill, at the last edge of sun, in the smell of crushed eucalyptus buttons, I stopped and read it.

Dear Friends—
How are you? It is so long a time! Just outside this village, which you know, I am living a quiet life. My husband did suffer a stroke and I moved him here to a house which Eigil gives us. He is like a child, he takes much care. The castle is as you saw it, no better—I see only Manon. But we have nothing and cannot choose. I had to sell even my little Ellebacken cottage, which I loved. But here where I grew up it is also beautiful. I walk and paint. Last month I had an exhibition in Copenhagen and sold nearly all. Often I wonder about you, if you have found your safe place. I wish much happiness to you both.

Fondly,
Astrid W/K

The other side of the card was a color photograph, taken from a high place, of a neat red-roofed village set between fields and woods at the edge of a tame sea. A boat harbor extended masonry arms into the water beyond warehouses and sheds. A little green island was afloat offshore.

Bregninge. I am related to it, or once thought I was. I know that estate, which includes two other villages, the harbor, the warehouses, a thousand acres or so of planted pinewoods, orchards, fields, and an English park modeled on that of Warwick Castle, where peacocks parade around the lawns under oaks that anywhere else in Denmark would have been cut down a century ago. I know the castle, too, a real *slot*, none of your mere thirty-bedroom manor houses, and I know some of its history, which is enough to put your pyloric caecum into spasm.

So that was where she ended. I was not really surprised. That was settled on Midsummer Night twenty years ago. She would now be sixty, Edith Patterson's age. A quiet life, looking after a helpless husband, in her one available safe place. She might live to be my age—ten more years of ebb—or Ben Alexander's, twenty. She might live, like her grandmother, to be nearly a hundred.

When I got to the house, Ruth was sunning in the protected front patio. "Isn't it a funny day?" she said. "It's so chilly when the sun goes under, and so warm when it's out."

"Bolts and jolts. What did Edith want?"

"She can't play for the shut-ins for a while. She and Tom are going somewhere."

No confidences, then. So be it.

"When do you want lunch?"

"Not right away, I guess. Can we wait till one? I'd like to go back down and work a little more."

"Fine," she said, pleased, and took the mail I handed her—without the postcard—and turned herself to pondering the needs of Boys' Town, the NAACP, and the Association for the American Indian.

I went down to the study and rummaged around in boxes until I found the diary I had kept, away back when I was sick and stuck in the sand and trying to winch myself out. It was written in three stenographic notebooks bound together with rubber bands that snapped when I stretched them. Thumbing the pages, I saw names I had entirely forgotten, places I didn't ever recall visiting, references to feelings I would have sworn I never felt. It was like a letter from a dead Joe Allston to the one who survives, and it dealt—I knew it did before I read it, that's why I went looking for it—with existential problems: Who am I? How to be? What is the meaning of everything?

I started to read from the beginning, and it began to come back. Some people, I am told, have memories like computers, nothing to do but punch the button and wait for the print-out. Mine is more like a Japanese library of the old style, without a card file or an indexing system or any systematic shelf plan. Nobody knows where anything is except the old geezer in felt slippers who has been shuffling up and down those stacks for sixty-nine years. When you hand him a problem he doesn't come back with a cartful and dump it before you, a jackpot of instant retrieval. He finds one thing, which reminds him of another, which leads him off to the annex, which directs him to the east wing, which sends him back two tiers from where he started. Bit by bit he finds you what you want, but like his boss who seems to be under pressure to examine his life, he takes his time.

Also, what he brings is not necessarily pleasant. It is a little like taking the top off the jar and letting the tarantula out, and not too unlike opening a grave. Alas, poor Allston. I knew him, Horatio. A fellow of infinite jest, but now strangely chapfallen.

Lunch interrupted me before I got past the first notebook. In the afternoon there were errands in town, some plants to be set out, some firewood to cut—routines, I realize, with which I fence my life in away from the mankillers. Then a shower, then a drink, then Cronkite like a ghostly cricket creakeen where a house was burned, then dinner, then the dishes, and finally the bedroom, which is where we really live. There, Ruth in bed and I in the big chair, two old parties in a warm well-lighted room, with the television standing by in case there should be something on worth watching, and the rest of the house dark and turned down in deference to that new American phenomenon, the shortage, we settled down for the evening, without interruption except when one or the other of us threw off old Catarrh, the Siamese, who at the age of ninety or so by human standards needs warmth too, and loves to creep up under your chin to sleep, and is never happier than when he is lying on your book.

Ruth is quiet and contented with her reading, but I am not. Until recently—until, in fact, the machinery began to show signs of wear—the Joe Allston sitting there reading the diary of his predecessor has been pretending to be Marcus Aurelius, or the Cicero of "De Senectute": stoic philosopher surprised by nothing, accepting everything, valuing only friendship, abstract integrity, and the cup that warms. *Nil admirari* and *memento mori* and all that. Take gratefully any pleasures the world provides, but don't curse God when they fail. Nobody in the universe ever promised you anything. Most things break, including hearts. The lessons of a life amount not to wisdom but to scar tissue and callus.

But it doesn't work indefinitely. Crucifixion can be discussed philosophically until they start driving the nails. Look at the way I was grumbling and whimpering down there with Ben this morning. The symptoms of failing vigor, the oncoming of age, have put me right back to where I was in 1954—which, come to think of it, was about where I was in 1924. Young, middle-aged, or getting old, Joe Allston has always been full of himself, uncertain, dismayed, dissatisfied with his life, his country, his civilization, his profession, and himself. He has always hunted himself in places where he has never been, he has always been trying to thread some needle with a string that was raveled at both ends. He has always been hungry for some continuity and assurance and sense of belonging, but has never had ancestors or descendants or place in the world. Little orphan Joe, what a sad case.

His unappeased presence in the diary and in the big chair makes the Joe Allston of recent years, the one the neighbors here think they know, look less like Marcus Aurelius than like a prosy Polonius. The stoicism he has pretended to is about as impressive as a telephone recording. His questions have never been answered and his hunger never satisfied. I only thought there had been some sort of accommodation because the spiritual epidermis, like the physical hide, thickens where it is rubbed.

There is even a question if it thickens enough. From here, it is apparent that that Danish excursion was the most romantic quest since Parsifal's, sure to end in a bloody nose. If you forget caution and start through the dark woods toward the dark tower, you are exposed, vulnerable, without guidance, and guilty. It may have been a water rat I speared, but ugh, it sounded like a baby's shriek. As for the maiden in distress, and Astrid *was* one, the dragon ate her. Here it is on the postcard.

If there is a lesson in that pilgrimage into the Gothic, it is a lesson misshapen, leaden, lightless, ugly as a toad in a drain, a real Grendel of a lesson left over from the time of trolls and demons. It leaves me no option but to scratch dead leaves over it as I scratched them over it twenty years ago. That seems the only method that will get us safely from infancy to senility. Was it the Boyg who advised Peer Gynt, "Roundabout, Peer, roundabout?" Or was it the Button Molder? Never mind.

One of the books I read in Denmark was *The Long Journey*, by Johannes V. Jensen, a patriotic chronicle about how the Scandinavians invented everything, first sex, then fire, then tools, then shelter, then agriculture, then bronze and gold, then iron, until the human race, put into gear by all that Nordic ingenuity, could be trusted to go forward on its own. Jensen got a Nobel Prize for his fable of civilization, and he persuaded some people, including some Scandinavian archaeologists. Not me. I like the Scandinavians as well as anybody else, and once went hunting my identity among them, but they didn't invent more than their share, and they are no monsters of goodness. Even now, when they have given up Viking raids and become the world's umpires and ombudsmen, they consort with evil like other folks, and confuse it with good like other folks. I didn't find what I went looking for in Denmark, but I found there was something rotten in that state, as elsewhere, and that the Danes like the rest of the world are attracted to evil, are involved in it, even feel dutiful toward it. If the ghost of Henry James came demanding copy, I could tell him a tale of New World innocence and Old World experience at least as instructive as *Daisy Miller*.

Having no traditions myself, I used to have a romantic view of tradition. I thought that time really does sift men's acts, that the good they do lives after them and gradually improves their descendants, and that the ill they do eventually writhes in pain and dies among its worshipers. That was real innocence. *Everything* we do lives after us. The future is not only now, as television assures me, it was also then, and Baal and Loki are as immortal as Jahveh and Baldr.

My mother was a Danish girl, an orphan and a runaway. She emigrated to America, all alone, at sixteen, worked as a hired girl, married a drunken brakeman who begot me and shortly got himself killed by a freight in the Sioux City yards, married again a couple of years later and was soon abandoned. Except for those brief spells of married bliss, she never had a house of her own. She lived, and I with her, in hot (and cold) third-story rooms and back-of-the-kitchen sheds in other people's houses, and she died of a fall down some dark cellar stairs when I was a freshman in college. Everything in the New World that she tied her hopes to, including me, gave way. I spent my childhood and youth being ashamed of her accent, her clumsiness, her squarehead name, her menial jobs. It used to shrivel me to put down, in the space marked MOTHER'S MAIDEN NAME. Ingeborg Heegaard. I never discovered until she was dead that she was a saint, and that realization, with all the self-loathing that came with it, put me into a tailspin that I didn't come out of for two years. Ulcers, nervous breakdowns, all the not so subtle psychosomatic punishments I visited on myself, went on till I learned how to scratch dead leaves over what I didn't want to see.

That was the way it was until my only son, Curtis, who had been nothing but anguish from the time he was breech-born, fell from or let go of his surfboard on the beach at La Jolla. He died an over-age beach bum, evading to the last any obligation to become what his mother and I tried to make or help him be, and like my mother's, his death lay down accusingly at my door. He was my only descendant, as she was my only ancestor, and I failed both. Chop, chop, there went both past and future. At fifty I had my second crisis—it is remarkable how apt bacteria and other agents of the moral sense can be, how readily they infect and afflict us when we need affliction. This time it was the myocarditis. But all the time while I was wondering if my clock would stop, I felt inside me somewhere, adjacent to or below the ailing heart, a hungry, thirsty, empty, sore, haunted sensation of being unfinished, random, and unattached, as if, even if the heart were working perfectly, there was nothing there for it to run.

Marcus Aurelius and all, I have never stopped feeling that way.

Sitting in the bedroom under three hundred watts of contemporary illumination, I found myself reading about the afternoon when Astrid's brother, Count Eigil Rødding, showed me his museum. Everything in it had been found on his estate. Dig anywhere on that island, and below the picnic plastics of the present you ran into the age of iron, and below that the age of bronze, and below that the age of polished stone, and below that the age of chipped stone, and still below that the age of antler and bone. All of it, straight down from the fourth millennium B.C., was undiluted Danish.

That impressed me, deracinated as I was. I suppose that an Indian on an Ohio mound might have the sense that down under him his own ancestors went in layers, generation below generation, all of them as native as the corn. But all other sorts of Americans, even those whose families have been on this continent for many generations, seem to me deprived, hanging around the national parks that enclose other people's archaeology, or else, like me, tourists in a private graveyard hunting hopefully for their own names.

All those sword blades rusted to brown pizzles, all those drinking skulls and bowls, all those horn spoons and horned helmets, all those bronze axes and stone spearheads and antler flensing tools, were nothing to me but curios. I wanted to *own* a past the way Rødding owned his. Though I was watchful with Astrid's brother, I envied him at least as much as I was suspicious of him. He had a lot of things I didn't especially covet and one I coveted very much: he belonged to something.

His prize exhibit was under a big bell jar on a table in the middle of the room. When it was first dug up, and the air hit it, it had begun to crumble, and Rødding had rushed it to Copenhagen to get the museum there to put it under glass. Deteriorated or not, it was recognizably human. It lay curled on its side with its knees drawn up, a small, shrunken man with a bent nose and high cheekbones. An odd, cocky, Robin Hood sort of leather hat was on its head. Rawhide cords bound its hands and feet, a rawhide strangling-cord was twisted into the neck under the ear. Its eyes were closed. On its mouth was what must have been the grimace it made when the cord was tightened, but it looked like a whimsical, knowing smile.

While we were looking at it and talking about it, Rødding for a joke claimed it as his ancestor. I looked at him—he figures as the Prince Orgulus, or Dragon Error, or maybe the windmill, of this romance—and damned if he didn't look like it, with the same little smirking smile. Shrink him and dry him out, and he could have been the relative that he claimed to be. Maybe, in fact, he was. That was what a real past could do for you.

Just about then I had an idea. I got up, avoiding Ruth's questioning look, and went out into the wind and down to the study. In the third album I looked through, I found it—a snapshot Ruth had taken of Karen Blixen sitting under a tree in her garden at Rungstedlund. Under her old garden hat her face was bird-sharp, leather-skinned. She was tiny, shrunken, her eyes as alive as snakes: as surely a witch as any old woman in one of her tales. In her hand she was holding a rune stone she had dug up only a few minutes before we arrived, and on her face was a look of glee, a smugness of secret knowledge, as if the murky world she visited every night on her broomstick had just sent her, in the cryptic markings on the stone, a daylight message that only she and her wizard and warlock friends could read. Sure enough, she looked like Rødding, and even more like that mummy of his. The same smile.

Which should not surprise me. Karen Blixen was a baroness, and related to Astrid and Astrid's brother. From all I ever saw of the Danish nobility, they are all cousins; they have been marrying one another for so long they look as much alike as so many Airedales. Still, it was a little spooky to have that lovely, subtle Danish writer looking back at me out of the snapshot with the same knowing, Old World smile that I had seen twenty years before on the face of a Bronze Age mummy from a peat bog.

I closed the study and went back. There was a big wind up. The live oak sawed and groaned, and the light fastened to its trunk glared up into threshing shadows. Petals from the wild plums in the woods below blew across the lighted dome of the tree. Going up the path was like being pounded from behind by pillows, and the wind tried to take the door away from me as I opened it. I came inside in a flurry of wind, fine rain, and plum blossoms. Ruth lowered her book to her lap and looked at me and laughed. Then she just sat there watching me like Little Red Riding Hood's grandmother—white hair, spectacles, Groucho Marx eyebrows, amused house-detective eyes.

"Where'd you go?"

"Down to the study."

"What for?"

"Look something up."

"Sounds as if the storm's finally coming in."

"Big wind. Not much rain yet."

A moment's silence, the widening smile. "You going to read some more now?"

"I thought I might. Why?"

"Then you'd better wipe the flowers off your glasses."

I removed my glasses and wiped the plum blossoms off and settled back down in the chair. She kept watching me.

"What is this you're reading so interestedly?"

I was already wishing I'd left the notebooks in the study, where I could have read them in the morning in privacy. I didn't suppose there was anything in them that couldn't be read to Ruth, because I am not a confider, even in myself. Nevertheless, ever since that postcard had showed up in the mail, I had had a half-irritable sense of wanting to be alone with what it revived.

"Papers," I said.

"What papers?"

"What papers? What papers are there? The only papers, the files, the evidence. Allston was here."

"It doesn't look like letters."

"You know why?" I said. "Because it isn't. It's a notebook—*three* notebooks."

"Notebooks about what?"

"It's a journal. Diary."

"Whose? Where'd you get it?"

"Mine. I got it out of a cardboard carton."

"I mean who wrote it?"

I settled deeper and found my place and became absorbed. "I did."

But she wasn't letting me get away with that. When her curiosity is up she can read your genetic code with the naked eye. "Come on," she said. "You don't keep a journal."

"I did this time."

"When?"

"Denmark."

"*Denmark?*"

I was getting a little exasperated at the quizzing. "*Ja*," I said. "*Det er ret.* What's wrong with keeping a journal in Denmark?"

She was still, and I went back to reading. But of course I didn't. I could feel her over there ruminative, abstracted, and unsatisfied, and when I cast a look across, there she was, propped against the pillows, her book lowered onto her stomach, one arm restraining old Catarrh, her eyes on me and her face wearing the impenetrable expression that means she is thinking, estimating, remembering, uncovering discrepancies, drawing conclusions. She made a little embarrassed sort of smile and blinked her eyes. "Read it to me?" she said.

She caught me by surprise. Normally she isn't much interested in all these papers she keeps me working at. So long as I disappear after breakfast, she can feel that she has done her duty and propped me up so that I can hold my own against deterioration. But of course she would be interested in any diary I kept in Denmark, and of course, for related reasons, I was not eager to read it to her, at least not until I had gone through it myself.

"It isn't anything," I said. "You know—blah-blah. Up this

morning betimes, and to the barber. Shave, thirty-five cents, newspaper, ten cents, miscellaneous, twenty-five cents."

She said in her soft Bryn Mawr whisper, "I was watching you while you read it."

"What?" I had heard her all right, but I have been trying for forty years to make her speak loud enough to *be* heard.

"I was watching you while you read it," she said in exactly the same voice.

I abandoned that line. "Don't be misled by my gales of laughter."

"It *matters* to you," she said; and then, in a tone almost accusatory, "You never told me you were keeping a journal then."

Which was true. Secret sin, furtive navel-picking. And unfair, I had to admit, even in the beginning. After all, Curtis was her son as well as mine, but it was my therapy that Danish trip was supposed to serve. The way I must have thought of it, she came along to look after me. And then that irruption of the irrational, that reversion into adolescence. We had never talked about it, we had only dropped it. Regret and guilt are selfish and secret emotions.

"It was a mistake," I said. "It isn't my kind of caper. It embarrasses me."

The look she was bending on me from the bed was troubled and troubling, steady, undisguised by any of the games we play. She wasn't sparring, or joking, or half joking. "Joe," she said, "why *not* aloud? Why not together?"

Very uncomfortably I said, "It really isn't anything. It's mostly just what we did abroad. Our trip to the Paris of the North. Danish castles from Kronborg to Knuthenborg. There's nothing else in it except some self-pity and some foolishness that I regret. And anyway, it's long gone now."

"Astrid and all that business?"

"Yes, some of that, I guess. I haven't read it clear through."

"And us."

"Us? Yes, naturally."

"Please? I think it might be good for us."

"Oh, hell," I said. "Here, the reason I dug it out, we got this today."

I scaled the postcard over onto the bed and she read it, taking a long time. She turned it over and studied the picture of Bregninge and then turned it back and read it again. "Oh dear," she said after about five minutes. "It makes you want to cry."

I said nothing.

"She was such a *nice* woman," Ruth said. "I liked her. I liked her as well as anybody I ever knew."

"I know. Or at least I thought so."

"I haven't thought about her for a long time."

"No."

"Why didn't you give me the card before?"

"I don't know. I just wanted to, sort of, look it up."

You can live with someone a long time and not have more than a few moments as exposed and intimate as that one. Ruth's face was full of questions, but I couldn't see any hardening or accusation there. Pleading, rather. She said softly and hesitantly, "Would it be . . . painful to read it?"

What could I say? Only that okay, sure, I'd walk out in the open without any clothes on, if that was what she wanted. And no, of course it wouldn't be painful. Why should it be? I flipped open the first notebook. "It probably won't make either of us particularly happy," I said. "It wasn't a very happy time. You want all that business about the *Stockholm*, too? That's where it starts."

"You took notes on that ghastly voyage?"

"Ghastly detail by ghastly detail. I lost my faith in God's justice when that ship ran into the *Andrea Doria* and it was the *Andrea Doria* that sank."

"What year was that?"

"When the *Stockholm* rammed the *Andrea Doria*?"

"No. When we went to Denmark?"

"Nineteen fifty-four." The odd tension and nakedness of the moment had passed. We were both being casual. "You want to *hear* this?"

"I'll be quiet. I was just getting oriented."

She laid aside her book, folded her hands around Catarrh and pulled him up against her, snuggled her back into the pillows, and looked expectant, like a child who has got her way and extracted one more bedtime story. She overdid it, on purpose, I suppose, and had to laugh. After a second, so did I. The woman is shrewd.

The soft, heavy wind slammed against the house. I heard hard rain at the windows. Nothing could have been snugger, or more secure, or more transitory.

"Getting oriented?" I said. "Aren't we all."

3

S.S. *Stockholm*, one day out, March 26:

It just struck me that if we hadn't taken off on this trip we would tonight be attending Robert Frost's eightieth birthday party, complete with personalities and tensions. Glad to be leaving all that behind for a while. Full of resolutions: look after myself, for a change. Get my health back. Forge in the smithy of my soul the uncreated conscience, etc. Settle some things. Read, absorb, learn, think. Sounds silly but probably isn't. Above all, relax. Learn to sleep again. Quit being such a puritan, file the point off the prick of conscience, quit crying mea culpa, quit beating the breast, quit pitying myself. *Accept.* The past is past, I can't do a thing about it. The future is none of my business. As Mr. Jefferson said, the world belongs to the living.

Very rough. Thanks to Dramamine, we remain vertical, but barely. Wind forty knots, which according to the Beaufort Scale of Winds on the bulletin board is a fresh gale. Approximately, it plucks the hair from your head. Bad luck at table—only survivors besides ourselves a pair of old Swedes. He has sold his Omaha grocery store and is taking his Minnesota-born wife back so they can live out their golden years in the village near Gøteborg that he last saw in 1905. Oh boy.

They are awkward and diffident, and would get chummy on the slightest invitation, but I know this kind from childhood—pious, censorious, opposed to smoking drinking cardplaying dancing movies books language thinking. They sit in lace-curtained parlors and *tsk-tsk* on an indrawn breath, they know every unwanted pregnancy in town sooner than the girl does, they want English teachers in Augustana College fired for assigning A *Farewell to*

33

Arms, they wrote the Volstead Act. And touching, in an exasperating sort of way.

Something happens to immigrants (I don't mean political exiles, who are another breed; I mean immigrants who left the old country they were at home in in order to better themselves in the land of opportunity). The trauma of exile petrifies them. Forever will they love, and the old sod be fair. They bring it all with them, in its 1890 or 1900 version, and they plant it in America without modification and then spend the ,rest of their lives defending it against change, while in the old country what they knew changes so as to be unrecognizable. I wouldn't want to be old Bertelson when he finds that in modern Sweden the Lutheran Church has become nothing but a registry of births and deaths, and that the sexual habits of young Swedes make the objectionable goings-on in Omaha lovers' lanes look like sandbox play.

And how their hound-dog eyes reproach me, otherwise quite a pleasant man, when I order a bottle of Pouilly-Fumé to go with the fish. I offer some to them, despite Ruth's eyebrows, and Mrs. Bertelson claps her hand over her glass as she might clap hands over her private parts if offered rape.

They are curious why worldlings like us should be going to Denmark, and when they learn from Ruth that we have no business there, but still are intending to stay for several months, and that my mother came from there and that we might look up the village where she was born, they instantly construe me as an ally. I too am fleeing Gomorrah, looking backward toward the good old ways. It irritates me to see myself in those two cracked distorting mirrors, standing in front of some thatched cottage filled with yearning thoughts and fulfillments.

Early to bed to read. So rough the bureau drawers keep falling out. I tie them shut with the rubber clothesline some well-wisher gave us for our drip-dry. The sentiments of *The Lonely Crowd* prove to be, as Huck Finn said of another book, interesting but tough, and I lay it aside to study Danish. Samples of the beauty of that language: *en smuk pige*, a pretty girl, *en blomst*, a flower. I make myself half sick practicing glottal stops, which crop up at

34

random in Danish sentences and make everything sound like hiccups, regurgitations, and death rattles.

March 27:

Wind fifty-two knots—whole gale. This knife blade of a ship, fast and unstable as a destroyer, wallows and heels and shudders through the enormous seas. The horizon tilts, sinks, rotates, lifts. Wind off the port bow, foredeck emptied and everything lashed down, now and then big waves coming aboard. Dining room nearly empty at breakfast. Don't know about noon—didn't go. Dinner ditto. Dramamine, Zwiebach, and yoghurt. Steward urges Rullemops, pickled herrings, as a seasickness cure, and I vomit him out of the cabin. Better now, but Ruth really miserable. Berths keep filling with bureau drawers despite all my rigging.

March 28, 29, 30:

There went a lost weekend, and we might lose the whole week. Wind now fifty-four knots, between a whole gale and a storm. Ruth stays in her berth, but I totter out, groggy with Dramamine and misled by that Lutheran conscience I seem to share with the Bertelsons, to try the gym, take a workout, get the blood moving and the gorge nailed down. The *Stockholm* is like a drunken elephant dancing—down by the bow, over to port, up by the stern, over to starboard, up by the bow. I make my way down to C deck like a marble bouncing down a pinball machine. The weights I work out on are one second as heavy as houses, and the next slack in my hands. I try a sauna and come out fast—too smothery. The masseur slaps his table, but I can't bear the thought of being mauled. Settle for a swim.

As I step into the pool's shallow end the ship begins its long shuddering lean to port, and the pool goes away: I pursue it down the slippery tiles. It stops, pasted against the far wall. The ship begins to roll back, returning water floods my feet and ankles, my calves. I crouch, ready to launch into a breast stroke, and hang on, here it comes! When the tidal wave has passed, I pick myself up out of the corner and get out of there. In all that place of dampness and shining tile, amid the machinery of physical fitness installed to make travelers happy, not a living creature except the lonely masseur and me.

March 31:

Today we should be debarking the Bertelsons at Gøteborg. God knows where we are—I doubt that the captain does—but we're a long way from Gøteborg. As for the Bertelsons' dream, that has been postponed to a better world. This is how:

The wind went down some today, and some of the groundhogs came out, including our other table mates: a cheerful Dane from Fyn, an apple and cherry grower who has been in Florida helping his brother with an orange grove, and a silent Norwegian who ate everything on the menu from Rullemops to mints. Both he and the Dane drank beer and *akvavit* with their dinner, scandalizing the Bertelsons. But the Bertelsons weren't driven away. Quelled, scared, out of their known place, they seemed to want to hang onto Ruth and me for safety. They even tagged along to the lounge, where dancing was announced, and watched us at the devil's work.

The devil's work was never so difficult. Try dancing on a hip-roofed barn in an earthquake. We slid into the chairs on every roll, and crosshatched our way uphill again, and were tilted forward and slid into the opposite chairs. The piano was bolted down, but the bench was not, and the piano player kept alternately sliding clear under his keyboard and then out beyond arm's reach. We could not have kept it up more than a few minutes at best, but the best didn't occur. On one of the *Stockholm*'s salmon leaps through the sea there was a wrench and rumble, the pianist yelped and fell sideways out of the way, and the piano slid ponderously down the deck and broke the leg of the silent Norwegian, belching and dozing among the wallflowers.

By the time we had the piano cornered and tied down, and a couple of stewards had come running with a stretcher and slipped and slid and teetered the Norwegian off to the infirmary, I became aware that Bertelson too was down, vomiting on the deck, with his wife trying to hold him back from sliding into his mess. So they carried him off too. The word a half hour later was that he had had a coronary, and was dead.

Oh, his poor wife! Ruth said when I told her. Yes. Oh, his poor wife. Oh, his poor dream. Oh, his poor fifty years of dull work with its deferred reward. Oh, his poor dim dependable unimaginative not very attractive life that was supposed to mature like a Treasury bill. Ah, Bertelson! Ah, humanity!

As I write this, Ruth is asleep, and whimpering with some sad dream. The bureau drawers come slowly out, stretching the rubber clothesline that holds them, and then, as the roll eases and starts the other way, are shot back into place like sluggish crossbow bolts. The wind is up again, as rough as it has been at any time on this miserable crossing. Nothing for me to do but lie and listen, not too confidently, to my heart, and be chased from side to side by things I don't want to think of but can't shut out. At least when I was seasick there wasn't that. They say you are never seasick in battle. The corollary is that you never battle when seasick. But who can stay seasick all the time?

April 1:
Bertelson just missed dying on April Fool's Day. With unseemly haste, urged by some consideration or other (no refrigeration?) the ship got rid of him before the day of fools was more than barely begun. They must have been sewing him into his sack before he was cold.

I had fallen asleep, finally, about three. Some time later I awoke with the panicked conviction that something was wrong. The ship's motion was different. She was not plunging forward with her straining roll, but wallowing with a horrible helplessness. I could not hear the engines, nor could I, when I stepped out of the berth, feel them in the floor. My watch said ten past five. At any minute I expected bells, shouts, cries of "To the lifeboats," and I almost shook Ruth awake to start her dressing. But first I decided to look outside.

The hall was brightly lighted, totally empty. Rows of closed doors. In robe and slippers I went up the companionway and into the lounge. It too blazed with light, it too was empty. The broken chairs had been taken away and the piano was once more bolted down, but not a soul, not a sound except the creaking of woodwork as the room warped and tilted to the heavy, helpless wallowing of the ship.

I went to the doors and looked out across the starboard rail. The ship's lights shone on the lifting, gray, foam-streaked side of a wave. I watched it rise and rise until it was high above the rail, and I felt the ship shrink and slide from it. I looked deep inside it, deeper than I wanted to look, and then it fell off somewhere, and the ship rolled so that I grabbed the doorframe, and the light spread out over the hissing crests of farther waves, an appalling turmoil of water, an uncreated waste without order or end or purpose, heaving and yelling through the dark that the ship's little brightness only made more total. And rain falling onto it, slashing at the glassy sides, while the wind blew a stiff spray flat off the crests. Whoever would know the age of the earth, Conrad says somewhere, should look upon the sea in storm. The age or disposition of the earth, he should have said.

Then out of the corner of my eye I saw the glint of moving oilskins out on the foredeck. A cluster of figures huddled out there, hanging onto each other or to the davits of a lifeboat, intent on something at their center. They hulked like conspirators, bent away from wind and rain, and in my scared condition I had the wild idea they were planning like a lot of Lord Jims to abandon ship and let all the pilgrims perish. For a minute or two they leaned and clung together. Then they fell back into a ragged line, two of them bent and lifted, and there went Bertelson down the plank and into that appalling sea.

There is no word for how instant his obliteration was. The second after they stooped, he was not. With hardly a pause the oilskinned figures started in, and I saw that two of them were supporting a third who sagged and staggered. Mrs. Bertelson. Why they let her watch that, God knows. Maybe, in her piety and wretchedness, she had insisted on seeing her husband go to God.

I fled ahead of them down the companionway and up to our own safe door. As I took hold of the knob I felt or heard the renewed throb of the engines, and by the time I was back in my berth the *Stockholm* was beginning once more to drive her nose into the seas.

So fast, so total an erasure. *Spurlos verloren.* And now this afternoon, with their raging efficiency or whatever it is, they've already got his wife out on the foredeck, wrapped in rugs and shot full of sedatives. The wind has dropped again, but not far, and the sea even in daylight is nothing she should be contemplating. There she sits, staring with dumb, drugged suffering at the North Atlantic. And a strange thing: now that she is stricken, people avoid her more than they did when she was only cowlike and uninteresting. Me too. Ruth sat by her for an hour and tried to talk to her, but I couldn't. What would I have said? I thought her husband foolish and bigoted and dull, and now that he is dead it would be hypocrisy to pretend differently.

I would like to be able to suffer fools more gladly. I am too likely to be contemptuous of people when their minds don't work at least as fast as mine. Curtis too, Curtis too. Maybe, whenever I am tempted to be snobbish, I can make myself remember the chaos and old night that Bertelson vanished into. Not even the most foolish and bigoted member of Lutheran Christendom deserves to be wiped out like that.

Also I can't forget that it was in the ocean—another and pleasanter ocean than this one, but part of the same element—that Curtis was knocked from or let go of his surfboard, and his last breath was water.

Agents, like publishers, get to be instant readers—they could carry the gospel of Evelyn Wood through the world. *Hamlet* in twelve minutes, Tolstoi in twenty. My eye, ranging down the page, saw something coming that I didn't want to get into—some of the breast beating and the Why, why, why, where did I begin to do it wrong, how did I manage to destroy the one person, besides Ruth, to whom I wished only to be kind and loving? I would have given him a kidney if he had needed it, they could have transplanted my heart. So I became his schoolmaster and his jailer and his judge.

I was not going to read all that to Ruth. Maybe I will go back and read it over, maybe I will read it many times, and maybe in tears, but I wasn't going to dump it on her. With only the most momentary hesitation, I flipped that page and turned it under, and when I glanced up briefly I saw that she understood exactly what I had done.

I went on reading, though what followed wasn't much more cheerful than what I had censored.

Once in college, trying to determine some optical truth or other, we taped distorting spectacles on a laboratory chicken and threw her some feed. At first she would cock her head, take aim, and miss a grain of corn by as much as an inch, but after a while she learned how to correct for the astigmatism we had imposed on her, and once she got the hang of it she was as accurate as ever with either eye.

Well, right now, while Ruth sleeps and I do not, and this queasy ship carries us through the undiminished seas, I feel like a grain of corn, with the Great Chicken of the Universe standing over me taking aim. I don't know whether she has binocular vision or not, she may be blind in both eyes for all I know. But she is not going to miss me when she pecks. I have made a point of not believing in distorting spectacles. Any hen worth a dollar can recover from them in a few hours. Bertelson probably thought he had her whammied with his sixty-five years of piety, and look what happened to him.

Moral: You can't trust optics, but you can depend on appetite.

Again I looked across at Ruth. She made a rueful, sympathetic smile, and her eyes were shiny. She obviously wanted to pat me and kiss me better. "Poor lamb," she said. "You were so miserable, and fighting yourself so. I guess I was so miserable myself on that voyage I didn't realize how bad it was for you."

Often I submit to her sympathy. I depend on it, in fact. But right then I chose to be flippant. "Despite all my efforts," I said. "I wore my bruised spirit in my buttonhole, and took frequent whiffs, and turned up my eyes, and you never noticed."

"But you didn't. You didn't let on to *me*. You kept it to yourself."

"And why not?" I said. "That's the beauty of a journal. That's where you meet the really sympathetic audience."

She understood that, too, and it annoyed her. She pulled Catarrh down from under her chin a little too impatiently, and had to disengage his claws from her dressing gown. "Why do you have to jeer?" she said. "Whenever you give away your feelings the least little bit, you have to jeer and cover up."

Trapped in my own role, I said, not very originally, "Beneath this harsh exterior beats a heart of stone."

She stared at me as if she couldn't believe me, and the longer she looked at me the more irritated she became. She is not a hard woman to exasperate, especially when I shy away from being comforted or mothered. "Sometimes I think you should take your own advice," she said.

"What advice?"

"To suffer fools more glady. Beginning with yourself."

Having said that, she obviously found herself furious. She startled herself, I think, with her own vehemence. I might easily have said something that would have wounded and frustrated her even more. After forty-five years we can still, if we let ourselves, bristle and bump one another around like a pair of stiff-legged dogs. Fortunately I played it light, for the fact was that I really hadn't intended to hurt her feelings. So I shrugged. "Maybe so."

She had no reason to go on, but as the injured party she had to have the last word. "I wish I understood you. You drive me wild, you really do. For a change we're doing something together, sort of reliving something, something as sad as it could possibly be, and important to us both, and you brought it all back so clearly, and I was interested, and touched, and then you have to start mugging and hoofing, and spoil it."

41

The telephone rang, and since Ruth was encumbered with the cat, I reached across to the bed table and answered it.

"Hello, Joe?"

Ben Alexander. On the telephone his voice is even wheezier, breezier, and louder than it is face to face.

"Present."

"Been thinking. Why wait for lunch? I want to have Tom and Edith up to dinner Friday. Can you and Ruth come?"

"Why, I guess so. Let me speak to the foreman." I put my hand over the mouthpiece and said to Ruth, "Ben wants us for dinner with the Pattersons Friday. Can we go?"

She checked the calendar and found nothing but a hair appointment. "Do you want to?"

"Do you?"

"Sure, I guess so. Why not? But you've been so funny lately about going out."

"I'm always ready for Ben's house, especially as long as he makes that Cabernet."

"That's probably it," she said, practically with a sniff. "All right, tell him yes."

I told him yes.

"Swell," he said. "Friday at seven."

Bang in my ear, as if he had tossed the instrument into its cradle from six feet away.

"That old rip," I said. "He's got more left at nearly eighty than most of us had at eighteen. Running around in his convertible. Why hasn't *he* got sore joints? Why doesn't *he* ever get tired?"

"What makes you think he doesn't?" Ruth said. "He's got that metal hip joint, he walks with a cane, his heart runs by electronics, he's alone, and probably lonely. Why do you think he's any luckier than you?"

"I didn't say he was luckier. I said he had more left than anybody his age should have. Sons of missionaries must learn early to get around God."

"Come on," she said, and let her hands fall and her shoulders

42

droop as if in defeat. "Come on, read some more before we get into a real fight."

"You don't want to hear any more."

"Of *course* I want to hear more!"

"The perils of the deep are nearly over," I said. "From here on it's less profound but with more local color."

April 3:
Gøteborg, two days late. In three hours ashore I discover that the solid ground of Sweden is as unstable as the North Atlantic. Doped with more than a week of Dramamine, I stand looking at statues and town halls and into store windows, and as I look they start to lean and roll. Which is maybe the way things look to Mrs. Bertelson, too. She is met by a couple of relatives and a representative of the Swedish-American Line and driven off the dock in a car. The Swedish-American Line man has to interpret—Mrs. B's in-laws have no English, and she can't understand their Swedish. Just before she got in the car she threw a desperate look back up at the ship and saw us at the rail. We waved. Her face worked. A word formed on her lips. *Good-by*, she said, probably not to us. Probably to Omaha, where the house and the grocery store were gone and couldn't be returned to, and to Minnesota, where her roots were cut, and to the only one who could have dealt with her problems for her, who had gone off that deck feet first, sewn into a sack, thirty-six hours before. *Good-by*. And vanished into a confusion hardly less than what he had gone into.

April 4, Hotel d'Angleterre:
Quiet run this morning down the Øresund in the rain, with Sweden dim on the left and Denmark dim on the right. Hamlet's castle at Helsingør loomed up awhile, guarding the narrows, and then a stretch of shore with villages and houses like Monopoly pieces among the leafless trees, and then Copenhagen, the harbor full of traffic, the Little Mermaid wet and cold on her rock, and finally we nudged and snuggled against a pier overhung with a

railed platform on which hundreds of people smiled and waved and held up signs: *Velkommen til Danmark. Velkommen Doktor Holger Hansen. Velkommen Onkel Oskar. Jeg Elsker Dig, Kristin Møllerup.*

The rain came down on them, half of them without umbrellas, and their wet faces shone, and they cheered and waved and held up their banners till the rain melted the paper and ran the paint. Altogether the healthiest, happiest people we have ever seen. We feel like something brought up by grappling hooks, but we are happy to accept their wavings and welcomings as if they were meant for us personally. Escaped from the deep. Praise the Lord.

As I write this, Ruth has gone hunting an *apothek* or some place where she can buy toothpaste and postcards. She is all recovered, I am still woozy. I sit here by the window overlooking the big square called Kongens Nytorv, nibbling Rullemops and drinking *akvavit*, and take a look at Copenhagen. The center of the square is all one leafless park. Across it I can see some copper spires, and some castle towers, and narrow streets winding away from the square. All around Kongens Nytorv crimson banners hang out the windows into the rain—some holiday, I assume— and a postman in a crimson coat is moving from door to door along the south side. Like the British, the Danes seem to have discovered the functions of crimson in a gray climate.

Bells are bonging the hour of four from a dozen steeples. Below me, people buy sausages from a street wagon. I pour another two fingers of cold *akvavit* and pick up another piece of slimy herring. I never much liked herring, but this is suddenly delicious. It goes with the *akvavit* in one of those subtle food-and-drink marriages like octopus, feta cheese, and ouzo in Greece. It is a form of instant naturalization. I am very glad to be here.

Just now the door opened and a maid, evidently expecting an empty room, started in. I said something in English. A wave of red washed upward from her neck, a blush so dark it looked painful, and she scrambled out, falling over her own feet. New, probably, a country girl just learning to make beds and scrub bathtubs and bring in morning coffee. I can't avoid the feeling that she is

44

just such a girl as my mother was when she first got up the courage—and what an act of courage it had to be—to spend her savings on a third-class ticket to America, all by herself. I have been half joking about going back to the village she came from—Bregninge, I don't even know what island it's on—but I'm sure now I will. Tomorrow we will start negotiations for a car, and call on the rental agent whose name we got from the cherry grower on the *Stockholm*. We will get maps, guidebooks, phrase books. Ruth swears she will not try to learn Danish, but that doesn't have to hinder me. Already I can say *Ja tak* and *vaer saa god* and *en smuk pige*, and I am getting pretty good at the glottal stop.

On the corner, carpenters are working on the second floor of a building. I watch a boy, an apprentice he has to be, come from the street with bottles of beer spread fanwise between the fingers of both hands. Eight bottles, he carries. He disappears under the scaffolding, reappears after a while on the second floor. The carpenters lay down their tools and each takes a beer. They pass the opener around, they hoist their bottles toward one another and tilt them to their mouths. They look like a bugle corps playing "To the Colors," and I accept their salute.

Velkommen, Onkel Yoe.

I slapped the notebook shut. "That's all for the night. I'm getting singer's nodules."

She didn't object. "All right. That was nice, We can read some more tomorrow night, and every night till we finish it. Unless it bothers you too much."

"It doesn't bother me."

"I'm afraid it does," she said. "It bothers me, too. But don't you think . . . I mean, this fits right in with the letters you're going through. Here's a whole piece of our life, a sort of strange interlude."

"Strange interlude is right." I stood up, and I guess she saw me wince.

"Hurt?"

"Just the old hinges."

"You shouldn't saw all that wood. I beg you and beg you, and still you go on working as if you were a young man. You could hire somebody to do that hard work."

"And then what would *I* do?" I said. I stood and listened to the rain hitting the windows in pattering gusts. "Minnie'll be tracking in more dirt tomorrow than she sweeps out."

"Oh, my Lord," Ruth said. "Tomorrow *is* Minnie's day, I'd forgotten. I meant to clear out that mess in the other bedroom."

My good wife is a cliché, the one who cleans up for the cleaning lady. And a good thing too, the cleaning lady being perceptibly slapdash.

The telephone rang again. Arching her eyebrows clear up into her bangs (who'd be calling at this hour, nearly ten o'clock?), Ruth answered it. "Yes," she said. "Just a moment, please."

Making don't-ask-me faces, she reached the instrument across. "Hello?" I said.

Female voice, breathless, hurried, young, apologetic, false. "Mr. Allston? I'm *terribly* sorry to be bothering you at home, and so late. Do you have a minute? You don't know me, my name is Anne McElvenny, I live in San Franscisco and I'm one of a group who act as hostesses and guides for State Department visitors. It's a Junior League thing. I'd like to ask you a favor, or a *question*."

"Ask away. Maybe I don't have the answer, but I can try."

"I *know!* It's nervy of me, but I thought maybe this is something you'd . . . and since he asked about you, and wondered if you weren't in the Bay Area. You know Césare Rulli."

"Of course. Is he in town?"

"*Yes.* For the last two days. He leaves tomorrow night. And you know him, so I don't have to tell you. He's such a *dynamo*, he's run through everything I had planned for him. I had such a list I thought we'd never get halfway through it, but . . . Well! We've done the City, and visited the bookstores, and had about six radio and TV interviews, and lunched with a lot of writers, and dined with the Italian consul—I'm calling from there, so I can plan tomorrow. I *know* he'd love to see you, if you'll be at home."

46

"Why, yes," I said. "We'd love to see him, too, if we aren't tied up. Just a minute while I look at the calendar."

The routine again, hand over mouthpiece, mouth down, sotto voce explanation. "Césare Rulli's in town, somebody wants to bring him down. Could we give them lunch?"

People who have lived together a long time are said to begin to look alike. They also respond alike to anything that challenges their routine. I could see my own sentiments pass across Ruth's face, followed by some of hers. First the automatic impulse to reject the intrusion as a threat to peace—a sort of Why can't they leave us alone? Then some rapid-eye-movement reconsiderations, neutral or only partly negative: what's on hand? have to shop? rainy day, everything will look its worst. On the other hand, Minnie's day, that's a plus. And a break in the daily round, good for Joe. And Césare *is* good company, and it's been a long time.

"We could take them out somewhere," I said.

"No, we should have him here. I'd like to see him, wouldn't you? But I'd hate to lose the whole afternoon. I'd like to get in a walk if it clears up. Ask her if they could be here by twelve-thirty."

"Looks fine," I said into the telephone. "Could you lunch with us? About twelve-thirty?"

"Oh, that will be lovely!" said Ms. McElvenny. "He'll be so pleased. But are you sure it's not a . . ."

"Not a bit. We'd be hurt if he didn't give us a chance at him."

"Oh, here he is now, just going by the door. Would you like to say hello?"

"Sure, put him on."

There he was, shouting in my ear. "Giuseppe! *Come va?* And what are you doing out here? I looked for you in New York, and they told me, and I didn't believe it. I thought you owned New York. *Cos' é successo?*"

"Césare," I said, "you ought to subscribe to *Publisher's Weekly.* I retired and we moved out here eight years ago."

He still refused to believe it. Retired? A *giovane* like me? Now what was it, really? Chased some girl out here, had I?

It amuses Césare to talk as if, every time we get together, we do nothing but pinch bottoms, follow Lollabrigidas and Lorens down alleys, and live the *dolce vita* with accommodating starlets, whereas in plain fact we have spent nearly every hour we ever had together sitting at a table at Downey's, where Césare will be most visible, conducting monologues with him as monologuist and me as monologuee, and consuming drinks for which, naturally and gracefully, he lets me pay. He always understood what agents are for, even though he was never more than briefly my client.

I held the telephone four inches from my ear and let him shout for a while. When he lulled, I said, "Well, that's great, it's great to hear your voice. We're delighted you called, and tickled you're coming for lunch. I know you're at a party now, so I won't hold onto you. We'll spill it all tomorrow, shall we? But better let me tell Ms. McElvenny how to get you here."

D'accordo. Va benissimo. A domani. Ciao, ciao, Giuseppe, arrivederla. He put her back on, and I gave her directions. She couldn't thank me enough. She knew it would make Mr. Rulli's trip, just to see us.

"Galloping sociability this week," I said as I put the telephone back.

"Is that so bad?" Ruth said. "I thought you liked Césare."

"No, it's not bad, and I do like Césare. I was just commenting on the way the calendar fills up."

"It's just as well," Ruth said. "You're getting such an automatic way of *evading* people. I should think you'd like seeing Césare. He's the liveliest person we know. He'll come into our quiet little backwater like a waterspout, and stir us up."

"And that's exactly what we need."

"What *you* need."

"And am perfectly happy to accept," I said. "I'll probably have more fun out of tomorrow's visitors than you will, since you have to cook."

"Yes," she said absently, already far ahead, already planning, forgetful of what she had started to say to me. "He's *such* an amusing man. He loves himself so he makes you love him too.

But I hope they have sense enough to leave by three-thirty or so. Then Minnie can get us cleaned up before she goes." In a couple of minutes she got out of bed. "Maybe I'll just go and clear out that bedroom right now," she said. "Then Minnie'll have more time to . . ."

Exit, murmuring and thinking ahead.

TWO

1

Pazienza.

The day that started hectic ends morose. I sit here grumbling to myself, while Ruth recuperates with a couple of aspirins and a heating pad. My impulse is to damn Césare, but he is not responsible, he was just being Césare. If I can't handle the sort of challenge that Césare makes to my chosen life, I had better choose another life.

It has poured all day, if the word "poured" can be used to describe rain that is not vertical but horizontal, mixed with leaves, branches, power failures, and fears for the windows. We awoke to the shaking and shuddering of the house. Ruth took one look outside and began to mourn. Going to the kitchen to make coffee, I discovered en route that the clerestory windows above the bookcase wall in the living room were leaking, and I spent half an hour on the stepladder taking down kachina dolls, papier-mâché Hindu gods, Hopi bowls, and other bric-a-brac from the drowned top shelf, sponging up a bowlful of water mixed with the cobwebs, dust, and dead flies that Minnie's house cleaning had left up there, setting a row of breadpans to catch the continuing drip, and removing from the shelves and propping open to dry most of the lifework of Joyce Carol Oates, Edwin O'Connor, Eugene O'Neill, and Katherine Anne Porter.

Then I got breakfast, which we ate as usual while listening to the "Today" show and watching the day develop outside the windows. It was not the day to entertain Italy's greatest novelist, the profound anatomist of passion, true heir of D'Annunzio, with a dash of Cellini and a dollop of Casanova. Not the day to entertain anybody. As we set to work to prepare his welcome we alter-

52

nated between anxiety that we might not be able to do right by him and a wan hope that he wouldn't come.

We are fond of Césare in spite of his books. His books are overrated, but that is because he is completely of his time, and his time overrates itself. He is neither the first nor the worst to make a career out of the verbal exploration of the various bodily orifices, genital, anal, and oral (not the moral orifices, he is less interested in those). Maybe if I were younger, and my hormones more active, I might appreciate his novels more. As it is, I have to think them compulsive, theatrical, and decadent even while I find Césare himself lively, amusing, and full of an attractive kind of Italian blarney. It is as much of an effort for me to flog my flagging sexual interest through one of his books as it perhaps was for him to flog himself through the writing of it. I suspect he much prefers the research to the writing. Nevertheless, in person he is engaging, the friendliest and best-natured of satyrs, far more fun than his books and far less repulsive than his audience. Though I grumbled a little about his coming, I was actually looking forward to it. News of the Rialto, and all that. It is possible to feel isolated even when you insist that that's what you want. It is also possible to feel that you should justify your retirement by showing off the putting green and paddle tennis court.

We used to do that sort of thing a lot. We had invented Eden, and owed it a PR job. Probably we thought we were adapting to one of those illusions they call a life style. We wanted our American plenty to show, but not *too* much. We wanted to make it clear that our tastes were simpler than our means would have permitted. We wanted to demonstrate that the rush to the suburbs and the country, when conducted by the right people, could be an enhancement of civilization, not an evasion of it. We had books, music, a garden, birds, country walks, friends. We were within ten minutes of a great university, with all it offered in intellectual and cultural weather, and less than an hour from the city that everybody in the world falls in love with. When we had Eastern or foreign visitors we watched them confidently for signs of envy. We wanted, maybe just a little desperately, to be thought terribly lucky.

Well, we were, we are. But at our age, seven or eight years make a difference. Since coming out here we have lost a few friends by their moving away, and one very dear one by death. Eden with graves is no longer Eden. Moreover, we have had an invasion from the Land of Nod. The place has been moved in on by junior executives whose upward mobility is always showing, whose new subdivisions scar the hills, and whose attitudes sometimes offend the godly. So as the people we knew back East die, or are institutionalized, or take themselves off to Tucson or Sarasota or Santa Barbara to estivate their last years away as we are doing here, our contacts here shrink, too. We have half given up the habit of mingling with our fellow man, and mingling, I suppose, is a little like sex. Use it or lose it. Like they say.

Result: we find it easier to stay home and watch television, or read, than go out, and these days when we entertain visitors we find them less a pleasure than an anxiety. I get smitten with the desire to make garden and patio worthy of admiring exclamations; Ruth cleans like Mrs. Craig and cooks as if Julia Child were coming to dine. We found ourselves preparing that way even for Césare, who could make a desert island lively. Why? I wonder. Maybe just friendship, a wish to show him a pleasant time. Maybe something else, a determination to send him back to his crumbling old palazzo on the Botteghe Oscure crying aloud for the felicity he left behind in California.

We were through breakfast by seven forty-five. By eight Ruth was in the kitchen with her glasses on and her cookbooks open, and I was out in the rain, doing my best not to blow away on every gust, trying to clean up the worst of the soggy leaves and trash that had eddied into the entrance. The plum blossoms of the night before were only a memory. This was no warm Hawaiian wind. This storm that had overtaken the first was straight down from the Aleutians.

Streaming water off my slicker, my beret soaked, I brought in wood and laid a fire. With chicken breasts amandine for the main

54

course, I decided to evoke Césare's appreciation with a good Green Hungarian, and put two bottles in to chill. To give a running start to Minnie, who was due at nine, I emptied all the wastebaskets and the garbage pail. When she didn't show up by nine, I went in and made the bed. Then I cleared some coat space in the front hall closet, and when my householder's eye was offended by the clutter of canes, umbrellas, and walking shoes stacked in there, I cleaned out the closet.

Nine-thirty, and no Minnie. Ruth, browning something in butter, compressed her lips and worked her black eyebrows at me significantly. "I thought maybe she could help with the cooking and serving," she said. "If she doesn't show up pretty soon she won't even have the house tidied up."

I started washing up her pots and pans, which she redirtied as fast as I washed them. By ten I had caught up with her, and the kitchen was filling with succulent smells, but still no Minnie. "She may not get here at all," I said. "There may be mud slides, washouts, down trees, all sorts of things. Maybe I'd better do the vacuuming. Then you can put her to work right away if she comes."

"Oh, if you would," Ruth said gratefully. Reaching to move something off the burner, she burned her wrist. Grinning with pain, she held still while I smeared the inch-long burn with ointment which I, suburban preparedness freak, had stowed in a drawer only days before.

The more any situation looks to Ruth like darkest tragedy, the more I am inclined to believe it can be dealt with. My contrariness, I suppose. At that point I was hearty and cheerful, and though I had been preparing just as anxiously as she had, I wished, from my superior calm, to reassure her.

"Take it easy," I told her. "Césare's never been known for his promptness. If he gets here at all, and he might not, he's sure to be late. There's plenty of time. Just do your cooking, and relax, and I'll go ahead and straighten up the house, and if worst comes to worst and we have no guests, we'll sit down together, just me and my Jo-John, and eat the chicken breasts amandine and drink a cold bottle of Green Hungarian together."

"I don't know," she said, and looked at me (or herself) and laughed. "If he doesn't come now, after getting us started on this, he'll never be welcome in *my* house again."

She had the lights on all over the house, to make things more cheerful that dark morning. I got out the vacuum cleaner and plugged it in and made one pass across the rug, and *pop*, the cleaner's howl died and all the lights went out.

"Oh, I *knew* it!" came Ruth's *cri de coeur* from the kitchen.

"Peace," I said, unruffled. "It's probably just the circuit breaker."

Leaving the vacuum where it stood, I went and inspected the panel on the kitchen wall. While I was craning up at it, looking for a breaker that was kinked, the lights flashed on, and the vacuum began to howl and flounder. I arrived just too late to keep it from bumping into the piano leg. As I shut it off and straightened it up Ruth came running, looking like Medea, and popped her finger in her mouth and rubbed it over the dented scar. The lights dimmed to a red pulse, flared up, and went out once more.

Unlighted, the room was gray and cold. The wind went past the plate glass absolutely flat, and rain like tracer bullets swept the tops of the live oaks below the terrace. I could barely see the valley or the country road; the hills opposite were only sodden, running outlines.

"What'll we *do?*" Ruth said.

"Haven't you got candles?"

"Oh, candles! How'm I going to *cook?* How'll we keep the house warm? What'll we do for water? We can't even flush the john."

True. There are handicaps to country living in an all-electric house whose water is pumped from a well, in a country where the winter ground is like soup, so that trees lie down across the power lines when the wind blows. Once last winter the power was off nearly all day, so long that Ruth and I paid three different calls, to people we didn't especially want to see, just to get to use a bathroom.

On the other hand, I was still feeling cheerful and competent. These little emergencies stir the blood. I cope, therefore I am.

"I'll light the fireplace," I said. "That'll both warm and cheer us. Johns—I don't know. What if I bring in some pails and kettles from the tank so we don't have to run down the pressure? Keep one flush in each john for the visitors. As for cooking, what is Sterno for?"

"Did you ever try to bake corn fingers with Sterno?" Ruth said. "Did you make an apricot soufflé with Sterno?"

"Maybe they'll just have to do without corn fingers and apricot soufflé."

"That would be quite a lunch. Chicken and salad."

"And wine. He's eaten a damned sight worse. At least let's see if we can keep the chicken warm."

I found two cans of Sterno, another fruit of my preparedness campaign, but no sign of the little tin stove to use them in. Ingenuity suggested tipping up a burner on the electric stove, setting a can of Sterno in the well under it, and tipping the burner back flat. Presto. I was congratulating myself and trying to cheer my determinedly gloomy wife when the door blew open and Minnie stamped in, wet-footed, wet-coated, hoo-hooing like a steamboat, with a wet cigarette pasted to her lower lip.

"Heyyyyy! Ain't *this* some'm!"

Every Tuesday morning she arrives at our door bursting with some dramatic tidings. Like any boiler or pressure tank, she must be eased of her burden gradually. She can't be hurried, she has to bubble and hiss herself quiet. Even on such a day as this we know better than to interrupt her show. As when on some hot mountain road a traveler hears the rumblings under the hood, and watches the temperature needle climb past the red and out of sight, and stops and opens the hood, and with handkerchief around hand makes darting stabs at the radiator cap to open it a little, but not too much, so the Allstons gave greetings to their cleaning lady, and waited for the jets of steam.

She kicked off her muddy shoes, she stripped off her raincoat and revealed the white nurse's nylon that gives her status as a professional and imparts a touch of class to the establishments she is willing to assist. Rumbling with phlegmy laughter, squinting against imaginary smoke from the cigarette that had been quenched in her run from car to door, she slid in stocking feet to the kitchen wastebasket and with a wet thumb and finger dropped the disintegrating cigarette in among the garbage.

"You know what I see on my way over? Ha-*ha!* Them creeps! Lessee if their zoning laws'll take care of *that* one!"

Them creeps are the junior executives and computer programmers who occupy the new subdivisions. It is Minnie's contention, with which in the main I agree, that they have ruined the hills by imposing their one-acre, one-house rigidities on land that used to be lived on comfortably by people who respected it. This morning, after waiting an hour while her husband Art dried out her wet distributor, she came over the hill past one of the new tracts just in time to see one of the bulldozed shelves let go its hold and slide smoothly down into the creek, leaving the aghast residents staring from the rain-swept edge of what had once been their front yard.

"Fence, trees, part of the lawn, the whole business," Minnie said. "I thought of callin' Art, and then I thought, What the hell, let 'em apply to Town Hall. *You* know, Mister Allston, if it was you, or the Pattersons, or somebody decent, Art'd be over in a minute to help. Jeez, it use to be a lot different around here. Everybody helped everybody else, everybody went to the same Christmas and New Year parties, there wasn't any difference except some people had a bigger house and maybe a couple horses in the pasture. And you *knew* people, you'd see things goin' on. Now everybody's behind a chain-link fence, you never see anybody even mowin' his lawn. But you'll see this guy for a while, you can look right in his parlor window. I wisht it would happen to the rest of them. Them creeps with their subdivisions and their tax hikes and their zoning! My God, you can't even build a henhouse without a permit—can't even keep hens, for hell's sake. Got to tie up your dog, can't do this, can't do that, can't keep horses because the neighbors object to all them *flies*. Then that same woman and her phony husband that have sunk all they got, and a lot more, in this place they've made too expensive for anybody to afford it, they go on down to Town Hall twice a month and pass some more laws so their fancy address won't get hurt by dogs and chickens and cluster housing and black people and Chicanos and students and hippies and federallyfinancedlowerincomehousing, all one word. That's their real scare. Honest to God, they cross themselves when they say it."

Ruth, with her unburned wrist holding up her bangs and her mouth in a rictus, said, "Yes. Well."

Minnie stowed her shoes and raincoat in the broom closet and stood up, grunting. "Might as well work in stocking feet, so's I won't mess up your floors. God, them people. You know what one of 'em said to me the other day—Mrs. Barnes, you know her? One of them white tennis dress ones with her legs naked clear to her behind? Runs into me on the road and stops me to ask about Mr. Patterson. Knows I work there. 'Mister Patterson don't look well,' she says. 'Looks so pale and thin,' she says. 'Well,' I says, 'he's just gettin' over an operation.' '*Is* he gettin' over it?' she wants to know. 'I heard it's terminal,' she says. 'I don't know where you heard that,' I says. 'Far as I know, he's gettin' along fine.' 'Well, I'm so glad to hear it,' she says, and then she says, like it hasn't been on her mind all the time, 'Oh, Minnie,' she says—who the hell ever give her the right to call me by my first name?—'Minnie,' she says, 'if anything *should* happen to Mister Patterson and they don't need you no more, I hope you'll keep me in mind. It's so hard to find reliable help,' she says, 'up here in the hills.' Sittin' there waitin' for him to die. Jesus."

"That's callous," Ruth said. "I can't imagine people being so callous. Minnie, I wonder . . ."

" 'Why don't you try East Palo Alto?' I ask her, and she says, 'Oh, I wouldn't *dare!* Bring a *black* into the hills?' she says. 'It would make me nervous, just knowin' they knew where we live.' 'Well, Mountain View or Sunnyvale then,' I says. 'There's plenty people need work.' But she don't like that any better. 'Chicanos?'

she says. 'Right when La Raza is suin' this town, right this very minute, tryin' to push a lowcosthousingproject on us and break down our zoning? I'd be just every bit as nervous hirin' a Chicano as I would a black.' 'Well, that's too bad,' I says to her, 'because you know what my last name is? Garcia.' That kind of scrambled her. 'Oh, but you're different,' she tries to say. 'I mean, you're *married* to Mister Garcia but you're not . . . And you *live* in the hills, you're a neighbor.' 'So was a lot of other Chicanos till you crowded them out,' I says. Oh boy, that's some kind of people. Nixon could of got his whole White House staff out of just one subdivision around here. I wish you could of seen them up there on the edge of that bank lookin' down to where their front yard had slid."

"I wish we had," Ruth said firmly. "I wish we had time to hear all about it. But we just haven't *got* time, I'm afraid. We're in a jam, Minnie. We've got people coming for lunch, and the power's off. You know how *that* is. You can't do *anything*. But we've got to, just the same. First thing, I guess you or Joe will have to bring in some buckets of water from the tank."

"Why sure," Minnie said. "Whyn't you say? You just tell me what you need done. Oh . . . hey." Her eyes were on me.

"What?" I said.

"I forgot to tell you. But if you got company comin', your culvert's plugged up and there's water runnin' all down your road. I just barely made it up."

The light came on, dimmed to a glow, fluttered, and went out —some forlorn last kiss of broken wires off in the wet hills. Ruth said in her crisis voice, "I suppose you've got to see what you can do. Minnie'll get me the water. But first bring me in two leaves for the table. Oh, damn, why didn't we say we'd take them out somewhere?"

"Maybe we couldn't get out," I said. "Maybe he can't get in. Relax. We'll make it."

"Oh, relax!" Ruth said. When she gets into one of those states she resents any attempt to soothe her. Only last-ditch desperation is permissible.

That was about eleven. Three quarters of an hour later I was still digging, blind with rain, my slicker threatening to lift me up like a hang glider, at the mound of leaves and gravel the flood-water had piled over the entrance to the culvert. Water pouring down against the pile was being deflected out into the road, to go sheeting down the asphalt toward the bottom, where a lake had covered the area between the eucalyptus trees. That culvert was obviously clogged too.

My feet were wet, my pants were soaked to the thighs. As usual, my hands had gone into their Raynaud's syndrome spasm in the cold and were white to the second joints of the fingers. For all that, the adobe mixed with leaves was so impossible to shovel that I finally had to get down and dig at the mass with my hands. Eventually I moved something that counted. The bottom fell out, the stream of water dove downward with a slurp, and across the road I heard the plug of mud and leaves shoot out into the gully. So. Emergency dealt with. I cope, therefore I am. I washed my numb hands in muddy ice water and stood up to shove them between the buttons of my slicker and into my armpits for warming. Then I heard a car at the foot of the hill.

It had already eased through the lake down there. Now, shifted down, it started fast up the road on which water was still sheeting, not yet cleared by my clearing of the culvert. It threw a bow wave like a power boat—a BMW, I saw, two people in it, blonde hair on the right, black behind the wheel, two faces staring out through the sweeping wiper blades. Césare and company, a half hour early. Ruth would be so pleased.

Leaning on my shovel, I stood aside, my face fixed for humorous comment, intending to wave them on when they slowed, with shouted assurances that I would be with them in a few minutes. But at the last moment something in the set of Césare's head and neck told me that he was not pausing in any downpour on any flooded hill for any workman in a muddy slicker leaning on a muddy shovel. I just had time to swing around as they passed. The splash drenched the back of my slicker and the unprotected back of my neck.

61

Almost contemplatively, assuring myself that I still had a half hour before my guests were due, I went on down to the bottom and cleared the culvert there to ease and drain the lake. Leaving the shovel in case further emergencies developed, I came back up the road littered with leaves, broken branches, and rocks loosened from above. To maintain feelings appropriate to a host, I did not allow myself to dwell on the State Department's exchange-of-persons program, nor yet on the volatile and romantic Italian temperament. Instead, I counted the steps it took me from the bottom culvert to the middle one—one hundred twelve—and from the middle one to the top—one hundred seventy-one. Two hundred eighty-three altogether.

Unseen, I got past the entrance and around to the bedroom door. But when I had peeled off my soaked and muddied clothes and stepped into the bathroom, my finger on the switch produced no light, and in the shower my turning of the knob gave rise to no more than a weak little old man's jet followed by a dribble. While I tried to get clean under that, I elaborated a fantasy in which I called Dr. Ben Alexander and had him come to examine the prostate of my plumbing system.

Finally I got half clean, though my hands continued numb, and at twelve-forty, only ten minutes after they had been invited for, but forty after their arrival, I went in to my guests. Things had obviously been a little strained in there. Ruth, who has a lot of doomed-queen, avenger-queen expressions, sometimes Medea, sometimes Clytemnestra, sometimes Lady Macbeth, gave me one that was more like Cassandra or Mary Queen of Scots. She was just handing a drink, probably the second or third, to Césare, who was peering out at the drowned hills and being reminded, not for the first time if my intuition was right, of Umbria.

Césare rushed to embrace me, crying to his gods that he had not recognized me on the hill. "How could I know? I saw you there, I thought, 'Poor devil, what some people must do to live.' But I could not stop, you understand, the road was a *torrente*. Or should I pretend that Ms. McElvenny was driving?"

I shook Ms. McElvenny's hand: she was a pussycat with half-inch eyelashes. "I knew who was driving," I said. "Remember the last time I saw you? You drove me down that corkscrew road from the American Academy to Trastevere. I didn't draw a breath all the way down. Once I looked back, just as we passed that little temple, the one with the fountains, and the gravel was still hanging in the air above the Villa Aurelia's gate. Then I looked down, and here came a Volkswagen bus that was going to meet us just at a curve where a fellow was washing his car in the road. And from farther down the roofs of the Regina Coeli were floating up toward us the way Fifth Avenue would float up at you if you did a half gainer off the Empire State. Nobody's going to be in any doubt who's driving, if you're at the wheel."

Césare was delighted. Said Ms. McElvenny the pussycat, "Can you picture what it's like to have him drive you down Jones Street?"

"Yes," I said. "Yes, I can. Exactly."

Ruth's eyes were asking accusingly, Where *were* you? Césare was simultaneously exclaiming about the *brutto tempo* and asking how I was and demanding to know how I found myself out here on the West Coast. I got myself a drink and offered to refill Ms. McElvenny. "I'm gonna drive," she said with a grin. The lights came on. Ruth breathed an excuse and darted for the kitchen. In the door she hung a moment. "Give me fifteen minutes?" she said, and vanished. There we were.

I inspected Ms. McElvenny. She was just the kind of pussycat that Césare collects. In fact, she too put me in mind of the last time we were in Rome, when an American girl came to me wanting me to get her an advance on her manuscript and be a reference in her application for a Guggenheim. She said she worked so well in Rome that she simply must stay another year. She intimated two or three times that she would do *anything* for the chance. I found myself unable to assist her as much as she wanted me to. Three days later I saw her at a table on the Via Veneto, smiling as any pussycat smiles who has just swallowed a bumblebee, while Italy's Greatest Novelist poured out to her, leaning head to head across the cloth, his best D'Annunzio monologue.

A version of which he was now giving me. Beside Césare Rulli, Ben Alexander would seem taciturn. He has an interest in everything that moves; only quiet things elude him. He cannot sit still. Sitting, he hitches a chair around like a milking stool. Standing, he hops and strides around with his impetuous limp, gained, he says, from a German bullet when he was with the partisans during the war. I make no judgment on where he spent the war or how he got his limp. Maybe he borrowed it from Lord Byron and liked it so well he forgot to return it. He is a fly in a bottle, a June bug against a screen. Where anyone else would simmer, he boils; where others boil, he erupts.

He didn't dwell long on the *brutto tempo* or the view that is like Umbria. He was instantly off on San Francisco, which he has of course fallen in love with: a world city, a city more of Europe than America, a place full of life, excitement, color, motion, a city that knows how to play. Apparently he and his pussycat had seen it all, including two or three topless-bottomless joints in North Beach that they took in after the consul's party.

"This that you live in is beautiful," he says with a sweeping gesture that makes Ms. McElvenny protect her sherry glass with both hands. "*Bella, bella*. Really, it *is* like Umbria. With cypresses it might be Tuscany. But I am curious, Giuseppe. Why do you live in the country? Why not in San Francisco?"

I said we were close enough. When we needed the City, which was no oftener than once a month, we could be there in less than an hour. Mostly we went for nothing more spectacular than to see an exhibition at one of the galleries or museums, or to walk in Golden Gate Park.

"Golden Gate Park?" says Césare to Ms. McElvenny. "Did we see that?"

"I didn't think it would be very high on your must list," says Ms. McElvenny.

The glance he gave her was of such melting warmth and promise and adoration that I expected I might out of pure discretion have to leave the room for a few minutes. "*Avevi ragione,*" Césare said. "You were right."

He tipped his glass to drink, and I saw his eyes fix on something across the room. There were the breadpans I had set out on top of the bookcase wall. Below, overlooked in the rush, were the collected works of Oates, O'Connor, O'Neill, and Katherine Anne. He limped across to inspect them, and after a moment of contemptuous scrutiny limped back.

"I didn't set them out to impress you with the competition," I said. "I set them out because the rain had leaked in and got them wet. Your own are farther along the shelf, nice and dry."

He grunted, regarding me across his raised glass. "So you like it better in the country. What do you do besides put pans under leaks and dig in the mud?"

"*Lavoriamo in giardino,*" I said. "*Leggiamo. Meditiamo. Di quando in quando facciamo una passeggiata.*"

"*Sei filosofo,*" Césare said. He studied me, tasting his drink with pursed lips, with the wincing, pleased, thoughtful expression of a horse drinking ice water. I half expected him to bob his nose in it. "Who are the literary people here? Who is there to talk to?"

I said there were writers up and down the Peninsula, but no literary life as he knew it, no taverns or pubs or sidewalk cafes where they gathered to talk shop and subvert each other's wives and girl friends. Publishers and agents were all in New York. The local writers operated by mail, a fine economical system.

Squinting in amusement, he called the pussycat's attention to me with a jerk of shoulder and eyebrow. "Look at him. He was once a man of the world, he had juice in him, he liked conversation, excitement, people, crowds, pretty women, literary discussion. Now he sits on a cow pad and consults the grass. He pretends to be on the shelf. Look, right over there is proof that on the shelf you can get all wet. You are not fair to your wife. She is an angel, I adore her, she should be out where things go on. She will look at you and grow dull, dull, dull! Listen. I wish you had been with us in San Francisco. Come back with us tonight, I'll stay over, we'll see something besides Golden Gate Park. You don't want to sit in this imitation Umbria and dig in the mud and struggle against uncivilized nature. That is the way to grow old."

It was "Up at a Villa—Down in the City" all over again. *Bang-whang-whang* went his drum, and *tootle-de-tootle* his fife. After I came in, he didn't once look outside again, though what was going on out there was spectacular and even frightening. Until Ruth announced lunch—she had lighted candles on the table, anticipating further trouble from Pacific Gas and Electric—he proselytized me on life in the city square. As if I were a high school student, and not a bright one at that, he literally construed me the word "civilization," and how it came from *civis*, and the word "urbanity," and how it came from *urbs*, and he suggested that, being the man I was, I could not rusticate myself without doing harm to the civilized world.

Since we were on that subject, one on which I have pondered, I reminded him of some other words: "arcadian," which had its own pleasant connotations, and "civility," which might once have characterized the *civis* but which seemed now to be forgotten there. I said if I had my choice I preferred to be suburbane. I said there were enough people around without my going hunting them. I preferred books. And as for pretty girls and *amore*, I quoted him Aldous Huxley to the effect that sooner or later everybody arrived at the point where he could not take yes for an answer. Miss Pussycat, sipping her barely touched sherry and keeping track of things behind her camel eyelashes, just about broke up over that one.

But Césare could not be diverted from his basic subject, women. He brought them to the table with him and developed them role by role: civilizers, comforters, handmaidens, houris, goddesses, objects of worship, homemakers, matriarchs. He made a speech worthy of an oil sheikh. Miss Pussycat watched and was fascinated, and likewise Minnie, stumbling around the table in her wiped-off but still wet shoes, bulging her white nylon as she thrust platters and bowls before people, her eyes on Césare's animated face and her thumb comfortably in the sauce.

But after he had run through his set pieces, Césare rather

tapered off. The plate that Minnie carried away from his place was only half cleaned. He drank his Green Hungarian without comment, almost impatiently. I had the distinct impression that he was more and more astonished that we had asked him down *en famille*. Why were there no other people, why had no one been invited in to meet him? Why, when we obviously were well enough off to choose, did we choose to eat like peasants in a kitchen, without the stimulation of guests? Why had we not understood that a famous novelist appreciated a larger audience? His eye once or twice wandered to Ms. McElvenny's. He yearned to be gone.

At two-thirty she took her cue, stood up from the coffee tray in the living room, and said they ought to leave. It was such a terrible day, bad for driving, and they had appointments. How lovely of us to let her come down and kibitz on our reunion. On departure, Césare embraced Ruth and then me, clapping my shoulders as if he were Anthony and I Enobarbas. When were we next coming to Rome? We must absolutely let him know. We must be pulled out of our retirement and restored to civilization. And for today, and the chance to see us even so briefly, *mille grazie*. And *arrivederci*. And *venga, venga a Roma*.

I held an umbrella over the two of them as we all ran for their car, and got myself wet all over again. As they grimaced and waved from behind their streaming windows and swashing wipers, I stood there like Little Boy Blue's tin soldier, waving them off. When I came in, I was depressed and irritable, and I have been that way ever since.

By working our heads off, we managed to give Césare the dullest two and a half hours he has had since arriving in America. Any lunch in the City, anything from fog cutters and Indonesian *saté* at Trader Vic's to a beer and a Polish sausage down at the Eagle, among the longshoremen by Pier 37, would have pleased him more. It did not occur to him, so busy was he talking up women and civilization, to comment on Ruth's food, which was better than anything he would have got in the City. He was not moved by the Green Hungarian, though it is so much better than the sulphurous Frascati he is used to that he should never know peace in Rome again. Nothing we provided him, including the company, was anything but a bore. His monologues were wasted on an empty house. He pities me, I saw it in his face.

One thing he did do—he impressed Minnie. "Ain't he a sky-rocket, though?" she said as we gathered to clean up. "What is he, Eyetalian?"

"He's a famous Italian novelist," Ruth said tightly. She was squeezing a headache between her brows. "Some people, including himself, have mentioned him for the Nobel Prize."

"Is that so?" Minnie said. "He talks like a writer, don't he? And don't he like the ladies! He never took his eye off his girl friend the whole time. Who's she? She don't sound Eyetalian."

"Ms. McElvenny is a San Francisco girl who will go far, and undoubtedly has," I said.

"Joe," said my weary wife, "you don't know a thing about it."

The hell I don't. I know Césare.

Now here I sit looking out into the dripping live oak, with somber afternoon fading to gloomy dusk outside, the study chilly because I haven't had the ambition to build a fire in my little Norwegian stove, and my spirits as gloomy as the evening and as chilly as the room. God *damn* that Roman cricket with his non-stop monologue and his pussycat and his *civis* and his *urbs*. He has managed to make me feel ten years older than I was yesterday —out of it, self-exiled, and without the courage of my convictions, without the grace to be content with what I chose.

Tonight, unless Ruth's headache alters the plan, I suppose I will have to read another installment of the journals of Joseph Allston, 1954. I am not sure I like Ruth's prescription any better than I like Césare's, and I find that I resent the assumption both of them make, that I have stopped, and am in need of repair. It irritates me to have people blowing out my gas line and testing my sparkplugs and feeling all over me for loose wires. I suppose Ruth thinks of me as that melancholy Half-Dane in need of comforting and mothering; maybe she also thinks of my life, which is also hers, as a sort of in-house soap opera. But mainly she yearns over me and knows things that I should do to become her old nice funny Joe again.

I can't see that Danish episode as an adventure, or a crisis survived, or a serious quest for anything definable. It was just another happening like today's luncheon, something I got into and got out of. And it reminds me too much of how little life changes: how, without dramatic events or high resolves, without tragedy, without even pathos, a reasonably endowed, reasonably well-intentioned man can walk through the world's great kitchen from end to end and arrive at the back door hungry.

2

April 7, Havnegade 13:

What am I after? Lost health? Lost content? Misplaced identity? Am I punishing myself? As a form of suicide, Denmark doesn't seem unpleasant, as a health resort it leaves room for improvement. Or maybe the Bertelsons were right in thinking me an ally. Maybe I do have this notion that the old country is simpler and better. But also, I knew before we came that it would probably be dull. Would I go back to live in the Middle West that I'm always defending against New York snobbery? Not for money. Yet here we are in Denmark, which you couldn't tell from Indiana at fifty paces, and the puritan in me keeps wanting to rub my nose in it, and every now and then shivers with the exquisite pleasure of the hair shirt.

Whether I'm after simplicity or after punishment, observe the irony of the place we've found to live in. The desk I am writing at is Empire, the drawing room I sit in is Louis Quinze. The steel engravings on the walls, all portraits of wigged gentlemen with swords, are either German barons related to the landlady's family, or Kings of France—Louis the Bald and Charles the Fat or vice versa—also related but by the sinister route. They go with the apartment, rented ancestors.

The whole situation is ridiculous. We have always been private people, but here we are sharing the apartment of an indigent countess, and I didn't even put up a fight. One thing, it's convenient: you can walk to any part of the old city in ten minutes. Another, it's more attractive, by a factor of ten, than anything else we looked at. Another, it's on the water—Havnegade means Harbor Street—and interesting things go on outside our windows. Three stories below, there is the street, then a cobbled quay, then a narrow dead-end canal, then a long warehouse island, then the main canal linking the free port with the south harbor. Seagoing ships whistle for the Knippelsbro, and as the bridge yawns open and a ship slides through, bicycles and cars back up both sides. The ship's funnels move with dignity behind a frieze of chimney pots and disappear beyond the Exchange building, above which twists up the green dragon's-tail spire that the Danes looted from the Swedes in some forgotten war.

The cobbles shine in the wet like pewter, the moving cars shine, the slickered backs of pedestrians and bicyclists shine. Girls in belted raincoats pedal along with their rain-stung faces turned sideward, and boys on bicycles shoot the traffic as if they were canoeists in a rapid.

Nevertheless, we must have been still doped with Dramamine to move in here. The countess retains the front studio-bedroom, we take the drawing room, dining room, and back bedroom. We share the kitchen and the one bath. At my time of life, bathroom lines! Hurry up, Countess, I'm in extremis. And one telephone for the two of us, in her room, naturally.

Are we sorry for her because her husband ran out on her? Do we pity a woman who once had everything and now has to share the little she has left with strangers? Maybe. Though she made her proposition with style. You'd have thought she was suggesting a fascinating social experiment instead of making the best of her humiliation.

Apart from the drawing room, the place is not even well furnished. The kitchen and bathroom primitive by American standards, the bedroom furnished in Early Goodwill. Bed I slept in last night a backbreaker, hollowed out by somebody with a most steatopygous behind. If it was once the bed of the countess' husband, then he must be a man of very peculiar proportions.

There will be more than backaches, I tell Ruth, but she thinks it will work. She and the countess liked each other on sight. "*Isn't* she lovely!" the countess said to me when Ruth was looking out the window with the agent. "I love people to look like that!" She says we will get along fine because we will be nice against one another. She will be nice against us, and she knows we will be nice against her. Well, Barkis is willin'. I have seen harder people to be nice against. The agent told us she was once one of the great beauties of Denmark, and so far as I can see, she still is, at forty or so. A husband who would run away from that should have his head carefully examined. But I don't need a share of her troubles, which seem considerable and a little mysterious, and neither do I want every move we make to be complicated by the feeling that she must be asked along. Nor do I want her around the apartment all the time. I feel too lousy, and she doesn't have a very good silencer.

Right now she and Ruth are out getting acquainted with the neighborhood greengrocers and bakers and butchers. I ducked, partly because I'm not feeling too well but also because I'm holding back from getting too chummy. Like this morning, when I went out to get tickets for Friday night's opera. What do I do? I buy three. What does the countess do? After a moment of surprise, almost of consternation, she accepts with pleasure. I have to learn to keep impulses like that under control.

Now here they come down the quay under their umbrellas, each with a bulging string shopping bag. Jabber jabber jabber. A woman's tongue, said the first American writer of any consequence, is the only edged tool that grows keener with constant use. Their wet umbrellas lean together, their bags bump, they are so blinded by talk that they stumble on the paving stones. For Ruth's sake I'm glad. I made no preparations for Denmark; I intend to look up no writers or publishers, even for social reasons. She can't have any great expectation of fun. A friend will help.

Ruth is small, the countess five nine or ten, with a vivid face and fine clear skin. She would be statuesque except that she is so animated. An almost feverish eagerness possesses her in conversation, she lights up even before you say anything. Everything is so funny, or so wonderful, or so nice. Maybe the strain of speaking English, in which she is fluent but not always correct, keeps her hyped up. Whatever it is, she couldn't be more cordial if we had just come ashore on the desert island from which she had been sending up hopeless smoke signals for ten years.

I have a good look at her from up here. She wears a kerchief on her head, but her heavy, smooth, dull gold hair is uncovered in front and gathered behind in a bun that looks as if it might weigh a kilo. Something in the way she moves. Is it breeding, or do they train them? American women who have what is called "bearing" look as if they'd learned it in model school and need a mirror for its constant reassurance. This one, in her tweed suit and sensible walking shoes and utilitarian raincoat, throws it away and still has it.

But sometimes as earthy as the stableman's daughter, and sometimes she mocks herself. When the agent mentioned the *havnefart*, the harbor tour that periodically comes up the canal, the English implications of the word struck her and she giggled. And when we were sitting talking, later, she noticed Ruth's shoes and cried out, "Oh, those tiny American feet!" and in frank envy stuck out her own number eights for contrast. She has a smile that would melt glass.

I watch them lean from the quay to inspect the plucked chickens held up by the man in the produce boat from Skagen moored at the dead end of the canal. They take one, then a slab of cheese, then six eggs that the Skagen man wraps individually in newspaper. The countess opens her purse. Ruth will not let her pay. Good.

Rain dimples the still canal. The cobbles shine, the deck of the Skagen boat is dark wet. Up and down it from bow to stern and back again runs a splendid black poodle, intensely interested in the life four feet from him on the quay. A sign hung from the rail amidships says *Hunden Bider*—the dog bites. Ruth, of course, animal lover and non-reader of Danish, reaches a hand across to pat him and is confronted by a raging mouthful of fangs. Hurt, she falls back, the countess volubly explaining. Really she is a handsome woman, and a true Dane: her cheeks glow in the rain like shined apples. They pass out of sight below me. In three minutes they will be at the door.

But I will bet that shortly we will have tea and then a drink together. Even money they will take that chicken into the kitchen and make a shared dinner of it. It's too wet and raw to go out, and can you see us letting her take her tray into her room, while we revel in the dining room over a *poulet rôti* and a bottle of Niersteiner *natur?* And tomorrow, in spite of my feeble efforts not to fraternize too much, this woman who spent her youth adorning royal balls and being ogled in theater boxes will share the second-row balcony with her new American friends, while thousands cheer.

I am just enough of an American democrat to get a kick out of the idea. Who dat tall extinguished-lookin' genman wid de testicle on his right eye, urinatin' up an down de aisle wid de countess?

Later:

As a prophet, I bat a thousand. We've had a gay dinner. The countess is good company, a giggler, full of stories, and when she dresses up in something besides her tweed suit she could be a princess in a fairy tale by the brothers Grimm. She is related to every castle in Denmark and most of those in Sweden and North Germany. Her family's estate is on Lolland, but she has spent a lot of time at Waldemarslot on the little island of Taasinge, and at a relative's *herregaard* on Fyn, near Odense. She used to see a lot of the royal family because her father was *Hofjaegermester*, master of the hunt, and an important business of his Lolland castle was growing hares, pheasants, grouse, chukars, and deer for the King's fall hunting parties. Another relative is Karen Blixen, who writes under the name of Isak Dinesen and who is the one person in Denmark I would like, out of sheer admiration, to meet. The countess says she will arrange it. Fraternizing like mad, we plan a lot of expeditions together as soon as our Rover arrives from England. See a lot of castles.

I gather that this leftover aristocracy has about lost its function and has been losing its lands for decades. They all marry their cousins for lack of anybody else suitable. Men mainly drunks, the countess suggests, and the women all witches. She herself has powers. Several times she has had second sight. She has a gift for quieting unruly or maddened horses, and once, while visiting relatives near Kassel, in Germany, she cured a boy of warts.

I learn from her how to *skaal* the lady on my left; until she has been *skaal'*ed she is not supposed to touch her wine. Look the lady deep in the eyes, hold the glass at the third vest button, raise it and drink, still holding her eyes, and then, still holding them, lower to the third vest button. It is an astonishingly intimate ritual. It taught me that I practically never look anybody that steadily in the eyes, especially a good-looking, amused, and amusing woman.

Coincidence department: Ruth mentioned that my mother came from Denmark. Oh, from where? asked the countess. I said some village named Bregninge. *Bregninge?* She said. Bregninge on Lolland? Oh, how funny! If it is that Bregninge, it is on our estate, where I grew up. Great, I said. That's another expedition for us when the car comes. Want to go back to Lolland?

But a cloud has come over our dinner party. The countess does not get along with her brother, hasn't seen him or written to him in years. It agitates her, obviously, even to talk about him. On the other hand his wife, who is Swedish and sad, is very nice. And the countess' grandmother is still alive, nearly a hundred years old. What if she wrote to Manon, her brother Eigil's wife, to see if she will invite us for luncheon or tea, so that the countess can see her grandmother and show us the castle, without running into her brother? We could stay at the little inn in Bregninge, on the shore.

Fine, sure. But notice one thing. The countess has a hundred stories, but none about herself, and she mentions every relative including some like her brother Eigil whom she won't speak to, but never her husband. And why haven't any of these rich castle-dwellers rescued her? Why does she have to take in lodgers?

People's private lives strike me as none of my business, and I have never developed the habit of fishing for them. I wait for the countess to volunteer something about her personal problems, but

75

so far she has not. Doesn't she trust us, after we have gone out of our way to be nice against her?

April 10? 11?:

This journal is already getting spasmodic, though it's the only halfway disciplined thing I do. Continue to feel lousy. Maybe, as Ruth keeps saying, I ought to take my ekg's down to some Danish doctor to see if the heart infection is really gone, as they assured me in New York it was. Every now and then she looks at me hard and asks me if I'm all right, and the mirror tells me I have a color like a two-week corpse.

Nevertheless I rather enjoy the routines we are developing and the sense of being totally out of touch with everything known. Up about seven (headache, backache), pick the milk and the countess' yoghurt off the back stairs, put the ice sign in the kitchen window, shave, and go out the front door, noisily enough so that the countess will hear me and get her clear shot at the bathroom.

The iron courtyard gates are already open. In the street the air damp and chilly. For a wonder not raining this morning—dim dawn under the clouds. Up the quay the Bornholm boat is unloading. Yawning people, bicycles, suitcases. At the corner, plasterers are mixing mortar on a square of plywood. Soon the apprentice will be sent for the first round of Tuborg *grøn* or Carlsberg *Hof*. During the day he will go out seven or eight times. In the U.S.A. this would be called drinking on the job.

At the bakery I take a number and stand in line with maids and housewives for brioches and *snegle*. Then back, carrying the warm fragrant sack through the thinning Bornholm crowd. The sun has burrowed into the overcast after one look at Denmark. A freighter comes up the canal, the Knippelsbro is rising, bicycles on the Amager side back up ten abreast.

New and fresh. Maybe living on the East River would be a little like this, but there wouldn't be the smell of warm baked goods and the scaled sheen of cobbles, and Gristede's would be no substitute for the clean little one-purpose Danish shops, each with its medieval symbol for a sign—bull's head for butcher, pretzel for baker, and so on.

We breakfast at the Empire desk by the front windows. When I laid the *snegle* down this morning and went into the kitchen to put the coffee on, I found the countess in her tweed suit—no robe-and-slippers sloppiness for her, even at seven-thirty—spooning brown sugar onto a bowl of yoghurt. Her back was toward me; somehow it looked depressed. I have hardly seen her since the night of the opera. That was Friday, this is Monday.

"*Har De sovet godt?*" I said.

She whirled, her face sharp and startled. Then her thousand-candlepower smile came on and lit up the gloomy kitchen. "You sounded so Danish!"

"The one-word Dane," I said. "*Et eneste ord.*"

"You see!" Since our first meeting she has taken the position that I am a linguistic prodigy and learn Danish with miraculous speed. (Danes in general are resigned to the fact that *nobody* can learn it except Danes.) She forgets that I heard it some in childhood, and she doesn't know that in college I was made to study Anglo-Saxon, which is curiously close in some ways. Also, when I learn a word I don't hide it under any bushel. "*Et eneste!*" she said in admiration. "Already you are saying a thing like that which some would never learn."

Our eyes splintered against each other, or against some common unspoken embarrassment, and she edged by me, brilliantly smiling, with her tray. Almost persuasive, the smile glowed back down the hall at me through the closing crack of her door. I saw it as a shield turned to cover a retreat.

A few days ago I was worried that we'd have her in our hair more than we wanted to. Now I wonder if we're to see her only in these strained, disappearing moments, like Emily Dickinson fleeing the sound of the door knocker.

What has the woman done? Why, in this city where she has been known and conspicuous all her life, did not one soul speak to Astrid Wredel-Krarup in the theater the other night? She ex-

77

pected it, we expected it. I had some idiotic notion of a brilliant procession of old friends and acquaintances. I was braced for introductions. I·suppose it was some such consideration that led us to dress up beyond the seats I'd been able to get—the ladies in long dresses, me in black tie. Moreover, the seats in the front row. ahead of us were unoccupied. We were as conspicuous as if we had been in a box.

Nothing. Not a visitor, not a flutter of fingers, not a smile. Eyes, yes. Heads leaning to whisper, yes. We were watched in the ten minutes we sat there before the lights went down. We were watched at intermission; and none of us wanted to get up and circulate. We were watched as we edged our way out with the crowd at the end, and I distinctly saw one couple note us and put people between us so that we wouldn't meet at the doors.

The opera was that Honegger thing, *Joan of Arc at the Stake*, in which the female lead neither says nor sings a word, just stands tied to a post in the middle of the stage, waiting for the dawn and the fire. It opened with an ominous line: *En hund hyler i natten* —a dog howls in the night—and because I was uneasy about the chill we seemed to have created, and wanted to kid things back to normal, I leaned toward the countess and whispered, "Hey, I understood that!"

In the dusk her eyes were large and brilliant. It was almost like *skaal*'ing the lady on your left. But she was not smiling. She gave the back of my hand a little pat. "You understand everything," she said.

But the fact was, I never understood another mumbling word. I didn't understand the woman beside me, or the people I caught trying not to be seen looking our way when the lights came up, any more than I understood what was going on on stage, where strange monsters out of some bestiary crept out of the woods and frolicked or mourned around Joan at her stake.

Neither of the ladies wanted to go to the D'Angleterre for a bite and a drink after the show. We walked home, talking more animatedly than we felt about the opera, and when we were back at the apartment the countess very soon said her thanks and good night and shut her door. For quite a while Ruth and I lay awake wondering what we had witnessed. Ruth had the impression that *we* had been stared at with hostility, simply because of the woman we were with. Mystery. The Danes are notably uncensorious, yet here is a woman whom all of Copenhagen cuts dead. We recollect that since we moved in with her nobody has rung her doorbell.

April 13:
Our Rover is on the free port dock. I spent the day persuading six thousand three hundred and eighteen petty bureaucrats that I don't intend to sell it in the black market but will guarantee to export it to the United States when we leave Denmark. And what is your business in Denmark, Mr. Allston? Tourist? Yes. And how long will you stay? Three or four *months?* Mmmm. The question stuck out of them in embossed letters: *why?* I told one particularly nosy gentleman that I was writing a book about Danish democracy, and that corked him.

April 17:
Two days lost to a raging migraine. I find myself thinking about the office. Homesick, the forsaken fire horse. This suspended life, this waiting for decent weather or for me to feel better, gets more tedious than I would have believed. A visit to one of the local specialized medics (a pleasant man, I must say, and a cultivated one, not just a mechanic who has studied medical Latin) assures me that my ekg is indeed back to normal. Can't lay any blame on the ticker. So I develop a migraine. Cunning of me.

The countess is our only drama. For a couple of days we didn't catch more than glimpses of her, because she had got a job doing some interior decorating and supervising the purchase of furniture and pictures for a French Embassy couple named La Derrière. She came out of her sober mood enough to giggle over that, and kept referring to them as Mrs. and Mrs. Behind. But mostly, when she hasn't been out, she has been shut up in her studio, presumably sketching and working. It seems unnatural and unfriendly to keep so separate. We wonder if she is being scrupulous about intruding on us, or if she is avoiding us because of that night at the theater.

This morning as we were having breakfast by the windows we heard her go down the hall to the kitchen and looked at each other. Shouldn't we ask her to join us? But I had barely pushed back my chair when her steps returned, positive and fast, and her door clicked shut. Such is our human complexity, we felt snubbed, at least I did. In her room the radio came on with its gobbledegook Danish news, most of which these days is about Senator McCarthy, a constant rebuke to our innocent assumption of American prestige in the world.

After lunch Ruth drove us (I was over the migraine, but feeling pale) up to Dyrehaven to try out the Rover. Though the sun was out, it was chilly. No leaves yet, and no flowers except some tulips. I begin to understand the disbelief of Danish bureaucrats when I tell them we came of our own free will to live in this country for several months.

We had come back and were having a cup of tea to warm up when the doorbell rang. Surprised looks, raised eyebrows. Thinking the countess must be out, I answered. There stood an elegant gentleman with his gray Homburg in one hand and his gloves in another. His head was baldish, but well brushed: the hat had creased the smooth fair hair above his ears. He had striking blue eyes, and the handsome regular features I will always associate with the Arrow Collar men of my youth. And he had a well-repaired but unmistakable harelip.

For a second I thought he must be some close relative of the countess', her brother maybe, and then I *knew* who he was. But he didn't know who I was. He was not prepared to see me. His eyes got hard, and popped a little, and he said something abrupt in Danish.

"Excuse me," I said. "Do you speak English?"

He did, perfectly, with a slight nasal cleft-palate whine. "Isn't this the apartment of the Grevinde Wredel-Krarup?"

"Yes," I said. "My wife and I share it. I'm not sure the countess is in."

80

But she was in. Her door opened and she stood in it, stiff and smiling. Her visitor made a return smile. "*God dag*, Astrid."

"*God dag*, Erik." Automatic as a traffic light, her smile turned on me. I doubt that she was aware of me as a person, she simply meant that traffic should move on. I stepped back, she opened her door wider, the visitor went in, the door closed, and I shut the outside door and returned to Ruth and my cooling tea.

She made her mouth soundlessly round. "Who?"

Just as soundlessly, I said, "Her husband."

"Oh-oh." We sat on, uncomfortable because their voices were audible through the double doors that connected her studio with the drawing room. After only three or four minutes Ruth said, "We'd better take a walk."

I said, "Ruthie, I'm pooped, I don't *need* a walk," but we *took* a walk, up to the Nyhavn and back around through Kongens Nytorv. There we had a beer and a *reje* sandwich in a sidewalk cafe where only the infrared reflectors in the canopy kept us from freezing to death. When we judged it was safe, we shuddered back home. No voices. But we had hardly got our coats off and highballs in our hands when there was a tap on the connecting door, and the countess' bright voice said, "Are you busy? May I come in?"

"I remember that evening," Ruth said. Her hand went slowly and regularly down Catarrh from his nose to the end of his tail. Without opening his eyes he arched against the petting. A purr like a snore broke out of him and ended in a glottal stop. "It was when we first began to find out something about her."

"Yes," I said. "But now that we know, don't you find all this a little long-winded?"

"Oh no, no, no! It brings it all back. It's as if it were happening to somebody else."

"I sometimes get the feeling my whole life happened to somebody else."

Ruth said, "I think you only get that feeling because you don't like to remember. You put things away and never look at them again. I want to hear every word of this."

"You don't expect me to read through the whole thing like some schoolmaster doing his annual rereading of Dickens?"

"I thought that's what we were going to do."

Rain like sand pattered at the window. I heard the clogged downspout by the door overflowing a heavy stream onto the bricks. I would have to get the leaves out of that before the next rain. "You want your pound of flesh," I said.

"Oh, Joe!"

"I told you, this isn't going to give either of us much pleasure."

"I didn't think that was the purpose."

"No?" I said. "What *was* the purpose?" But after a second or two in which we looked at each other with that baffled, stubborn expression that people who have been a long time married often wear when they are reading each other's minds, I started reading again. My problem was the opposite of what I said it was. In our relationship with Astrid Wredel-Krarup, and in the recollections that the diary brought back, I wasn't quite spectator enough.

She sat down but wouldn't take a drink. She was at once more statuesque and more nervous than usual. She couldn't keep her hands still. Finally, with a little laugh, she took one in the other and stopped its jittering, and holding them so, manacling herself, she lifted her shoulders and said, "You saw my husband."

"I didn't know," I said. "I thought he might be."

"I have not seen him since many months. He has not lived here since the day the war ended. Now he asks to come back."

After a cautious interval, Ruth said, "And what do you think?"

She provoked a surprisingly fierce response. "*Think?* In such matters I do not *think*. I do not live in my head. I live down here." She slapped her hand melodramatically against her belt, or below it. "Ever, all my life. I feel better than most people think."

I smiled, Ruth frowned, the countess had no idea what she had said.

"You don't *feel* you want him back," Ruth said.

The countess bent her head, heavy with smooth hair, and pondered. Then she raised her face, made an apologetic smile, and said, "I am feeling many things at once. Excuse me, please. I know I should not bring this to you, it is nothing of yours. But I could not—sit in there any longer."

Ruth's pleasant opaque look said to me that I'd better get out and let the women deal with this, but the countess read the look as clearly as I did. She reached a hand as if to hold me in my chair. "No, please." We sat uncomfortably, liking her, sympathetic with her in her troubles, as humanly curious as the next couple, and not quite sure she could be trusted. Ruth was murmuring that of course she should come to us, what were friends for?

"You know about him, of course," the countess said.

She drew a blank. "You mean that he's left you?" Ruth said.

"Oh, that was only the finish! Someone must have told you that he was a quisling."

If anybody had told us that, it would have explained a great deal, but who would have? She was the only person in Copenhagen we knew.

"At the opera, you could not help seeing," the countess said. "It was an embarrassing for you, I am sorry. I should not have tried. But I thought, maybe because I was with *you*. And I had not been out like that, to the theater, since before the war ended."

I figured on my mental fingers. "Really? That's nine years."

"Yes." A shrug. "The cinema only, where it is dark and no one has a face." Not quite intending to, I caught her eye. It was clear, steady, and serious. She had a look as patient as sculpture. Up till then I had never seen her unprotected by the smile and the excessive animation. But, my God, nine *years*.

"I wish you to know," she said, sitting straight in the gilded French chair. "During the Occupation, German officers came here—relatives, cousins of some degree. I suppose they thought, because of Erik? I don't know. Possibly they were bored and lonely in a country where they were hated and avoided. Perhaps their mothers had told them to call, or being gentlemen, they thought they understood what was correct. They understood nothing. I said to them, 'I am a Dane, I love my country. Put on other clothes and I will receive you for your family's sake, but in that uniform I will not let you in.'"

"But your husband did let them in."

"Not here. I did never know what he did. They accused him of all things—collaborating, giving informations, spying. Once something made me think Goering had bought him."

"Goering?" I said. "Why? How?"

"Because he tried to buy *me*. In Kassel, where we have relatives. We are all related, there is some Schimmelman and Knuth in all of us a generation or two back. I had to go to Germany for an operation on my knee. He came to my hospital room. I never asked him to sit down, he understood that much, he was standing the whole time. It was not spying he wanted, only to be accepted. That swine. If more of us would act like Erik, he said, and say in public that the Germans were behaving very well. It was the first time I was sure that Erik had been what at home they were saying he was. I was furious. I planned to get a gun and murder that fat Goering if he came to me again."

She stopped, halted, I suppose, by the skepticism in my face. "Oh, I did," she said. "I got the gun. I have it still. But he never came back. Only that once, to tell me how generous the Germans were prepared to be if we would accept them. They didn't want to have to be harsh. You have heard how on the first day of the invasion they ran down the flag before the royal palace, and the King with his own hands ran it up again. They left it there, it flew throughout the war. They wanted our good will. Erik's they had. He hated the socialist Danish government that squeezed the landed families, and he was educated in Germany. He was always bitter, and he caught the Nazi disease."

With two fingers she touched her upper lip. "You saw that he . . ."

"Yes."

"When he was a little boy his mother would never kiss him

84

She would not let him walk beside her. He must come behind as if he did not belong to her. She hated it that he was marked."

"Ugh," Ruth said. "No wonder he was bitter."

"But that wouldn't necessarily make him pro-German," I said.

"Ah, if I understood why! Most of us hated the Germans, the longer the war went on the more we hated them. We were ashamed that the Danes didn't fight, as the Norwegians did. Later, when the underground was organized, there were explosions, and sabotage, and shootings, and we were glad. Many people tried to get away to Sweden in small boats, or across the ice one winter when the Øresund froze. Some were caught and shot. People like Erik were blamed. I have been spitted on, can you believe that? Twice the partisans tried to kill Erik. The second time, only a day or two before the war finally ended, they shot him down on the steps of the D'Angleterre. Only the police who were there saved his life. That was the last day I had a husband. First he went to the hospital and then he went to prison. Two years."

She pronounced the terminal s the way my mother used to, as if its sound were really s, not z—a sharp, hissing, unpleasant sound. Two yearss. Trying to imagine what her life had been during that time, I was thinking that two years from the end of the war brought us only to 1947. What about the other seven years since the German army broke up along the Schleswig-Holstein border? But the countess was still pouring.

"They took Erik's estate on Falster and even my place at Hornbaek, that was not his but mine. They left me only this apartment and my little cottage at Ellebacken. I did not like it that my husband was a quisling, but he was my husband, what should I do? I sold my silver, my dishings, many pictures, furnitures, all things, to pay his fine. From prison he wrote me pitiful letters, Get me out, save me. I went over and over to government offices. Some people told me I should be in prison too. I went to relatives who might have influence, they didn't dare do anything. I went to the King, I said we would leave the country. But those in power did not want Erik out of the country. They wanted him where his

85

punishment would be plain. When they had insisted on that long enough, they let him go."

She seemed to have finished. "Then did he come back?" Ruth prompted.

Sidelong flash of eyes. "I thought he would not be able to find work. I said I would support us with my designs. While he was in prison I lived by making designs for prints and wallpaper for Illums Bolighus—I had a friend there who would not tell who made them. But, you know, they released Erik and he came here for his clothes and went straight away with that woman he met during the war."

Ruth made a nasal sound of female indignation and solidarity. As for me, I was uncomfortable. It always embarrasses me to have people confess or pour out their troubles. I never know what to say. I always feel a little like the man who fixed cats for a living, and who was asked why he filled his shopwindow with clocks. What would *you* put in the window? I left it empty.

"So!" the countess said. "Now. Now he would come back. Something has happened with his woman, I don't know—she has gone to someone else, or he has tired of her. He says it is I who have been his wife all along. He was not pleased that I did not ask him to move straight in. How could I, even if I wanted to? You are here."

"But my goodness!" Ruth said. "If you'd like us to make room, you only have to . . ."

"Oh no, no, no, no. I would not have him. He is such a child. He shouted, you must have heard. He says I am not loyal, I have no sympathy for his suffering."

"We didn't hear anything," Ruth said. "We were out for a walk."

Just then I thought of something to put in the window. "Would you like that drink now?"

Brilliant suggestion. The countess turned on her smile and it stayed on. Her angry flush faded away. Her humiliating story told, she was back to her old gaiety and animation. She reminds me in some ways of Ginger Gilbert, a girl I used to know in the begin-

86

ning of the twenties, a game one, sassy, the original peppy date. If I should say, "Handsprings, anyone?" I have the feeling she would cartwheel around the room. That aspect of her goes oddly with the statuesque bearing and the unmistakable stigmata of breeding.

"Yes!" she said. "Pleass! A strong one!"

When I brought the three glasses in from the kitchen, she and Ruth were just parting from a sisterly hug. I handed the countess her drink. "Vaer saa god."

"Tak!"

She took the glass with her left hand, and with an impulsive, whole-bodied gesture she leaned against me and squeezed her right arm around my waist. She surprised me.

"You are both so good!" she cried. "Oh, I am so glad you came here! It is so lovely to have friends!"

To keep the tableau from getting too corny I assumed a most rigtig stance, with the glass at the third vest button, and skaal'ed her, gazing deep, deep into her peerless eyes.

3

I closed the notebook and laid it aside and went to the closet for my pajamas. Ruth did not protest. She lay petting Catarrh, watching his hair lift with static. I was buttoning the pajama coat when she said, "It's funny, you keep speaking of her as 'the countess.'"

"That's what she was. I'm a plain American boy, I don't go around calling the nobility by their first names. I'm like Minnie. Their status is what impresses me, not their names. That Eyetalian. The countess."

"I called her by her first name after the first day or so."

"Well, I didn't, after two or three months. Ever. She called me Mr. Allston and I gave her back the full business. When I tried Danish, I didn't *Du* her, I *De*-ed her."

"Yes." She handed me the limp cat. "Here, Catarrh had better go out. Put him out the front so he can get to the flower bed without getting wet."

I carried him to the front door and set him out in the entry surrounded by the drip and splash of rain. He stood with his back humped and then made a bolt to get back in, but I blocked him with my foot. "Go on and do your business," I said, "and when you're done, come in the cat door even if you do have to wet your feet. Don't stand around the bedroom door yowling."

He looked up at me as if he hated my guts. His eyes were as blue as Erik Wredel-Krarup's, and his lip was cleft. I shut the door on him.

In the bedroom Ruth had turned off the bed light and settled down. I snapped off the reading lamp by the chair and stood in the dark listening to the uninterrupted rain. Then I crawled into bed and put my arm around Ruth, soft and familiar, and without turning she laid her hand on my hand and squeezed. "Thanks, darling."

"*Hvorfor?*" I said, bemused by what we have been remembering, and oddly dim in the sight from looking down some roads not taken.

There is a feeling part of us that does not grow old at all. If we could peel off the callus, and wanted to, there we would be, untouched by time, unwithered, vulnerable, afflicted and volatile and blind to consequence, a set of twitches as beyond control as an adolescent's erections. It is this feeling creature that Ruth keeps wistfully trying to expose in me. To have me admit to yearnings and anguishes, even if they threatened her, would allow her to forgive and pity me, and since she has trouble getting me to hold still for outward affection, forgiveness and pity are not unimportant. If she can do that small thing, after years of failing to make me over into what she wishes I were, she can devote herself unselfishly to me without fear that she is pounding sand down a rathole. Catching me with my feelings showing would give her power over me as surely as if she had collected my nail parings and tufts of my hair.

Is this unjust? Obviously. In protecting myself against circumstances, or against myself, I pretend to protect myself against her.

What I felt while reading that diary, and what I somehow can't tell her or talk about with her, is how much has been lost, how much is changed, since 1954. I really *am* getting old. It comes as a shock to realize that I am just killing time till time gets around to killing me. It is not arthritis and the other ailments. Ben exaggerates those. It is just the general comprehension that nothing is building, everything is running down, there are no more chances for improvement. One of these days the pump will quit, or the sugar in the gas tank will kill the engine in a puff of smelly smoke, or the pipes will burst, or the long-undernourished brain will begin to show signs of its starvation.

I don't suppose Ruth would bear my senility any more happily than my death, and I certainly don't wish for her the job I have seen some wives saddled with, the care of a shuffling invalid, a vegetable whose time has come, whose tie is always smeared and whose zipper is always unzipped and who is always mistaking the PG&E man, come to read the meter, for a son who died years ago, or a brother who has been in his grave for forty years. What the countess has come to, actually. The trouble is that the feelings do not die. I remember Ruth when we brought her and her baby home from the hospital, her fine bones, her small wracked healing body, the tightness of her arms around my neck in the bed made suddenly roomier by the eviction of that intruder between us. And I remember my gurgling son, fat and broad-faced, happy despite a full diaper, and how he laughed and reached out his hands when I played at knocking him over with a pillow. I remember too much. I remember a futile life. Yet if I turn away from it and die, Ruth loses her lifework all at once. If I only lose my buttons, she can go on managing me, sadly but with the satisfaction of love, duty, and selflessness. It is something women get for being durable. I don't envy them.

I have put away a bottle of pills, as who hasn't, but nobody can guarantee that when the time comes he will have the wit to take them, or even remember where he hid them. Ben Alexander, with his pacemaker, has an advantage that he brags of. He has only to disconnect a wire, or so he says. He can't be betrayed by senility and forgetfulness, as I can, for when life is on a jack like a telephone there is a good chance that accident will sooner or later disconnect it even if forethought fails to. The end is the same: not even a dial tone.

I suppose I had no real chance, once I had let her know that the journal existed, of not reading it to Ruth, or at least letting her read it. She is an exorcist at heart. She believes in cleansings and purifications, and she has a dangerous theory of complete honesty in marriage. When we had been married no more than twelve hours, she told me she had made a vow never to go to sleep on a quarrel. It must be settled before we closed our eyes. Since my impulse is to close my eyes on the quarrel and sleep it off, our systems have not always meshed. What often happens is that I back down in order to avoid all that soul searching that she likes, thereby committing some dishonesties she is unaware of. I doubt that she could ever believe that a man who resists her management and does not tell her all he knows can really love her as she wants to be loved and as I am sure she loves me. Yet I do. She is the woman I share the world with, and I can imagine wanting to share it with no one else.

I could hand her these notebooks and tell her to read them herself, but then I refuse the marital communion her soul craves. If I burn the things and declare that I will not be henpecked into spilling guts I no longer acknowledge, then I burn into her a conviction that certain aspects of the Danish episode were more important than in fact they were—that they left great scars on my soul. They didn't. Denmark was only one of those queer little adventures that the life-tourist runs into—a circus where you saw a man crawl through a ten-inch pipe, a side show where the fat lady's stuffing came out, a trapeze act where the acrobat flinched and refused a jump he knew would kill him.

No, Denmark did no more than thicken the callus. It was something I survived. Left to myself, I would deal with it (I tell myself) as Catarrh deals with his leavings in the flower bed.

THREE

1

Ruth strikes a lot of people as a cute lively little lady, bright, cultivated, interested in people, a good listener and a chatterbox of a
talker. Some of them overlook the Presbyterian missionary in her,
some of them fail to see the Salvation Army lass, most of them
have never seen the shrew. They all know the warmth and sympathy she feels for all sorts of human misfortune or cussedness,
but even Ben Alexander, until he had acted as her doctor for a
couple of years, failed to comprehend the anxious tension that
both holds her together and threatens to warp her out of shape.
And nobody but me knows the little girl of about six who is
buried in her, as ineradicable as the uneasy adolescent who is
buried in me. Tell me a story, Daddy. Tell about when you were a
teenager of fifty. Tell about Denmark, where you were so sad.

She was already in bed, without a book, waiting, when I came
into the bedroom after turning down the thermostats and
switching off the lights. The storm had blown itself out in the afternoon, but the clogged downspout was still dripping through
whatever clogged it, and big regular drops *thunked* against the
turned tin at the bottom. She had me go out and stuff a wash-
cloth into the spout to kill the noise, and when I came in she was
all business. "Well," she said. "Where were we?"

A good question.

I got into the chair and opened up the second notebook and
found where we had left off the night before. "I told you I'm a
bum diarist," I said. "There's nothing here for ten pages but quotations from the wise men."

"Read them. Isn't it important to know what you were thinking
about?"

"Is it? It looks pretty gloomy from here."

"Still."

"All right. Here's Thucydides: 'Having done what men could, they suffered what men must.' "

She said doubtfully, "I guess I don't . . ."

"Having lived as long as they could, they died. Having fought as long as they could, they were killed. We should all have it engraved on our tombstones. Maybe you'll like this one better. This is from Marcus Aurelius:

> "And as for thy life, consider what it is; a wind; not one constant wind neither, but every moment of an hour let out, and sucked in again. . . . And also what it is to die, and how if a man shall consider this by itself alone, to die, and separate from it in his mind all those things which with it usually represent themselves unto us, he can conceive it no otherwise, than as a work of nature, and he that fears any work of nature is a very child. . . . What art thou, that better and divine part excepted, but as Epictetus said well, a wretched soul, appointed to carry a carcass up and down?"

I flipped the page and glanced up. Ruth was staring at me, frowning. "Why would you write down something as morbid as that?"

"What's morbid about it?" I said. "It isn't very cheerful, maybe, but it's wisdom. I suppose it struck me because I was a little tired of carrying the carcass up and down."

She continued to stare at me for what seemed a long time—four or five heartbeats, I suppose. Then she folded back the covers and jumped out of bed and wrapped her arms around my head, hugging my face into her breasts.

"Why, Ruthie," I said when she eased up and let me breathe.

"I didn't know you were that . . . I thought you were just tired out!"

"Well, I survived." I pulled her down in my lap and we had a little cuddle. The cheek I kissed was wet. "Oh, now, come on," I said.

"You ought to *tell* me more!"

"I wonder. Look what even a hint does to you."

"But when I think of the *difference* it might have made!"

"Yes," I said. "It might have made you so anxious about me

you'd have driven me off the Knippelsbro. Now why don't you hop back into bed before you get cold." The fact was, I had pulled her down on me when I was kinked, and my knee was twisted and my hip ready to pop out of joint. If she had been sorry for me another minute she'd have broken me up like a Tinker Toy.

Ah, me, the complexity of being married to a woman you dearly love and automatically resist. I inevitably evade her management. I even evade her sympathy and affection, or meet them with my guard up. Martial is the anagram for marital. The grapple is everything, and I don't mean the sex grapple that so obsesses the seventies. That is only the signature for something much more complicated.

"All right, that's better," I said when she was back under the covers. "Ready for more gloomy wisdom?"

"I guess."

"Here's something from Kazantzakis: 'When a Greek travels through Greece, his journey becomes converted . . . into a laborious search to find his duty.' "

"That's you, for sure."

"Duty? Me? I follow pleasures and grails and lines of least resistance."

"Like fun. I never saw anybody so set on finding his duty as you. You're like somebody hunting for the key to his house that he's hidden somewhere, when he comes home at night and can't get in."

"All right, if you say so. I never deny what I wish was true. So here's another one from Kazantzakis: 'Never return to success; return to failure.' And still another one: 'Cursed be he whose thirst is quenched.' "

"I like those a lot better than Marcus Aurelius," Ruth said. "They're more like you, for one thing."

"Never disparage Marcus Aurelius," I said. "Did you know he was one of the earliest environmentalists? You could quote him to the Sierra Club. Here he says, 'That which is not good for the beehive cannot be good for the bee,' and under that, in Allston's crabbed hand, is written, 'The world suffers from an increment of excrement,' which you might render into the vernacular as 'The world is full of shit.'"

That dried up any excess sympathy that might have been yearning toward the surface. "You know I don't like that word," she said. "Are there a lot more of these quotations?"

"Pages."

"What were you doing, making notes on everything in Penguin Books?"

"Looking for the house key. Want to skip the rest?"

"All right. I get the idea."

I flipped pages until I came to solid scribbling again. "So. There's been a gap. It's now May 13. The Allstons have just returned from a ten-day automobile trip to escape the Danish rain. They have driven (in the rain) through Hamburg and Hannover, with one splendid evening in a wine cellar in Celle. They have circumnavigated the East German border and traversed (in the rain) the Romantic Road through towns named Dinkelsbühl and Rothenburg, with mottoes and scriptures on their gables and Riemenschneider altarpieces in their churches. They have driven (in the rain) through a lot of blossoming apple trees to Innsbruck, where the Inn was full. Remember that green glass river, and the way the streets were full of lilacs and horse chestnuts blown off by a storm? Remember the Munich company that was singing *Così Fan Tutte* in the opera house? Then back (in the rain) through the Rhine-Mosel country, a fine experience because 1953 had been one of the best vintage years in history, and even the dollar-a-liter grocery store wine was marvelous. And so back to Copenhagen (in the rain) with the Rover's boot full of smuggled wine to beat the Danish taxes, and the old lady quaking all the way for fear they'd be thrown in jail. We rejoin them in the apartment on Havnegade, in the company of their interesting but troubled friend the Countess Astrid Wredel-Krarup, abandoned wife of the celebrated quisling."

"Idiot," Ruth said. "Read."

"Cursed be he whose thirst is quenched," I said.

2

May 13, Havnegade 13:

Hugs and kisses for Ruth, none for me this time, when we get back. It is surprising how much it feels like coming home, and it gives me qualms that a pair of tourists should be as important in anyone's life as we seem to be in the countess'. The poor damned woman has probably not talked to anybody but tradesmen and Mr. and Mrs. Behind since we left. And that's the condition she's been in for nearly nine years. Why doesn't she emigrate?

One thing she's done. She's been in touch with her sister-in-law back at the old castle, and we're invited down on May 20. Her wicked brother will not be at home—a shame, I'd like to see what real wickedness looks like. We will stay in the castle, which will give Ruthie a thrill. As for me, I will be able to take my mauve face into Bregninge village, if this turns out to be the right Bregninge (there's one on Taasinge, too, and maybe others in other places), and see it reflected in the window of a thatched cottage. Maybe that will exorcise my yearning for visits to the ethnic and cultural source. Once that's over, I can take Ruth down to Italy, where she'd like to be, where the food is good and the wine is cheap, and exchange my hair shirt for something more seasonable.

May 16:

Two mornings now we've got the countess to bring in her yoghurt and join us at breakfast. This morning, as we sat looking out at the harbor, it struck us all that the light was singularly bright, that there was not a cloud visible, and that the cheeks of bicyclists waiting for the Knippelsbro were pink with sun, not purple with rainy cold.

"We have to *go* somewhere!" Ruth said.

Denmark was all before us, where to choose. The countess said, hesitating, "Would you like to see my little Ellebacken cottage? We could carry a picnic. If it is really warm we can swim—it is on the shore. And oh!" She is an atom under constant bombardment, no thought goes by without knocking off an *oh*. "Oh, you did want to meet Karen Blixen. Her house is by Rungstedlund, on the way. Shall I telephone?"

Ruth said automatically, "How does she feel . . . I mean about your husband, and . . ."

"We have that in common," the countess said a little grimly. "In Africa, in the first war, *her* husband sympathized with the Germans."

When she is excited she has an extraordinarily vivid face. She jumped up and went into her room, leaving the door open. After a couple of minutes, exclamations, questions, chirps began to blow through the open door like straw from in front of a fan. I understood two words of it: *ja* and *farvel*. Blazing with pleasure, she came back.

"Oh, it works so right! She asks us to take our picnic in her garden. She will give us the first strawberries out of her *mistbaenk*— how do you say? Hotbed? Do you not think she is a great writer? And she will like you because you are both so nice. Oh, I am so glad I can take you to her!" She stopped, looking at my face. "But is it too much? Are you well enough?"

I said I felt fine, which was only a medium-gray lie.

About ten, with the top down, we pulled out of the courtyard into a miraculously soft, warm, windless day. A few clouds as soft as cats had crept in to sit around the horizon, but they did not stir, just sat. The Østerbrogade was bumper to bumper with cars and bicycles. Weekday, workday, be damned. Father Rain had left town, and all of Copenhagen was headed for the beaches, shedding clothes as it went. The Irish priests who Christianized this country, and the Lutherans who undertook the maintenance contract, never had much effect. Danes on a sunny day are unreconstructed pagans headed for a festival—May Day, I suppose, delayed a couple of weeks by wet grounds.

Cars with Swedish plates, full of roaring young people, kept coming down the left side of the road, inviting me to play chicken. Cursing, I took to the ditches and woods and gave them the road. The sun always brought them, the countess said. Coming from prohibition country, they started getting drunk on the Hälsingborg–Helsingør ferry. By the time they had been in Copenhagen an hour, they would be overturning launches on the *havnefart,* and the Danish women would have to carry clubs. Those Swedes, they are so *rigtig,* but when they have drunk some things they will follow you right up your own stairs.

The sun shone on us, the soft air flowed over us, the Øresund was very blue. I said, "A couple of days of this, and I might throw away my crutches and follow you myself."

She is not prim. She gave me something like a leer. "Ah, it would not do if you were to get feeling too well!"

Impenetrable smile from Ruth.

"Oh, impenetrable!" Ruth said. "What is this 'impenetrable' business?"

"I read what it says in the book," I said. "My glaciers began retreating and you were jealous, a little. Or so I evidently thought."

"So you thought. All right, go on."

We were out of the worst traffic. Suburbs, gardened houses, glimpses of sea: the Danish Riviera. The countess was telling about how they used to sail here, before the war. Then down the Øresund came a white ship, standing only a little way out from shore. "Isn't that . . ." Ruth said. "Yes, it is! It's the *Stockholm!*"

We could see passengers crowding the rail in the sun, watching Denmark flow past. They had it so much better than we had had it, limping seasickly in through the rain two days late, that I gave them a certain Italian gesture. "Anathema," I said. "The Yankee curse on all of you."

The countess affected to be hurt that I did not like the ship that had brought us to Denmark.

"Anathema," I said. "A bunch of damned Swedes." We were all silly with sun.

Then we came to a stretch of beechwoods, and the light changed. Everything went palely green and gold. Between the smooth gray trunks the grass was starred with white anemones or hepaticas. The leaves passing over our heads were tiny, delicate, tender as pale green flowers, a tinted mist that in a couple of days would be a green roof. Fairies must have been invented in a spring beechwood. The ladies exclaimed and fell silent. At the far edge I made a quick U-turn and came back through. We rolled slowly with our heads tipped back, and at the edge turned again and came through a third time. Druidical magic.

Ruth, looking a little trembly, said, "I never knew you to do a thing like that before. That was lovely."

The countess too. "Mr. Allston is not the way Americans are supposed to be," she said. "Why is he not loud and insensitive? Why does he not think all things can be bought for money? Why does he respond to beautiful things? Why is he so nice?"

"Nice" is her nicest word. It is a fine thing to be admired by two attractive women on a spring day, with the top down. I felt like boxing my ankles. Shucks, girls, it was nothing. Velkommen, countess. Glad to do it.

A little farther on she directed me in a drive toward a house covered with ivy. "Karen said she would be in the garden," she said, and led us around past a glassed-in porch with light sunny colors and wicker furniture. Outside, big overhanging trees, just leafing out. Tulip beds, about gone by. Lilacs darkly budded but not yet quite popped into flower. At the back of the garden a thatched cottage with a squat chimney, and on the chimney a stork's nest.

A woman in a floppy hat stood up beside a raised, slanted hotbed. She had a trowel in one hand and a stone or clod in the other. She was small and thin. It was impossible to imagine this little creature leaving a dinner party to go out and shoot a couple of lions prowling the yard, or assisting at Kikuyu childbirths, or doctoring the great bloody wounds of Masai warriors, though I knew from *Out of Africa* that she had done those things and more. She was brown-faced and brown-handed, as if Kenya had permanently altered her Danish skin. Though she was smiling, no teeth showed in her smile: she merely bent her lips. Her eyes were dark, alive, and noticing. She stood very still. Witch, for sure. Shape-shifter. If you held a mirror behind her it would reflect not a little brown woman but a monkey, one of those ambiguous old-woman monkeys of her tales, or perhaps a still bird with a curved bill.

We were hardly introduced before, with the air of disclosing a delicious secret, she opened her hand and showed us what she had just dug up while planting a flower—a flattened cylinder of stone six inches long, marked with the crooked letters of a dead alphabet. Just as she showed it to us, the stork came back to its nest with a sun-darkening spread of wings. Karen Blixen glanced up. "Ah, old friend."

They were two of a kind, as beady-eyed and as capable of stillness. Knew each other in Africa, no doubt, and in a lot of sabbatical doings. I looked for the broomstick, but the stork had hidden it among the nest twigs as she flew in.

Picnic on the grass. By witchcraft or otherwise, Karen Blixen produced the only salad we have had in Denmark that wasn't composed of hothouse cucumbers. Also a very eucharist of strawberries out of her hotbed. Her talk was all of Africa. Listening to her bring it to life, monumentally primitive and powerful, I remembered the passage in *Out of Africa* in which a line of elephants emerges one by one out of the mist, as if being created before the eyes of the watcher.

"You loved Africa," I said to her.

She gave me a dark, alert look. Her cheeks were wrinkled in fine parallel lines. She appeared to have no cheekbones at all, and her eyes looked too big for her face. A bird's face, really. For the first time I became aware that she must be nearly seventy.

"It was life," she said.

I made a motion that included the hedged, protected, breezeless garden and the old chimneyed house in its overcoat of ivy: inherited country place, probably complete with all the lost loves, crimes, and whispers from the past that she has written into her stories. "And what's this, then?" I asked.

"This? This is safety."

I had the nerve to argue with her. "Is it bad to have a place to come back to?" I said. "An American, or at least one kind of American, would envy you. His parents or grandparents were immigrants, uprooted. He was born in transit, he has lived in fifty houses in fifteen places. When he moves, he doesn't move back, he moves on. No accumulations. No traditions. A civilization without attics."

"Or rubbish piles," said Karen Blixen. "Or dungeons. Or ghosts."

"Or rune stones."

She continued to regard me with her dark eyes, interested. "You feel this."

As if anxious to explain me, the countess said, "You know, Karen, Mr. Allston's mother was Danish—from Bregninge, can you imagine? We go there next week, all three of us, to see if that is his safe place."

She had taken off her scarf, and the sun was on her smooth hair. If Karen Blixen was a witch, the countess was a Lorelei, and not unclairvoyant herself. I had never said anything to her about why I had an impulse to see my mother's village. My safe place?

Karen Blixen said, "Have you and Eigil decided to be friends, then?"

"He will not be there. It is a chance to see Grandmamá and Manon."

"Eigil is his father's son, isn't that the trouble?"

I thought the countess flushed a little, but she looked back steadily into Karen Blixen's look until the look was withdrawn. The old woman sat ruminating on the rune stone. It was remarkable how witchlike, how malicious and gleeful, her face could be. *Click*, went Ruth's camera. I hope she caught that expression.

"I hope you'll forgive me," she said in confusion. "I couldn't resist."

"I don't mind," the old woman said. To me she said, "It's too bad you don't know Eigil Rødding. *There* is an accumulation, if you like accumulations. *There* is a house with an attic."

Not sure whether she was baiting the countess or simply making conversation, I thought I might turn the subject aside. "If it weren't for houses with attics, where would you have got your marvelous Gothic tales?"

"Of course. But you are not writing stories, I take it."

"No."

"You expect some revelation? You think you may recognize something? You expect that closing a link with your mother's past will make you feel safer in some way?"

"I'm not so compulsive about it as we're making it sound. I'm just sort of curious."

"You don't expect to reverse your mother's emigration and come back to Denmark to live?"

"Oh no."

"Why not?"

She caught me out. I said honestly, "I guess I'd find it too small and tame."

When she smiled widely, her wrinkled cheeks puckered up into pleats of brown skin. Under the floppy hat her eyes looked black, without pupils. "But *very* safe," she said. "Denmark is full of retired sea captains growing roses. It is full of people like me. But you won't find Bregninge like that. That whole estate uses the past to create the future. Astrid's father was a man of great talent, and her brother has inherited a good deal of it." She glanced at the countess with affectionate malice. "I leave Astrid out of it. Her talents are different from theirs."

"Karen, please, it is not funny," the countess said.

"The old count was the Doctor Faustus of genetics," Karen Blixen said. "Trees, flowers, hybrid fruits like those of your American Burbank. Also game and hunting dogs and much else. It was said of him that if he needed dogs with long legs and webbed feet for running in swamps, he could start with a pair of dachshunds and in a little while produce you hounds as tall as giraffes, with feet like paddles. It is good that Eigil has inherited his father's gifts, because some of the experiments involved species that do not breed quickly like mice or guinea pigs, and so take many years. How would you go about a genetic experiment with elephants, say? It is not quite like fruit flies."

The countess had grown obviously sullen; she did not like this talk about her father and brother at all. Karen Blixen studied her, lightly smiling, her expression about fifty-fifty malice and affection. "Astrid is sensitive about some of this science, and she can tell good from evil, she thinks—that is one gift her brother lacks. As I grow older I wonder who is right. I do know one thing. Evil, if it exists, is not all lumpy and ugly like a toad. It is often more attractive than what people call good. Eigil disgusts his sister because he follows their father's practice of seducing peasant girls. It is naughty of him, surely. But is it evil? Who would say that for sure except a virtuous sister? The fact is, Eigil could not be uninteresting if he tried. If you were to meet him, you might find him fascinating."

"Alas," I said. "He won't be at home when we call."

The witch woman was rubbing the rune stone along the side of her nose the way I have seen pipe smokers polish the bowls of their pipes. Abstractedly she studied the childish scratches of the runes. Quick as mice, her eyes darted to the countess, who was sulky, and to me, who was uncomfortable. "Your mother was from Bregninge. Tell me about her."

"Nothing much to tell. She was an orphan. She lived with a peasant family and did farm work—thinned sugar beets and cleaned cow byres and so on."

"How old when she emigrated?"

"Sixteen."

Raised eyebrows. "That young. Why?"

"I don't know. It wasn't in character for her to do such a thing. She wasn't really adventurous. When I'd ask her, she'd put me off. Said she just wanted to see something new."

"She was not, as they say, in trouble?"

"Oh no, I'm sure not."

"But she was running away."

"I used to wonder if she wasn't. She would never say."

"From the old count, do you suppose?"

Now there was a thought.

"Karen," the countess said furiously, "this is simply unkind!"

"My dear, look on it as a story," her cousin said. To me she said, "It pains Astrid to hear these things spoken of, but they *are* part of a story, and stories are part of the accumulation you think will tell you something. Stories last better than the people who lived them. Hamlet is only a tattered shadow up here in Helsingør, but on Shakespeare's pages he is immortal. Now. What I am saying isn't as fantastic as it sounds. Sixteen-year-old Danish peasant girls don't run off to America for nothing, and she lived on the estate of a man famous for chasing peasant girls, as for much else. But since she ran away, and escaped, there is not much of a story. I would turn it around if I were writing it. Suppose she didn't have the courage or the money to do what your mother did. Suppose she was trapped, or suppose even that she found the old count irresistible—and why wouldn't she? Suppose she didn't quite escape, or escaped only after she had been seduced and was pregnant. Then you, though born in America, would come back here hunting for your safe place, as Astrid says, and find that you were Astrid's half brother, and a sort of cousin to me. It takes only a little twisting to make your return take on possibilities and become part of a Gothic tale."

"I give it to you."

She nodded, holding the rune stone to her cheek and smiling the smile that showed no teeth. "For Astrid's sake I will decline it. She has always been terrified that I will write about her family."

"There's a catch, too," I said. "I wasn't born until four years after my mother landed in America. There goes my only hope of a distinguished pedigree."

The countess stood up, and as she did so, the stork left its nest and flapped off low over the tops of the trees. We watched it go. "Well!" said the countess with her brilliant smile. "If we are to go on to Ellebacken we must begin."

Karen Blixen didn't try to keep us. But she held my eyes a moment, her smart wrinkled face like the smiling face of a Greek kouros, and said, "If you find it possible, come and see me again after you have been to Ørebyslot. I am curious to know what a returning pilgrim would find."

We had driven all the way to Helsingør and beyond, and were looking through the Ellebacken cottage and throwing open windows to air the musty house, and wondering if the sound was warm enough for a swim, before the countess was quite herself again. It is a place that expresses her—ten acres or so of wood and pasture, a clearing of unmown grass, a walk guarded by cypresses, a half-timbered thatched cottage as picturesque as something in a drawing. As a matter of fact, I had seen it in a drawing, one of hers. This was the place, apparently, where she and her husband used to be closest and happiest. She said he liked to play at mowing the grass and chopping wood, like the Kaiser at Doom. Before the war, they spent many weekends here. Since her life blew up, she has managed to come only two or three times a year. She offered us the use of the place, an offer which I took to be a transparent hope that we will come and bring her with us.

A swim in the sound, very chilly. But a new side to the countess. For one thing, when reduced to a bathing suit she is more seductive than I would ever have guessed; the plain clothing and the erect bearing are a form of disguise. For another thing, she was not kidding when she said she lives in her body, not in her head. She frolicked in that ice water like some Valkyrie, and she swam out until her head disappeared in the chop of little waves. She could have swum to Sweden, I suppose. As for me, I got blue and goose-pimpled and had to come out. So of course Ruth and the countess worried about me, and built up a fire in the fireplace, and made tea, and clucked over me like a pair of over-healthy hens.

Long past time to quit this. Very, very late. A long time ago I heard all the clocks in Copenhagen strike two, each making its own guess. It took the hour about fifteen minutes to ricochet from the Raadhus tower to the last lost church steeple out on Amager. Ruth sleeps in the other bed like a tired dog, and here I sit in my backbreaking oriole's nest, wide awake in spite of the pill I took at eleven. If I take another one soon, I may get three or four hours of sleep.

This day, though the most interesting we have spent in Denmark, has been too long. I have a beaut of a sunburn—nose, skull, forearms, back of the neck—but it's nothing to some of the cases we saw on the way home, when fifty thousand Danes were retreating through a red sunset in complete disorder, a Dunkirk.

Notice: just thinking the word "beach," I think disaster. When I should be sleeping, I am dragged back to that grubby van in that dusty arroyo near La Jolla where Curt lived with his silly surfboard and his dreary girl in his raffish community of streak-haired mind-blown demigods and demigoddesses, disciples of sun and kicks. Intent upon what? Rebellions? Repudiations? Apathies? Boredoms? Fears, panics, terrors? Or just on Now, on the galvanic twitches of the eternal pointless present? What is that life style (that jargon term) except a substitute for a life?

And what is mine, that is what troubles me. Curt's repudiations let the air out of my confidence that I know what my job, my principles, my vote, my admirations, my friends, and my marriage are all about. I am as unsure of myself as I ever was of him. And I know why. In rejecting me he destroyed my compass, he pulled my plug, he drained me. He was the continuity my life and effort were spent to establish. I have been guilty of making first Ruth and then Curtis into barricades behind which I could take shelter. But why couldn't he have understood the hunger and love and panic, the trembling and the cold sweats and the sleeplessness, the times when I looked at him sleeping, as a child, and was overwhelmed by my responsibility to him and his dearness to me? Who broke it, he or I?

Fell or let go? Did he eventually bore himself with the

aimlessness to which, maybe, my anxious demands on him drove him? Did he try for too big a wave, and if so why? To show me something?

Christ, even in my regret I can't leave him alone.

It is a pitful, grubby little story any way you read it. The saga of an immigrant family, a succession of orphans, that began in flight on the island of Lolland in 1901 and ended fifty-two years later (in flight?) on the beach at La Jolla, on the western or suicide edge of the New World. Fifty-two years from wooden shoes and hope to barefoot kicks, fear, and silence; and in between, Joseph Allston, the bright overachiever, his mother's joy and treasure, his son's alien overseer.

Safety, Karen Blixen says in scorn. She resents rusting unburnished when she wants to shine in use. She pretends to think her life in words, which has made her an international figure, is meagerer than the life of action she once lived. Nevertheless she came home in the end. Echoes of the turtle and snail persist even in her, she carries her safety on her back. Safety is a legitimate human desire—isn't it?—and home, says old wise man Robert Frost, is where, when you have to go there, they have to take you in. Safety is a mutual matter. Do I hate the thought of Curt's death more because he never fulfilled himself, or more because he never fulfilled me? Did he know how gladly we would have opened our door, how carefully we would have avoided making his return a humiliation of his pride? And do I know for sure that I could have been wise and open? Do I think right now that I could have kept my temper and my tongue? Which is deeper, a father's love or a disappointed father's contempt?

The Danes have a name for the energy and ambition that they ridicule in the Americans and fear in the Germans. *Albuer*, elbows. They call our overgrown cars, with their toothy chrome grilles, Dollargrins. Of course they speak from weakness and probably envy; their humor is underdog humor, a put-down of what is more powerful than they. I wonder if it was an underdog world, a small-power world where little could be expected of him, that Curt was hunting when he spent a summer here in

Copenhagen a few years ago? Or was it only the tales of how compliant the Danish girls are that drew him? Why did he live in a furnished room on the Nyhavn, supposed to be the roughest waterfront in Europe? Was he hunting safety in that cave, a place where he fitted in? Who is the waif and orphan here? And do *I* really think there is something reassuring I might find in this mousehole of a country?

What should a little Kafka animal do? Hide in the hole and hear the Enemy digging toward him, or run out of the hole into the fearful open? What did the Europeans gain by Columbus? The illusion of freedom, I suppose. But did they gain or lose when they gave up the tentative safety of countries and cultures where the rules were as well known as the dangers, and had been tailored to the dangers, and went raiding in a virgin continent that was neither country nor culture, and isn't yet, and may never be, and yet has never given up the dangerous illusion of infinite possibility? What good did it all do, if we end in confusion and purposelessness on the far Pacific shore of America, or come creeping back to our origins looking for something we have lost and can't name?

No sooner do I ask that than I have to admit that what brought my mother and a lot of others to the New World was precisely the hope of safety, not any lust for freedom. What do I want, a drawbridge between the continents, across which the cultures and hence the generations can meet, and pass, and meet again?

The fact is, I don't know what I want, or should ever have wanted, and I don't ever expect to know. What I would settle for right now is the ability to fall asleep.

3

That was the end of the second notebook. I had read right through the breast-beating part, instead of skipping it as I had done the night before, and I think I did so because I wanted Ruth to listen to it, I felt the compulsion to declare myself unmistakably, no matter how it troubled her, no matter how it troubled me. For a while after I stopped, we sat there. She turned her face toward me, her serious, still pretty face with its pert unfaded eyebrows under the white hair. She is as lucky in her skin, which doesn't wrinkle, as she is in her figure, which hasn't changed two pounds' worth in forty years. She is one of those whom old college friends would recognize at once; I am not. We looked at one another, and then she looked down and picked absently at a knot in the mohair throw that covered her. With her eyes on the knot she said, "You've never got over it."

"No, I guess not."

"Why not, Joe? It's been over twenty years. I loved him, too, I thought I couldn't bear it when he died. But I have. It's the only way. It's not healthy to go on grieving forever."

"You're forgetting I wrote this journal only six months or so after."

"I heard how you read it."

"Yes? Well . . . sure it bothers me. It was the worst thing that ever happened to us. If you can finally bear it, all that proves is that you're a born survivor and I'm not."

"What do you mean by that?"

"I don't know. Nothing. Maybe just that women are more durable, they're made for surviving and holding things together. Anyway it's not his death, or not only his death."

111

"What then? Do you still feel guilty about all the clashes you had?"

"That, sure. I don't suppose I'll ever get over blaming myself. I should have been wiser, somehow. But that's not all of it, either."

"Then what?"

She is ever one to talk it out. What? Good God, what not? But it was I who had provoked this dialogue.

"The way the world wags," I said. "The difference between what we'd like to be and what we're able to be. How to respect myself when I know I'm confused and cowardly. How to respect a world where nothing I believe in is valued. How to live and grow old inside a head I'm contemptuous of, in a culture I despise."

"You mustn't," Ruth said, ready to cry. "Even if it was as bad as you say, you have to go on living, and you can't blame either yourself or him just for the way things *are*. He agreed with you, don't you know that? He despised it, and himself too, as much as . . . You *taught* him to."

"So don't tell me I'm not to blame for anything. The hell of it is, I despised his way of despising it more than I despised *it*. If he'd really fought against the things he hated, some way or other, do you think I wouldn't have been with him? But he just quit. He turned belly up. And he was on the side of the future, his way won. In twenty years everything he stood for has taken over. He was prophetic. The counterculture. The pleasure principle. Now. Wow. Junk everything good along with the bad. History is an exploded science, civility is a dirty word, self-restraint is not only unhealthy, it's a laugh. Manners are hypocrisy, responsibility means you've sold out, adolescence lasts into the seventies, or will. And it's okay to lush on the money civilization so long as you hate it. So then the money civilization gets the word and adjusts itself to the new market and sells itself in a new package to its despisers and lushes."

"He'd have come around."

"I wish I thought so."

"Anyway, what is it you're complaining about? You used to say the world is at least fifty-one per cent in our favor or we couldn't live in it."

"Sometimes fifty-one per cent doesn't seem quite enough. Also, sometimes it's all you should take. My problem with Curt was that he wanted to take eighty-five per cent while keeping his right to gripe. It doesn't do any good to pretend that he *didn't* lush. He never learned the responsibility of giving something in exchange for what he took. If I come down out of the hills with foxtails in my beard, crying, 'Woe, woe unto this people!' I have to include him among the enemy. I can't see any other possibility."

"You could forgive him."

"I forgave him long ago."

"Did you? He might have had something to forgive us for, too."

"Ah, Ruthie." We looked at each other across fifteen feet of our last mutual sanctuary, she in the bed one or both of us will probably die in, I in the chair where the survivor will sit and wait to wear out. "What do you think?" I said. "If he'd lived, would he finally have joined us? If he'd been alive these last twenty years would we have made it up, and been friends?"

"I think so," Ruth said. "I have to think so."

"Maybe you're right," I said—I just dropped it, I didn't want any more of it. I stood up, and found that I was so stiff I almost couldn't stand. My toes, ankles, knees, hips, ground bone against bone. My finger joints were sore and hot to the touch as I casually washed them in air. Ruth watched me until I went to the bathroom, where out of her sight I took an allopurinal and an indocin. She watched me in silence as I went through the bedroom on my way to the kitchen to get a glass of milk to counteract the corrosiveness of the painkiller. I came back, and she watched me in silence as I undressed. I went to bed gloomy.

FOUR

1

Today, among other junk mail, there was a questionnaire from some research outfit, addressed apparently to a sampling of senior citizens and wishing to know intimate things about my self-esteem. It is their hypothesis that a decline in self-esteem is responsible for many of the overt symptoms of aging. God knows where they got my name. Ben Alexander, maybe; his finger is in all those pies, and always stirring.

I looked at some of the questions and threw the thing in the fireplace. Another of those socio-psycho-physiological studies suitable for computerizing conclusions already known to anyone over fifty. Who was ever in any doubt that the self-esteem of the elderly declines in this society which indicates in every possible way that it does not value the old in the slightest, finds them an expense and an embarrassment, laughs at their experience, evades their problems, isolates them in hospitals and Sunshine Cities, and generally ignores them except when soliciting their votes or ripping off their handbags and their Social Security checks? And which has a chilling capacity to look straight at them and never see them. The poor old senior citizen has two choices, assuming he is well enough off to have any choices at all. He can retire from that hostile culture to the shore of some shuffleboard court in a balmy climate, or he can shrink in his self-esteem and gradually become the cipher he is constantly reminded he is.

What bothered me about Césare Rulli's visit if not the lacerations it left on my self-esteem?

The responses that I feel more and more when we step out into the unsafe surrounding world are doubled and tripled every time we go down to the Stanford campus, as we did yesterday afternoon to hear the Guarneri Quartet. Inside the hall, all's well. Music is a great democratizer. There are as many white and gray heads in the audience as dark or blond ones. Attitudes are suspended in favor of appreciation, you see a few people you know, you are smiled and waved at, you feel the solidarity of common tastes and interests you have spent your life acquiring, and you participate, even though an outsider, in the community of the university.

But go outside after the concert and you step out of security into hazard, out of the culture into the counterculture. All around the terrace the young roam, or sprawl, or lounge. White Plaza has a sort of bazaar, a stretch of blankets and quilts and plastic groundcloths on which are displayed belts, handbags, macramé flowerpot hangers, and other kinds of the junk that Gertrude Stein called "ugly things all made by hand." The wives, children, and dogs of the artists tend them and sleep among them. Students pour back and forth, or sit arguing at the union's tables, or read propped against trees. They are not hostile and contemptuous as they were a few years ago; they just don't see you. They will move their feet off a table if you sit down at it, or pull in their legs if you fall over them. They don't seem offended that you exist, only surprised. It is unsafe to approach a swinging door too close behind one of them. If you get there first, and pause to hold it open for them, they bolt on through with an alert, sidelong, surprised look, both puzzled and offended, as if your act of courtesy had been a trap they had just managed to evade.

In the plaza and along the walks, their ten-speed bicycles come up behind you silently and swiftly, and without bell or warning whiz by you within two feet at twenty miles an hour, leaving you with a cold shock of adrenalin in your guts and a weakness in your knees, and in your head a vision of your humiliated old carcass lying on the pavement, pants torn, knees bloody, arms broken, glasses smashed. You wonder if they'd notice you *then.*

"What do you expect?" Ruth asks, getting quite exercised over my grumblings. "They've got their own concerns, why should they notice you or me? Do you expect them to whisper to each other, 'Who's that distinguished-looking couple that just went by?' Do you think they should stand aside and pull their forelocks at you?"

"Oh, for Christ's sake," I said.

"It's just your vanity."

"Okay, it's just my vanity. The fact remains that every time I come into this plaza I feel self-conscious, and uneasy, and like a freak—an *ignored* freak. And I resent being made to feel like a freak by a bunch of *real* freaks, self-made."

"I wish you weren't so prejudiced," she said hopelessly. "It would do you good to have more contact with young people. You need it even more than they do."

"Yes?" I said. "How do you make these contacts? It wasn't the old who declared that feud."

"Feud! What feud? I'll bet if you'd just accept one of those invitations to talk to classes you'd find out there isn't any feud at all. That destructive phase is all past, everybody keeps telling us. It went out with Vietnam. These are just healthy normal kids going about their business in a place where they have every right to feel at home and you and I don't."

"They obviously do and I obviously don't," I said. "Come on, let's get out of here and take our walk."

"It might be good for you," Ruth said.

Maybe good for me, but not comfortable. That spell of mucking out my culvert in the rain just about fixed me. I limped and hobbled—maybe exaggerating just a little for Ruth's benefit, to emphasize my legitimacy as an oldster. Her response was not sympathetic, though I thought I detected doubt in her glances now and then, and caught her just about ready to ask if I felt well enough to go on.

Actually I was enjoying it, in spite of the rheumatiz. We walked all around the hill where the older faculty houses are, and all the way, in the big opulent yards, the mimosa made yellow globes among the other trees—pure forsythia-yellow, the true color of spring—and there were whiffs of daphne, and manure, and mushroom compost, and the pleasant sight of gardeners working. The briskness of the air got us to walking faster than I really wanted to. I wanted to saunter and savor, because this was clearly not the country of the young, this was civilization of a pleasant and reassuring kind, the kind I have been trying to earn citizenship in ever since I was old enough to know what I wanted.

We rounded the hill and came down along Frenchman's Creek, running a steady little stream after the rains, and pooling above old weirs. There we overtook Bruce and Rosie Bliven, bundled up in overcoats and armed with canes and walking with brittle briskness.

They have lived on the campus ever since he retired as editor of the *New Republic* many years ago. Since retiring, he has had about three heart attacks and written about five books, and it is a cinch that at eighty-five or whatever he is he still contemplates five books more, and may be halfway through the next one. His last Christmas letter contained a line that should be engraved above every geriatric door. He says that when asked if he feels like an old man he replies that he does not, he feels like a young man with something the matter with him. He has a sweet humorous face and an innocent resilience that make me ashamed of myself. As an apologist for old age he is better than Ben Alexander, even. And Rosie can make you feel good at a hundred yards, just by the sight of her. Bruce says she is always trying to help old ladies of sixty down steps.

We chatted awhile under the pepper trees and parted, and they went back up along the creek with their canes, talking as if they had just met after long separation and had a lot to catch up on.

"Aren't they a cute pair," Ruth said.

I thought I detected a monitory tone. "Mellowed by age," I said.

"Oh, come on!" she said impatiently. "You can admire them without getting off on the young again."

"Brace yourself," I said. "Here come a couple."

They came toward us arm in arm, the girl sashaying out and swinging her long skirts as if in a square dance, and turning to look up into her companion's mat of whiskers with a teasing sort of adoration. As we came close they both looked at us directly, and smiled, and said softly, "Hello."

Startled, we replied. They passed on. Ruth was ready to pop with self-righteousness. "What about the surly young?" she said. "How about that feud?"

But I defused her with a reasonable response. "That's all it takes," I said. "That's all it would ever have taken. They noticed us, they were civil, they appeared to be closely related to the human species. God bless them, if they'll act human they can wear all the granny dresses and whiskers their little hearts desire."

"All you need is one pretty girl to speak to you, or one boy to act respectful, and you melt."

"Was she pretty? In that getup, who could tell? But okay, you're absolutely right. I'm a pushover. Just let them beware of undermining my self-esteem, that's all. Now how about heading home? I'm cold, and my toe joints are killing me."

"Ah, poor lamb, I've walked you too far." She took my arm, perhaps remembering the way the girl had swung on the elbow of her boy friend. "But don't you *like* this? Don't you like walking down here where something is going on and there's more to see than leaves to be swept up or wood to be cut? I wish you'd talk to a class, if they ask you again. I might even try to audit something, if they'd let me."

"The innocence of age," I said. "If you were black, sure. Since you're female, fine. If you were blind, deaf, crippled, absolutely. But if you're old, you're up against discrimination that doesn't even know it's discrimination. You'd just better stay out of it."

"Oh pooh. At least I don't go around with a chip on my shoulder."

"Speaking of which," I said, "did you ever *see* anybody put a chip on his shoulder and dare somebody else to knock it off? Where do we get clichés like that? *Tom Sawyer* or some place, I suppose. Maybe once, down in some Mississippi woodyard, somebody made his dare like that, and forever after we have no way to express challenge but that stupid metaphor."

"Please," she said. "Not another tirade about what's wrong

with the world. Can't we just finish our walk in peace, and enjoy it, and maybe come down again? Will you? With or without a chip on your shoulder?"

"Sure, why not? So long as we stay away from that plaza."

"All right, let's do it," she said. She was being bright and chatty and unchallenging, and she hung onto my arm. "What's in to-night's installment of the journal?"

"I don't know. I guess the ancestral castle of Øreby."

"Is it . . . unhappy? Will it bother you? Because if it does, we don't have to do it."

"I don't mind."

"Good. Don't you sort of like having it ahead of us? Something to look forward to in the evenings?"

"If that's the way you want it, that's the way I like it."

"Just so it doesn't depress you and make you gloomy. You scare me when you get the way you were last night, lashing out at every-thing, including yourself. You know you don't believe everything you said."

I was not so sure of that as she was, but I wasn't in a mood to be contrary. "Put it down to historical queasiness," I said. "I al-ways did get a little seasick riding backwards."

Seasick or not, we were at it again after dinner, summing up a day or a life.

2

May 21, Ørebyslot, Lolland:

As she usually is when I get around to communing with my *Geist*, Ruth is asleep, this time in a canopied four-poster, a real *lit du roi*, the duplicate of the one I am in. The room is enormous—two rooms, actually, two of about twenty in this wing—with casement windows through which come stray tree- and cloud-interrupted streaks of moonlight and a smell of lilacs and lindens. As the trees outside move in a night wind, the moonlight sneaks across the room and touches Ruth's bed, and then scoots back to the windows as if afraid it might have awakened her. Fat chance. As for me, I hunch here under a dinky forty-watt bulb (why are Europeans, even in castles, so scared of adequate lighting?) with no more likelihood of sleeping than of understanding what's been going on.

What was going on at lunch, for example? The countess promised to explain later, but we haven't seen her since. And what aborted dinner—the old lady's illness, as advertised, or something else? And who is Miss Weibull? Most of all, why did I, fifty years old, out of shape, out of practice, just recovering from a long spell of illness, accept the challenge of the werewolf who runs this place, and try to beat his brains out on the tennis court? He comes on me like Sir Kay the Seneschal coming on the Connecticut Yankee, and says to me, "Fair Sir, will ye just?" and instead of saying, "What are you giving me? Get along back to your circus or I'll report you," I take him on. My hand is blistered, the skin is peeled off the bottoms of my feet, and I am already so stiff that if I tried to get out of bed I would break in two. I deserve a coronary, as Ruth did not fail to point out while we were eating the dinner that Room Service brought up.

But I have made my pilgrimage to my mother's cottage. It was as meaningless as I knew it would be. The cultural vitamin deficiency is not appeased by nibbling the clay and plaster of the old home. The cultural amputee is still trying to scratch the itch in the missing limb.

Well, set it down.

We got here about eleven. The castle, to Ruth's mild disappointment, is not Gothic, with turrets, but Dutch Renaissance, with stepped gables. Wicked brother, as promised, not at home. Greeted by his wife, Manon—tall, skinny, strained, all angles, with a sweet puckered face that looks as if she is always trying to remind herself not to forget something, and little black dots of eyes like a Laurencin drawing.

In the vast front hall, tinkling with the sound of a fountain around which Thorwaldsen-type nymphs clustered, in the presence of a brawny maid and a couple of Chinese jars that probably concealed elves, dwarves, or the forty thieves, she and the countess fell into each other's arms. The maid picked up our bags and led Ruth and me up the stairs, while the countess called after us, "Oh, come straight down, as soon as you have finished your washings! Gerda will unpack you. I must show you this castle where I grew up!"

All pleasure for her, apparently. No bad associations, only delight at being back home in the grandeur to which she has grown unaccustomed to being accustomed. We did come straight down, after Ruth had made a quick inspection of our ducal suite, and were shown the castle, thus:

Drawing rooms, three, each grander than the last, all ornate and gilded, French as to furniture and Beauvais as to tapestries, these last bearing the usual representations of stag hunts, successful, and Arcadian picnics, topless.

Music room: square Bechstein, celestina inlaid with mother-of-pearl, gilt velvet-seated chairs, exhausted cello case prostrate on a banquette.

Ballroom: a basketball court overhung with crystal chandeliers, french doors all down one side reflecting their slant light across the parquetry and showing us reaches of lawn and roses outside.

Conservatory (orangerie?): a jungle of steamy plants from which a Rousseau tiger might have looked out—might *be* looking out now that everybody but me is asleep.

Billiard room: two tables. Around the room trophies of the chase—stuffed pheasants and grouse, a rhino head, a cape buffalo head, a long row of stag heads labeled as to year and slayer. Some of these the King's and the King's father's. Lion and leopard skins on the floor, a narwhal horn spiraling up like some sort of rocket from an onyx launching pad.

Now the library, famous for works on horticulture and game management, here probably still called venery—everything from medieval herbals and bestiaries to contemporary learned journals in four languages. It seemed to me that these books made both Manon and the countess nervous; they stood back, politely giving me, the visiting book man, plenty of time to examine and admire, but showing a transparent willingness to pass on. Having no expertise in either horticulture or game management, and seeing them hover there trying not to hurry me, I put back the volume whose binding I had been admiring, and said, "These are impressive, but over my head. I've got other imperatives." Oh, what? they said. So I plucked from the shelf a Goethe in German and read them the last line of *Faust: "Das Ewig-Weibliche zieht uns hinan."* Manon managed to take that piece of japery as a compliment to her, and the countess gave me a snickering look that said Mr. Allston was *sehr kavalier*, and Ruth gave me another sort of look, asking me in effect who I thought I was, Little Lord Fauntleroy?

Whom we met as soon as we started out of the library—a pale, pretty, solemn little Swedish baron of about ten, a nephew of Manon's, on his way in to read Duns Scotus or something else light. He wore blue serge short pants and an Eton collar and jacket, and he was the quietest, politest, most watchful little boy I ever saw in my life. I asked him if he spoke English and he squeaked, "*Lillebit.*"

Ruthie was enjoying the tour, and the ladies chattered, and I came along on my leash. Through a quickly opened door we were given a glimpse of a great pantry, with a board where lights went on to indicate what room was calling, and a receding warren of subsocial rooms and kitchens and such—the only rooms, I supposed, that my mother might ever have seen, if she had seen those. Then we tiptoed respectfully into the dining room, a hollow cave with satiny sideboards, heavy silver, a table forty feet long with three great bowls of lilacs spaced along it, and walls covered with the usual wigged ancestors and muddy Danish landscapes. I was tempted to ask why the Dutch should have produced a regiment of great painters, while their close relatives up the North Sea coast, with the same blood, weather, light, sky, and architecture, never produced a one. But since the countess is herself a sort of artist, I admired the silver instead.

The countess was happily recalling dinners in this room with a thousand candles and four wines, times when the King had come down to hunt. Then, she said to me, you would have seen some *skaal*'ing! Privately I thought the room too grand to have any fun in, and much too big for the present party. The table was set only at one end—seven places.

The countess noted the number, too. "Who is coming?" she asked Manon.

"Grandmamá. She shouldn't, but she wants to see you and to greet your friends. And of course Bertil."

The countess' eyes were on the seventh plate; then they came up and met Manon's. That was a speaking look if I ever heard one, though I didn't understand the words. The countess' mouth tightened till she was white around the lips. Manon lifted a thin sweatered shoulder. The butler came in and announced lunch.

There was little masculine company to distribute, just Little Lord Fauntleroy and me. We waited. After several minutes a woman, not especially young but very pregnant, came carrying her great belly before her from one of the parlors. She had a broad, healthy-looking face and a way of smiling slyly to herself. I thought she was faking a composure she didn't quite possess.

Manon thrust out her lips into a nervous pucker and blinked her round eyes. In Danish she said to the woman, "You remember Astrid."

The woman gave what can only be called a scornful snort. In that room, in that context, it was an extraordinary response.

"*Naturligvis*" she said. "*Velkommen.*" Her eyes touched the eyes of the countess for just an instant. A complex expression passed across her face and was covered over by the careful sly smile.

"*God dag*," the countess said—oh, icy.

"And these are Astrid's friends, Mr. and Mrs. Allston."

"*God dag*," the woman said. And we said.

"Miss Weibull," Manon said.

I had an immediate semaphore from Ruth, which said, with flapping red flags, DO NOT SAY ANYTHING! DO NOT, REPEAT DO NOT, ASK HER WHO HER HUSBAND IS OR WHAT HE DOES. DO NOT SAY ANYTHING BEYOND ROUTINE POLITENESS. TAKE CARE. BE ALERT. SHUT UP.

She assumes that I have all the acuteness of a mongoloid, and so she stands on tiptoe and wigwags wildly enough to catch the attention of everyone within a half mile, and unless I give her back a signal as obvious as her own, she believes I have not only missed the original situation that set her to signaling but have somehow overlooked the fact that she is now up on the table flapping her arms.

In this case I carefully did not look at her. I smiled at the countess, who was stony, with an angry flush around her eyes, and at Manon, skinny and nervous and maintaining her sweet vague expression. Then I finally did look across at Ruth and widen my eyes slightly so she could relax. With her help, I managed not to say to this Miss Weibull, HOW COME YOU'RE A MISS, BUT EIGHT MONTHS ALONG? OLD DANISH CUSTOM, EH? HA-HA.

Ruth said fiercely from the bed, "Just remember the times when I've saved you from making a fool of yourself! And some of the times when I haven't succeeded!"

"You overreacted," I said. "You generally do, because you take

126

it for granted I can't see what's under my nose. You started this truth party, now hold still and see yourself as others see you."

"Unless I'd warned you, you'd never have known anything was wrong."

"I wrote this journal that very night, didn't I? Wouldn't you say I'm aware that something is wrong?"

"*After* I warned you. Anyway, you didn't know *what* was wrong."

"Don't tell me you did."

"I think so. Part of it, anyway."

"I think you found out just the way I did, and *when* I did."

"Well, do we have to quarrel about it?"

"No. So why did you start quarreling?"

"I? *You* started it."

I counted ten, then ten more. She saw me doing it, and was furious. Finally I said, "Listen, if there's anything more ridiculous than two people seventy years old . . ."

"Speak for yourself!"

". . . or nearly seventy, bickering about who knew what twenty years ago, then it can only be the same two old fools bickering about who started the bicker."

"All right, but . . ."

"No buts. Peace, perturbèd spirit."

"Oh, I hate that condescending phrase!"

"Condescending?" I said. "Who said it? Prince Hamlet to his father's ghost?"

"Oh, go on and read. And I hope you get through that luncheon pretty soon. There were more important things happening than that luncheon."

"I read what it says in the book," I said. "What it says in the book is what seemed important to me at the time. If you don't like it, write your own diary."

"I wish I had. Then there might be a way of checking on yours."

We were still standing, waiting. I kept expecting Manon to tell us to sit down, but she didn't. Beside me this mysterious Miss

Weibull stood flat-footedly, breathing hard. She had that faked composure, but she didn't have the look of the quality. Governess who had got in trouble? But governess to whom? There were no children around except Bertil, who was only a visitor. But not family either. One of Count Eigil's peasant girls? You didn't bring those into the castle, or at least I assumed you didn't. Those could be left in the hayloft with their dresses up around their necks.

The countess hated her being there, Manon was resigned to her being there, and Miss Weibull was damned well going to be there whether they liked it or not. The most obvious thing about all of it was that all three seemed to believe they were concealing what was perfectly obvious. Also, the more I looked at Miss Weibull the more I saw that she was pretty old to be in the condition she was in. She had to be around forty, about the countess' age.

Like people at a funeral before the preacher enters, we waited, and smiled, and said nothing, and were desperately bright. The bowls of lilacs spaced down the table filled the room with their scent. Now, I grew up among lilacs, I am a lilac lover, and group silences that go on too long make me nervous. So I said to Miss Weibull, most politely, "Aren't the lilacs marvelous?"

"*Jeg taler ikke Engelsk,*" said Miss Weibull.

Put on my mettle, I sniffed deeply and appreciatively, rolled my eyes, looked pointedly at the lilacs, sniffed again, and placed a hand over my heart. I searched my mind in vain for the Danish word for lilacs, and had to fall back on something less precise. "*Smukke Blomster,*" I said. I suppose I felt an obligation to make her feel at home.

Most curiously she looked at me. I have been looked at that way by cows watching me climb through a barbed wire fence. "*Ah, oui,*" she said. Across the table, as if on signal, the countess and Manon straightened their backs. Ruth was about to start her semaphore again, but what had I done? Praised the lilacs.

Then their three pairs of eyes turned sideward, and I looked where they were looking. Here came Grandmamá on a servant's arm.

She was so old she would have had to be dated by carbon 14. Conforming to the rule that old ladies should give up primary colors and return to the pastels of babyhood, she wore a dusty-pink jersey dress that hung on her like a sweater on a gate. She was thin and brittle. Veins and tendons stood out on the backs of her blotchy hands. Below the sagging jersey dress, which came to mid-calf, her stockings drooped on unpadded bone. The skin had shrunk on her skull, which looked no bigger than a monkey's, and the shrinkage had all gathered into wrinkles. Her face was a spiderweb with eyes.

As we might have watched George Arliss making an entrance, we watched her slide and shuffle toward us. Her eyes were fixed straight ahead on something miles away, disdaining to look for the obstacles her feet felt for. For all her decrepitude she was fiercely erect, and I had one of those little thrills of sensation that sometimes come with martial music. Pride, she had. If the servant had withdrawn his arm, she would have fallen on her back, not on her face. She looked like one of those Milles ghosts, running on her heels toward eternity.

The servant was careful and slow. The old lady's shuffling foot reached the edge of the Chinese rug and felt, inched, slid up over it. Then as she brought the rear foot up over the edge to meet the front one, she brought her eyes down from whatever horizon they were fixed on, and took us all in in one look. It may have been intended as a greeting; it felt as peremptory as a bullwhip.

Manon and the countess jumped to help the servant get her into the chair at the head of the table. Supported by six hands, she teetered and sank, and went the last four inches with a bump. She clenched her claws on the chair arms while the servant lifted chair and all into place. Only then, her difficult entrance accomplished, she turned her cheek up to the countess, who bent and kissed it. There was a flurry of bird sounds, much pressing of hands. When the countess left her and came around—widely around—Miss Weibull to place herself on my other side, her eyes were wet.

Manon stood with her hand on the old lady's shoulder. Solicitous and gentle, she bent and said, "Grandmamá, here are Astrid's friends, Mr. and Mrs. Allston."

The old red-rimmed eyes touched Ruth and then me, a glance

surprisingly steady, though her whole head shook. She crossed an arm across her breast and laid a hand on Manon's, still on her shoulder. I liked that gesture, as I liked the tears in the countess' eyes. Aristocracy humanized. Three affectionate women. "You are very welcome here," the old lady said in English.

Across the table the little baron, with perfect timing, pulled out Manon's chair. She came, he nudged her into place and turned to Ruth. As for me, I was torn between the countess and Miss Weibull, and had to elect Miss Weibull as being on my right and *enceinte* at that. When I got her bulk shoved up to the table against the resisting pile of the rug, the countess had seated herself. She gave me a blank, pleasant, annoyed smile as I edged in between them.

It did not begin as the liveliest luncheon I ever attended. Manon was quiet, the countess nearly mute. Ruth tried, in English, to catechize the little baron. The old lady dabbled and picked at her food, Miss Weibull ate heartily for two. There was fruit soup, then a great salad of the shrimps they dip up from among the sea grass in these brackish estuaries, then a mousse and that universal Danish addiction, marzipan cookies. And, praise God, wine. As soon as I properly could, I *skaal'*ed the lady on my left and got her to melt a little. Then I went on and *skaal'*ed all the rest of the ladies in turn. I didn't know whether I was supposed to or not, but there was no one else to do it—the little baron didn't even have a wineglass—and I thought we could all use a drink. It was a strange sensation holding the eyes of the old countess, like peering through the cobwebbed window of an abandoned house and meeting the eyes of something alive looking out. I also gazed into the eyes of Miss Weibull, as enigmatic and impenetrable as marbles.

Ruth remarked on how humiliating it was for Americans, but how pleasant, to travel in a country where it seemed everyone spoke English. (And who was it who had refused to try to learn Danish?) Manon repeated something Astrid's father used to say— that if a Dane fell into the sea and washed up to the south, he would have to know German; if he washed up to the west, English or French; if to the north or east, Norwegian, Swedish, Finnish, or Russian. So every Dane was compelled to prepare for the day when he fell into the sea.

The countess, coming out of her sulks, claimed that if Mr. Allston fell into the sea he would come up speaking anything he needed to, and Manon said ah, but that was because he was really a Dane, and to the old lady she explained that Mr. Allston's mother had been born in Bregninge, wasn't that interesting?

The old lady's head wobbled back on its scrawny stem. "Here?"

"Here in Bregninge, yes."

"What family? Are we related?"

"Oh no," I said. "She worked on one of the farms."

"One of our peasants?"

In that room, the word "peasants" had a nasty arrogant sound, and I wasn't exactly taken with the "our," either.

"Yes," I said.

But they were too polite to expose their prejudices even if they had them, as perhaps they didn't. The old lady looked at me with interest out of her wrinkles, and quavered, "Where is she now? What was her name? Have you come to visit your relatives?"

"She died years ago," I told her. "Both of her parents died of smallpox when she was an infant. I never heard her mention any other relatives. Her name was Ingeborg Heegaard."

I became aware that Miss Weibull had turned her head and stopped chewing and was watching me with interest. Why? She spoke *ikke Engelsk* and couldn't have understood anything I said. But she spoke some French, evidently, which was interesting. She must have fallen in the sea only once. I found myself giving her a token smile in passing, while I paid attention to the old lady, who was sorting through the drawers of her mind and not finding what she was looking for.

"No," she said, "I remember no one by that name."

"I'm sure the family had run out," I said. "She was brought up by some people named Sverdrup."

It was as if I had broken wind. For a split second—*et øjeblik* as they say in Denmark—the table froze. At least the old lady and

Manon did, and I had the strong impression that the countess did, though I was turned away from her. Miss Weibull was *very* interested.

A moment only, and then people were breathing again, the table was casual, my faux pas was ignored out of existence, had never happened. Whatever it was. "Yes," the old lady was saying as if the conversation had never broken down, "it must be fascinating to visit where she came from. It must be very different from America. And your father, who was he?"

I suppose I was feeling bruised and aggrieved and bewildered. Somewhat sullenly, I said that he was a brakeman on the Chicago, Milwaukee and St. Paul, and got a stiff look from Ruth.

Manon motioned the servant, who brought around fingerbowls with sprays of lilac in them. The old lady paddled and dabbled and touched her puckered lips with her napkin, Manon laid her napkin on the table. Signals went around among those people in a way that Ruth should study, and before I knew we had ended our conversation the servant was at the back of the old lady's chair and Manon was there helping to hoist her to her feet. Stiff between their lifting hands, and looking like death, she said to me, "We must talk again. It has been . . . very pleasant. Now I must ask that you excuse me. I tire easily these days. Please make yourselves entirely at home. I am happy to have you here."

They started her out, and I turned just in time to run into another of those speaking looks that the countess was directing at Manon, who was looking back over her shoulder as she moved. At once the countess smiled, and Manon smiled. Manon said, "Perhaps Mr. and Mrs. Allston will want to rest. Or to walk. Perhaps they will lend you to me for an hour."

Of course, we said. As you wish. Don't worry about us.

Miss Weibull was planted where I had landed her as we rose. It is hard to tell about pregnant women, their bloat makes it impossible to see them as they really are, but I thought she might once have been a quite splendid animal, and there was no doubt at all about her interest in me. She laid a finger upright against her pursed lips and said through it, "Ingeborg Heegaard. . . . *De? Elle était . . . ?*"

"My mother. *Min moder*. Yes."

Miss Weibull wagged her head, her pondering finger still at her lips. Her eyes grew wide and round, the way eyes do when their owners are about to go *boo* at children. *"Hun var min moders veninde!"* she said with an air of great conviction, and some sort of triumph, and maybe a dash of malice, and glanced sidelong at the countess as if she might say more. But she didn't. She turned, smiling her sly smile, and steered her belly out of the room. That left Ruth, the countess, the little baron, and me.

"What in God's name," I said.

The countess was upset. "It is complicated. It is incredible. I will explain you sometimes. Later."

"What does *veninde* mean—friend?"

"Yes."

"And who is Miss Weibull?"

"Her mother was a Sverdrup."

"That reminds me of the Arab proverb: Ask a mule who his father was, and he'll always say, 'My mother was a horse.' "

"Joe," Ruth said.

The countess was really upset. "Can you wait? Pleass? I will explain all things. Later."

"I wonder if we *should* wait," I said. "I don't want to be rude, but it seems I already have been. I've said something unforgivable. Shouldn't we just leave?"

"No, pleass!" She put her hand on my arm and shook me. "You must not feel so! It is only . . . Pleass, you must not think of leaving, Manon and Grandmamá would be miserable. I too. Listen! You wanted to see your mother's house. If it was the Sverdrup cottage, I can tell you. It is at the end of the entrance drive, the very end, before you go down the hill on the church path. You should see the church too, it is old and quite good. Perhaps both of you?"

"I think I'll lie down for a while," Ruth said. She never looked less happy.

"Yes!" the countess said. She was frantic to get us out of her hair. "A little nap, you will feel better. And *you* take a walk, and make no worries. Eh? We will talk later. I will come to your room after I have seen Manon.''

Smiling to grin my bark off, she put her arm around reluctant Ruth, who went along as if up gallows hill. She was trying to send me some signal, but her machinery was so shorted out I could not tell what she was trying to say. There I was, alone with the little baron, who had been taking this all in, more interested than his training would quite let him be. I winked at him, took a *krone* out of my pocket, showed it to him, snapped my fingers, and opened my empty hand.

A half-suspicious, wavering smile. He reached out and opened my other hand, and while he was looking for the coin there, I took it out of his ear. He fished among his pocketful of English and came up with a word. "Again!" Or maybe it was *igen*. Related languages have these happy correspondences.

So I disappeared a few more *kroner* for him and finally showed him how it was done. When I left for my walk he was standing in the middle of that regal dining room trying to snap a coin up the sleeve of his Eton jacket.

The castle's drive is a good mile long, absolutely straight, nearly level along the crest of the ridge, and bordered all the way by flowering lindens. They filled the air with sweetness and dropped sticky liquor onto the gravel and now and then onto me. It began to drizzle before I had gone a hundred yards. The view down the slope to the right, through the English park with its big spaced oaks and bursts of rhododendron and lawns that ran down to the very edge of the sea, was dim and romantic.

I saw it, or tried to see it, with my mother's eyes. She had lived at the end of this lane, and undoubtedly walked along it sometimes, and stood back respectfully when the great folks from the castle passed. And dreamed, maybe. And had friends to whom she talked about what she'd like to do and be, and what she'd like to see. Miss Weibull's mother, one of the Sverdrups. And then one day she had gone down to the little harbor almost corked by its green island, and taken the ferry to Copenhagen, and like a bewildered animal crowded aboard an immigrant boat, and voyaged to

America. There was something that made the women of the castle tighten their mouths and straighten their backs, and my mother was somehow part of it. And in I come, into this Old World shenanigan, like Miss Connie Coincidence herself. Incredible, the countess said. I guess. But not by any means intelligible.

The upper side of the drive is all one big planting of pines, with lines of shelter trees between the rows—a future forest as neat as a vegetable garden. Straight ahead of me the spire of a stone church rose above the trees, and short of the church, set in a green meadow at the end of the pine planting, was the cottage.

It was an absolutely standard Danish farm cottage, stuccoed, with a red tile roof and eyebrow dormers, but it looked exceptionally tidied up. A neat fence enclosed a small neat yard, with flower beds inside the fence and a snowball bush in bloom on each side of the doorway. The barn behind the cottage stood open, two goats were tethered among the dandelions at the side, red cattle were grazing at the far end of the meadow. It didn't look like the hardship and poverty one was driven to flee from; it looked like a postcard. Wet by the fine rain, the meadow was so green it hurt the eyes.

Not knowing what to expect, I had visualized nothing, and though I looked the place over most curiously, there was no pang of recognition. I had no impulse to go in the gate and knock on the door. What would I have said? "I'd like to see Ingeborg Heegaard's room, please, the one she slept in sixty years ago?" Ridiculous. And yet my mother's name was still known in that house. Why would Miss Weibull remember the name of a friend of her mother's who had left the country before Miss Weibull was born?

I was walking slowly, rubbernecking. Just as I passed the gate, the cottage door opened and a girl appeared in it. A wench, a buxom one, Aphrodite in stocking feet, still yawning from her nap, her hands reaching back up under her blouse to fasten her undone brassiere. Staring at me, curious and bold, she finished hooking herself together and settled herself into her harness with a wriggle. She reminded me of Miss Weibull—and why not? This was the Sverdrup house, they were probably related.

I touched my beret to the blowzy hoyden in the doorway. "*God dag.*"

Already in the midst of another yawn, she tried to cut it off with her hand, and produced a smothered laugh. "*God dag.*" Bubbling with her silly laugh—at what? something about my American clothes? the beret I wore against the drizzle? the mere fact that I was a stranger?—she watched me pass by. That was my visit to my mother's childhood place, that was the pilgrimage to the source. Not worth the price of admission.

When the drive turned down toward the village, I followed the path that kept on through a green hollow and up the church hill. The church was very old. Its doors of built-up planks were grayed and weathered, the grain so raised that it half effaced the carving. Inside the vestibule, hardly bigger than the hall of an ordinary house, was an enormous poor box made from a section of the trunk of an oak. It was four feet across, hooped around with five or six bands of heavy iron, and fitted with an iron lid. Through the lid on each side came an iron hoop as thick as my finger, and in each hoop was a hand-wrought padlock the size of a good-sized lobster. The coin slot was three inches long and a quarter inch wide, suitable for the coppers of giants.

The thing looked as if it had been made to withstand Viking raiders—too heavy to lift, too strong to smash with battle-axes. As I stood inspecting it, a wispy young man in a black robe and an Elizabethan ruff came into the vestibule from the church. He stopped, surprised: a Danish clergyman who finds anybody in his church these days is bound to be surprised. He spoke to me and I replied. Then there seemed nothing more to say. After a questioning moment he went softly through the door and outside.

In a spirit of scientific research I fished out of my pocket the *krone* I had been snapping up my sleeve for the little baron and dropped it into the slot of the poor box. It fell with a dry sound on wood. No giant coppers in there, nothing at all in there, evidently. I wondered how often they took off the manhole cover to collect the loot. I imagined the thin young clergyman in his ruff coming out with foot-long keys on an iron ring, unlocking the massive padlocks one after the other, prying up the ponderous lid, and reaching in to scrape up a button, a couple of Tuborg caps, and—with a shout of triumph—my single *krone*.

At least the poor box, armored like Fort Knox, made poverty authentic and tangible, as the Sverdrup cottage did not. It made more plausible the flight of my mother, at an age no greater than that of the wench who now perhaps slept in her room. It said something about meagerness and lack of generosity and feudal limitation, it radiated suspicion in the very act of soliciting alms.

Inside, though, the church said something entirely different. It was small, clean, painted white, the prototype of dozens of little Lutheran churches I have seen in the Middle West except that it was built of stone and that the altar under its grayish lace was more high church. But what took my eye was the ships' models hanging on wires from the ceiling. There must have been a dozen of them, three-masters, trawlers, even one white passenger ship with rows of portholes. Each had a card tacked to it, detailing the shipwreck from which its grateful maker had been saved. Here was none of the mean charity expressed by the poor box. Each one of these lovely things was a prayer of thanksgiving. I was reminded of Karen Blixen's remark that Denmark was full of retired sea captains growing roses. Maybe poor old Bertelson, headed for the Swedish village of his childhood, had something after all. Whatever it was to me (nothing), this placid island in its landlocked sea was for the makers of these models the ultimate safe place.

Ambiguous church, speaking simultaneously of deprivation and sanctuary. Its antiphonal voices may well have come from different periods, different ages even, the place seemed so old. As I went around reading the cards on the hanging models, I came to a little bare cell to the right of the front door, with a long horizontal slit in the wall facing the altar, and a little door that opened to the outside. This was the medieval leper chapel, where the afflicted and dying could hear and see the mass without offending the sight of their families and friends. I make a practice of trying to imagine myself into human situations, but when I tried to imagine myself into that ten-by-twelve cell with other noseless, fingerless, suppurating sufferers, and to ponder what consolation I might get from crowding to a crack in the wall to hear somebody in a starched ruff preach God's mercy, I found myself wanting to be out in the air.

So out of the church and down the hill and up again to the linden lane. At its end, a mile away, the ivied front and stepped gables of the castle sat like a barricade—absolute destination, utter terminus, total power. No ambiguity there.

The Sverdrup cottage, as I passed it, showed no sign of life, but when I was a couple of hundred yards down the drive, I heard a door close and looked back to see a man come out the gate and turn my way. I went on, not hurrying. The drizzle had stopped, there were ragged clouds dispersing out over the sea beyond the reaches of vivid lawn. The lane steamed.

The man behind me was walking faster than I was: I could hear his gritting steps on the gravel. Then just inside the iron gates, where the drive looped to circle before the doorway and enclose a medallion of impeccable lawn, I glanced back again, and he motioned with his arm and called to me. "*Du!*"

I stopped, and he came up—hard eye, hard mouth, bushy sandy eyebrows. Younger than I, vigorous mid-forties, probably, in a corduroy jacket and jodhpurs and an Ascot tie. He looked me up and down. His contemptuous "*Du!*" and his arrogant air annoyed me, so I looked *him* up and down, too. Even without the resemblance —something about the eyes and the shape of the head—it would have been clear who he was. The wicked brother. I had seen him before plenty of times, without the feudal trappings—a muscular bulldozer, a pusher-around.

"*Hvad behøver Du?*"

Some way to greet a guest. "I don't *behøver* anything," I said. "I was taking a walk."

At once he tossed his head back and laughed. In English he said, "Of course, of course. You're the one with Astrid." Not

"Sorry, we have to be careful of trespassers," not, "Oh yes, glad to see you, I'm Eigil Rødding." Just, "Of course, you're the one with Astrid."

I was ready to tell him I was not "the one" with anybody, and suggest where he could put his castle, and go to pack our bags. On top of the disturbing conclusion of lunch, his greeting about used up my eagerness to be entertained by the nobility. But my irritation, which I did not hide, amused him. Well, well, his look said. Feisty, eh? Eat me alive, will you? He had a thick neck inside his Ascot scarf, and his thighs and calves bulged his jodhpurs. His eyes had come from some other gene than the one from which the Countess got hers. His were yellow.

"So," he said, with his hands in his pockets, "American, are you? How are you enjoying Denmark?"

"Charming country," I said.

"Been here before?"

"No."

"You and your wife are living with Astrid."

"Yes."

"That must be cosy."

"We've become very good friends."

It seemed he withheld comment. With his hands shoved down in his pockets and his shoulders pushed high, he watched the flight of some starlings off the gable and eventually turned his yellow eyes back on me. His accent he had learned in England. I don't suppose he had had to learn there the upper-class manner which is never unintentionally rude. He jerked his head toward the castle. "The ladies taking good care of you?"

"They've been very hospitable."

He understood me; he grinned like a wolf. "I was unable to greet you."

"Yes," I said. "We understood you weren't at home."

That made him laugh out loud. "I was instructed not to be."

Since he was obviously a man who had never taken instruction in his life, especially not from his women, there seemed nothing for me to say. Teetering in his jodhpur boots, clenching his hands inside his pockets, rolling his corduroy shoulders, he appeared at once abstracted and impatient, itchy with the need to be doing something. He looked me over again, this time without hostility.

"What do you do?"

I told him I was a literary agent.

"Really? That's interesting." (His tone said it was not.) "Where?"

I didn't ask him where he thought anybody *would* be a literary agent. I only said mildly that it was a tribe found only in mid-town Manhattan.

Out of a clear sky he said, "I don't suppose you play tennis."

Fair Sir, will ye just? I had to smile, it was so knight-errant of him. "Why would you suppose that?" I said.

Another appraisal of my parts and my pallor, and he said bluntly, "You don't look like a tennis player. Are you?"

"I guess I don't know what tennis players look like," I said. "I used to play some."

"How about a game now?"

"This minute?"

"Why not? It isn't going to rain any more. There aren't many tennis players on this island, I have to pick up a game when I can find it."

And what if the selected opponent doesn't want to serve your lordship's convenience? "I didn't bring a racket or any clothes," I said.

Wrong response. He said, "That's no problem. How big is your foot?" and stuck his foot down beside mine. "Looks about right. Come along."

"No," I said. "Thanks very much, but I haven't played in months. I'm all out of shape."

He had already started to drag me off. Now he stopped. "Well," he said, "of course it's up to you. You know your capacities better than I do."

That did it. If I were in shape, if I hadn't been sick . . . oh, the hell with caution. Come death, come dishonor, I wanted to put Von Stroheim down. At once my hesitation transformed itself

into an ambush. Shedding crocodile tears, smiling in self-deprecia-
tion—one may smile, and smile, and be a villain; at least I'm sure
it may be so in Denmark—I said, "It's only that I don't know if I
could give you a game. But if you're willing to take a chance . . ."

"Better a slow game than none at all," says this Eigil Rødding.

I hadn't had a racket in my hand since last summer, I hadn't
played in even a club tournament in six or seven years. But if I
couldn't summon up enough of what used to be there to make
Eigil work for his exercise, I would eat three fuzzy new Slazenger
tennis balls.

So fifteen minutes after he intercepted me at his castle gate, I
was warming up with him on a damp clay court near the stables,
and thinking, *Mistake, mistake!* I felt old and stiff, the balls were
heavy, the racket unfamiliar and too big in the handle. There was
no whip in my shots, the opposite base line looked fifty yards
away. There I sat with my little paws on my chest, waiting to be
run over.

Because he was no dub. I suspect he was used to beating anybody in Denmark except maybe Torben Ulrik. He hit his forehand
with a lot of juice on it, and it came off the damp clay whizzing.
When I sent a floater over to his backhand, he wound up and exploded on it, a real old Western-grip broken-arm backhand of a
kind I hadn't seen since Wilmer Allison and Johnny Van Ryn
were winning the national doubles. It went down the line like a
rocket and bruised the fence.

I kept scrambling, knocking them back off the rim and the handle or not getting them back at all. Eigil liked to score off you, he
shot for the lines and corners even when warming up. I did get a
little warm chasing balls. But little by little something began to
come back, I hit a few forehands that felt right, I found that I
could at least chip my backhand and control it. And when I went
up to try a volley or two, and old Eigil threw me up a lob, I hit
that one exactly where I wanted to—into the corner, where Eigil
could chase it for a change.

There was no point in delaying it. I was already getting winded.
"Any time," I said.

He stopped in mid-court and spun his racket.

"Rough," I said.

He bent and looked. "Smooth. I'll serve. Want any particular side?"

"This is fine."

He tried a couple of serves, and I got a look at them. Twist, with a sharp kick to the backhand. A juicehead all the way. So I moved to the left and a little back to give myself room, and he aced me with a sliced one into the forehand corner. In the odd court I moved up, thinking I'd try taking it on the rise, and he gave me one high on the backhand that I couldn't handle.

I lost the game at love, won only one point on my own service, and lost the third game, also at love. Time for the Seventh Cavalry to come riding down the Little Big Horn.

Both his forehand and his backhand were hot as a firecracker, but it seemed to me he had to hit them close to his body, it seemed to me that, like a lot of topspin players, he might not be able to *reach*. So I served wide to his forehand and came up, and sure enough, high weak return, easy lay-away volley. I tried the same thing in the odd court, and same result. Right then I began to think I could take him if I didn't burst a blood vessel with all that running. If I stayed back, his ground strokes would murder me. But he was used to hitting them deep; I didn't think he could consistently put them at my feet as I came up, and if he didn't get them at my feet they came over high, begging to be swatted. And I must say that when he fed me one of those shoulder-high returns, it *was* a pleasure to see him strain and lunge, or go smoking off in the wrong direction when he anticipated wrong.

I wasn't able to break him back, and he took the first set 6–3. By the time I stepped up to the line to serve the first game of the second set I had a blister forming at the base of my thumb, I was soaked with sweat, and my feet in Eigil's too big sneakers were red hot. But I was damned well going to take him, and I did. We went with service through the fifth game, and then I broke him with a net cord shot and a sliced backhand down the line—God, I loved myself. Then all I had to do was hold service and I had him, 6–4.

Enough. Quit with honor. I had been running on the sides of my feet for ten games. I went straight to the grass at the side of the court and sat down and took off one shoe and sock. A big flap of skin was peeled off the ball of the foot, with red meat exposed underneath. "What is it?" Eigil was saying, smacking the top of the net with his racket. "We can't stop now, a set apiece!"

"I'll have to default," I said, and held up my scalped foot. You never saw such disappointment. He was raging with it, like a high school quarterback whose coach won't send him in in the last two minutes to pull out the game. Of course he had won, since I couldn't continue. But the score was dead even, and he had had to run his tongue out. I was willing to settle for that. I flopped on my back on the lawn, tasting brass, my lungs burning, my heart pounding, and my feet on fire—and if the truth were told, thankful to my feet for getting me out of more.

Eigil took two towels off the net post, yanked one around his neck, and came over and dropped one to me. Oddly, his disappointment was over. He was elated, exhilarated by combat, full of chivalry and sportsmanship. His face was red and happy. "You know, you're too modest by half," he said, panting. "You really *are* a tennis player."

"Was," I said. I felt like dying.

"You're amazing for your age. Were you ever ranked?"

"Long time ago. Never higher than the third ten."

"But in the United States, that's *tremendous*. I used to follow these things in the Spalding Tennis Annual. Who were the number one people in your years?"

"Tilden?" I said. "Johnny Doeg? Ellsworth Vines? Riggs? Don Budge?"

"Did you ever play them?"

I mopped my face and neck and flopped my head to look at him. He sat on the grass, towel around his neck, eager and enthusiastic, an admirer. In a minute he would ask for my autograph. Instead of being upset that I had split with him, he apparently

143

had this fantasy of having held his own against an American internationalist with a houseful of cups.

"Played some of 'em," I said. "Never beat any of 'em." But I didn't have the heart to deflate him completely. "After college I only played in tournaments for a few years. In my senior year my partner and I won the national intercollegiate doubles, that was why I was ranked."

"Yes, doubles!" old Eigil says. "I could tell you're a splendid doubles player. The way you punch a volley, the way you hit your overhead. I need to play more with people who play your game, serve and volley. Why don't you stay a month and we'll play every day."

I think he meant it. I was almost sorry to remind him that we were leaving in the morning, and that even if we weren't, I wouldn't be able to play on those feet for at least week. There we sat, pouring sweat and rehashing shots, a couple of locker-room jocks. I have to admit that I've always enjoyed the company of jocks more than that of the literary intellectuals and hyperthyroid geniuses among whom, unhappy one, I earned my living. Also, I hadn't had any company but that of women since we landed in Denmark, more than six weeks ago. I found myself half liking the bugger. Quite plainly he was delighted with me.

After we showered he found me some Band-Aids to patch my feet. Then nothing would do but I must see the estate. I said that my wife, whom I had left at two o'clock, would wonder what had happened to me. Promptly he called the castle and told somebody that Mr. Allston would be in around seven.

My feelings were mixed. My mind's eye kept wandering to the bottle of scotch in my suitcase—I knew that Ruth would expect to hold a note-comparing session over it before dinner. Instead, here I was hobnobbing with the hobgoblin. I wondered where *he* would go for dinner, since we were pre-empting his castle. Lonely service in the library, with smoking jacket, brandy, and cigar? A tray in the kitchen? To the stable to eat with the horses? To Bregninge Inn for *Koldt bord* and beer? A good old-fashioned Dracula picnic in some local graveyard?

It seemed to me he was being pretty good-natured in the face of his sister's non-fraternization policy. I enjoyed talking to him. He had been around—England, where he was educated, and Italy, some, and France and Germany a good deal, and the United States once, with an agricultural mission. He remembered Decorah, Iowa, for some reason. He knew a lot of people and had read books and knew what went on. I had to admit that once he got past his impulse to throw me out as a trespasser he had been good company.

See the estate? All right, why not? He said it was the most scientifically run estate in Denmark, perhaps in the world. The very compulsiveness of his brag made me curious. And I supposed that he was the one who had got Miss Weibull pregnant, but who she was, and what she was doing in the castle, and why the countess was so implacable against him for what was, in emancipated Denmark, surely no mortal sin—those were things a man might find out.

Okay, let's go. How would you say that in Danish? Having fallen into this particular sea, I found myself without the linguistic wherewithal. Without a Danish word I climbed into the Volkswagen parked outside the stables, and we toured the farm.

It isn't a farm, it's an economy. In an hour and a half of whizzing around an area about the size of Delaware, he showed me wheat fields, beet fields, truck gardens, three different varieties of hybrid corn he's experimenting with, and a battery of greenhouses. Also pine plantings, cherry orchards, apple orchards, game coverts, and pastures. Also pigpens, cow stables, henhouses, pheasant and grouse hatcheries, and kennels full of German short-haired pointers and English setters. Also a sawmill, smokehouse, dairy, cheese factory, and refrigerated fruit warehouse. There are two other villages besides Bregninge on the estate, and he owns the port and all its facilities; for all I know, he may have a private merchant fleet. And he is no raw material producer only. Everything he grows, he processes, except the cherries, which are shipped to Amager to be made into Cherry Heering, and the sugar beets, which go, I think he said, to Kiel.

I heard a good deal about confiscatory taxes and a government that lay in wait until a landowner died and then came down on the heirs. I gathered that things had shrunk sharply when his father died in the 1930s. But he had a bit left. At the hour we went around, there was hardly a working soul in sight. He had everything mechanized, even automated. The peasants who used to work on the place must all be up in Copenhagen on welfare (my mother got out just in time).

Crops grow by blueprint. The pigs come off the belt line within a pound of their bacon weight. While the milking machines relieve them of their day's production, the cows can contemplate on the stanchions by their heads the charts that reveal their intake in grain and ensilage and their output in milk and butterfat. No contented cows there. Stakhanovized cows. No tickee, no laundly. Any cow that doesn't keep up her statistics is schnitzel.

Everything clean, nothing smelly, nothing wasted. The straw that most Danish farmers burn in their fields, Eigil bales and uses for fuel to heat his greenhouses, which produce the year round. Now I know where those hard little tomatoes come from, and those incessant cucumbers. He is proud of the hay-burning furnace, which he designed himself.

"You've got a lot to be proud of," I said, and meant it. "You and your father. I understand he was called the Doctor Faustus of genetics."

His shoulder bumped mine, he twisted around in the cramped seat. "Where did you hear that?"

"Karen Blixen, I think."

"Oh, you've met *her*."

"Last week."

"Better her than some others," Eigil said sourly. "At least she's intelligent."

"She said he was a very talented man."

"Was he not," Eigil said, looking straight ahead down the lane. "And they hounded him as if he were the Antichrist. He was the greatest man in Denmark, a century ahead of his time. Do you believe that?"

Without half trying, he seemed to have worked himself into a rage. I said mildly that I knew nothing about his father, or next to nothing, but had no reason to think he wasn't exactly what Eigil said he was. Nevertheless, as an unsuccessful father myself, I almost resented so much filial loyalty. Would Curtis have defended me if someone had questioned my intelligence or integrity? I doubted it. But then I wasn't the Doctor Faustus of anything, either.

"All those rhododendrons you saw in the park are his hybrids," Eigil said. "Half the roses—did you get taken into the rose garden out beyond the ballroom terrace? Those pointers in the kennels are desired all over the world—that's the finest strain anywhere. We grow and ship two varieties of apples he developed. So it goes, all over the estate. He *made* things, new things. He improved what he found. People talk about Mendel. My father looked through windows that Mendel didn't even know were there."

We were rolling softly along a dirt road between scrub woods and a pasture fenced with woven wire. From the woods, pheasants and grouse and what I took to be chukars watched us without flying. The pasture on the other side was humped with dozens of feeding hares as big as dogs. Everything was as Eigil said—nature improved, cultivated as carefully as his bacon hogs and pine plantings. Even the scrub woods were carefully *cultivated* scrub woods, the perfect game covert. And then as we rolled slowly and he talked about his father, with his eyes straight ahead and his jaw bunched up, he stepped suddenly on the brake. A buck, or stag I suppose they would call him, had just stepped out onto the bank of a ditch a hundred yards ahead.

"Khhhhh!" Eigil said in his throat. "There's that bastard with the bad horns!" He cramped the Volkswagen around in two quick moves, and we were accelerating out the way we had come in.

As soon as we turned behind a screen of trees, he put his foot to the floor. We zipped around behind the stables and pulled up in a cloud of gravel next to the room where we had showered. Eigil jumped out, leaving the door open and the motor running. In a minute he came running back with a little Mannlicher in his hand. "Hold this!" he said, and shoved it at me. Off again, like Crazy Horse on his way to intercept Custer.

Of course the stag was gone when we got there, and five minutes of careful prowling failed to flush him. I was glad. I am not much on killing things, and I didn't need a lesson in selective breeding.

"I ought to get back," I said as soon as we got to the car again —me walking on the sides of my feet, my hips, knees, and shoulder already stiff. The trees on that lane were fuzzy with sprouts clear to the ground, like the legs of some chickens, and peasants had harvested these sprouts for faggots year after year, leaving an extraordinary stubble of cut sprouts out of which grew new green ones. Never waste anything. Make faggots of your prunings, and make a business of making faggots.

Eigil looked at the sun, bedding down in high clouds over the Baltic. "It's not quite six-thirty. There's time to show you the museum. Are you interested in archaeology?"

I thought I'd better be, as the quickest way of closing out the tour. "I don't know anything about the archaeology of Denmark, but sure, I'd like to see it, if you have time. Just a quick look, and then I'll have to go and dress."

Going back, we circled down to the shore, through the village, and up the hill to the lane of lindens. As we passed the Sverdrup cottage, the girl I had seen was picking flowers in the yard. Eigil lifted his hand in casual greeting from the wheel, and she gawped after us as we headed toward the castle. I had an impulse to tell him my mother had lived in that house. Then I remembered that when I first saw him he had been coming out of it. Why not, he owned it. Visit from the landlord. Nevertheless, there was Miss Weibull, upon whom I suspected him of having exercised a few *droits de seigneur*, and she lived in that house, or once did. I decided that instead of revealing my family history I would praise the lane of lindens. Naturally they turned out to have been planted by Eigil's father.

The museum was a long half-timbered cottage beyond the stables, three rooms full of the kind of stuff that quickly gives me museum feet and strabismus: tools, weapons, utensils, skulls, bones, a complete record of all the Danish horizons from the antler-and-bone culture to the Iron Age. Seems that Danish places whose names end in -inge are invariably old, and therefore often rich archaeologically. Bregninge, according to Eigil, has been continuously inhabited since at least 4000 B.C. "All Danes," he said with a grin. "There's no evidence of any immigrations or invasions. These people raided other tribes, but they don't seem to have been raided. *My* tribe. Except for an occasional captive woman, an essentially unmixed strain for six thousand years. You can imagine what that meant to my father."

I let it be assumed that I could. Still wearing his sidelong smile, Eigil took hold of a cloth that covered something the shape of a big bird cage. "Here, let me introduce my first known ancestor," he said, and pulled off the cloth. Inside was this mummy his peat diggers had found. Its hands and feet were tied, and it had been strangled with a thong. The museum in Copenhagen thinks it was an executed prisoner of war or criminal, but Eigil thinks it was a sacrifice to keep the fields fertile. "What's more logical?" he says. "This was hundreds of years before the invention of manure. In any case, I don't want him to be a prisoner of war, because then he couldn't have been my ancestor. Don't you think we look alike?"

Simpering, he posed beside the bell jar, and by God, he did look a little like the mummy. I wondered if perhaps I did, but I didn't want to ask. Because that thing was more likely to be my ancestor than his. My folks undoubtedly belonged to the class that got strangled, his to the class that did the strangling.

"You're better looking," I said. "The breed has improved since the Bronze Age."

Several times this afternoon I noticed his way of looking at me hard when I said something, as if he suspected double meanings. He is not a man who understands playfulness, I think, in spite of his competitive instincts. But there had not been a trace of hostility in him since the tennis. Knock heads with him and he was

your pal. In fact, he had a look of eagerness, a certain impet-
uousness of explanation and argument, as if he wouldn't mind
converting me to something. To what? Membership in a six-
thousand-year-old strain of Homo sapiens? He didn't know, but I
already had at least a guest card in that club.

"You'd be surprised," he said. "There can't have been much
change, especially in families like mine. We got a shot of Prussian
and Hanoverian in the last couple of centuries, but that didn't
greatly dilute us. We're one of the rare examples of selective
breeding of humans over a long period. First a pure type like this
one, without mongrelization, and then a naturally selected superior class from that type—the biggest, strongest, most intelligent
—and then the aristocratic practice of seldom breeding outside
that class, at least officially. Aristocracies are always essentially endogamous. If we had used the same intelligence in breeding ourselves that we use to breed cows or pointers, we'd have a race of
supermen. I am not necessarily being smug when I say my family
and my class come as close as you're likely to find. Even as it is,
with infusions of Wendish and Polish and German and Swedish
blood, we come close to being a pure strain, and unlike primitive
endogamous groups, we have kept records. This was something
that fascinated my father."

I was thinking of the countess' remark that the men of her class
were all drunks and the women all witches, and remembering
vague sophomore biology courses which spoke of inbreeding and
exhaustion. "You know a lot more about it than I do," I said,
"but as an American I have to stand up for hybrid vigor."

His eyebrows went up and his finger went up, he backed me
against a case of old bones—relatives of ours, no doubt—and said,
"Hybrid vigor, exactly. It's a fact, it exists, it can be demonstrated.
But it's too accidental. America will be ten thousand years
developing an American type as pure as that fellow there with the
string around his neck, and while you're developing the pure type
you'll have other results of mongrelization besides hybrid vigor. *If
it could only be done scientifically*, that was what my father always said. He didn't mean play Hitler, he was not interested in ty-

rannical eugenics or Brave New Worlds. He meant only that if there could be a controlled experiment over a good many generations, a demonstration clear enough to show the superiority of method over accident. When Darwin said that man is a wild species, he meant just that—nobody ever domesticated it or bred it scientifically for quality."

"What about the Egyptian royal line?"

"All right. Brother-sister incest through hundreds of years. But who was keeping track of the experiment? Who made the kind of records that I make on my Holsteins? What Pharaoh ever won a Best of Breed ribbon at a fair? And who would permit any such experiment now? Sentimental outrage, Lutheran horror. It would hurt no one, it would move the human race a quantum jump forward. But *nej, nej,* thou shalt not. They would crucify anyone who suggested it, especially since Hitler gave it racist and fascist connotations. Eh?"

"I guess," I said.

"We need to know so many things we are prevented from finding out," Eigil said, pinning me against the bone case. "It takes many generations to develop the qualities you want, without bad recessive traits. You breed dogs for decades to get the carriage, coat, docility, ferocity, intelligence, nose, whatever it is you're after. If you could once get it pure, you could inbreed forever without bad results. But no line is pure enough, and so your dogs after a while show, say, hysteric traits, excessive nervousness, that sort of thing. Then you have to breed out for a generation or sometimes two. Not mongrelize—you don't let your bitches run in the woods and get mounted by anything that catches them at the right time. You pick another good line that has strength where yours has this weakness, and when you've got it firmly built into your mixed strain, you turn back, you exchange exogamy for endogamy again. Think what it would mean to the human race if we had an elegant and incontrovertible experiment to show the transmission of certain traits in human beings. You would be on the way to eliminating physical defects, heritable diseases, even ugliness. Mendel thought everything could be explained by peas. I know some people these days who think fruit flies will provide all the answers. But there is no alternative to experimenting with the animal itself."

I eased away from the case and flexed my blistered hand and looked at the blisters to suggest a change of topic. He was really on his pulpit, and preaching. "I don't know," I said. "I'm not sure I *want* my gene pool manipulated. You know what I miss on this marvelous estate of yours?"

"What?" He had expended his vehemence, he was grinning again. His eyes were as yellow as amber.

"Wild things," I said. "Little cottontails or gophers or snakes or moles or raccoons or polecats that could breed in the hedges and live in spite of you. Holsteins and short-haired pointers are nice, but a little predictable."

Curious, smiling, he searched my eyes, trying to understand me and probably making it all too complex and difficult. "Why would I permit them?" he said. "Why should they be allowed to eat what might feed my cows or hares or game birds or deer?"

"You were all set to shoot that buck with the bad horns," I said. "How do you know he doesn't have everything else a deer ought to have—size, strength, speed, a good digestion, virility, everything but good horns? How do you know for sure that shooting him won't *weaken* the strain?"

The smile remained on his square face, with a shadow of amused forgiveness in it. "But I raise them for *trophies*," he said.

There was an old Morris Minor parked in the drive when we walked to the front of the castle. Eigil gave it a glance. "The doctor. I suppose my grandmother isn't digesting well." He stood there in his jodhpurs and corduroy, country squire, feudal lord, smiling and shaking his head regretfully. He put out his hand and gave my poor blistered mitt a hearty crushing. "I'm going to have to write Astrid a thank-you note. I had no idea what she was bringing, or I would have insisted on being at home."

"I'm glad you didn't entirely vanish," I said. "I've enjoyed the afternoon."

"So have I. Immensely. I'm sorry I didn't meet your wife. Perhaps you'll both come again, without Astrid so that we won't have to play these silly games."

Embarrassed, I said, "I don't understand anything about that, and don't particularly want to. I hope you see that in the circumstances we . . ."

"Of course. But come again, please. I hope your feet don't trouble you too much. I took advantage of you. But I want you to know, that was the best tennis I've had for a long time."

We parted, mutually complimentary. He went away somewhere, and I rang the bell and was admitted by the brawny maid, who was obviously agitated. I couldn't understand a word of her Danish, but she kept looking up the stairs, so I started up, to be met halfway by Ruth, crying, Oh, where have you *been*, I've been going out of my *mind!* You shouldn't have stayed out so long, what have you been doing? Etc. Turns out the old countess was no sooner steered back to her rooms than she had a seizure of some kind, stroke, heart attack, nobody seemed to know. She might be dead or alive at this moment. Manon and the countess were with her, dinner was canceled, they would send something up.

In the circumstances I didn't want to ring for ice. We had a couple of warm scotches and water while I told her what I had been doing, and with whom. She looked at my hand and my skinned feet and lamented. She wondered that *I* hadn't had a heart attack, what on earth was I thinking of, how could I *dream* of playing tennis, the way I had been feeling? Shortly the maid knocked and wheeled in a tea cart with dinner on it, and a good dinner, too, with a good cold bottle of Mosel, and over it we speculated a long while about this feud between the countess and her brother, and about Miss Weibull, and discussed my adventures down the lane and among the fields and woods and on the courts of honor.

We kept expecting the countess to come and let us know what was going on, but it got to be ten-thirty, and then eleven, without a sign of her. Ruth kissed me a trembling, helpless kiss and went off to her canopied four-poster and after a while I heard that she was asleep.

And here I sit, with thirty great wounds, of the least of which an emir would have died, scratching in a God damn notebook. Why? Do I think I'll forget this? I can smell the lilacs that breathe up through the open casements, and watch the moonlight chase timidly back and forth across the Aubusson rug, advancing to Ruth's bed, scurrying back, creeping out again. Outside it is not really dark; we are getting close to the time of the white nights, when there is no true darkness, but only some hours of dusk. The sky now is either filled with moonlight or is the same predawn gray that it was when I looked out before going to bed.

The moonlight ventures out, reaches, stretches, dimly trembles on the bedclothes, on the darkness of Ruth's hair, the paleness of her face. I hope she is dreaming something gorgeous, her first night in an authentic castle.

FIVE

1

Ruth has had no luck finding anyone to substitute for Edith Patterson at the convalescent home. This morning at breakfast she braced *me*. How about coming down and talking to the old folks about contemporary writers? I would be surprised how much they read and how responsive they were.

I said what if I couldn't think of a contemporary writer I wanted to talk about.

"Oh, for heaven's sake, don't be that way! There are dozens."

I said name one.

She looked at me pretty stormily. It is her opinion that my distaste for many kinds of contemporary novelists, including the critic-intellectuals, the mythologizers, the fantasizers, the black humorists, the absurds, the grotesques, and the sexualizers, is as pigheaded as my prejudices against the young. She is of course right, I wouldn't argue with her. By definition a prejudice is a principle that its owner does not intend to examine. Which does not prove it is wrong. And what a comforting thing it is.

"How would I discuss the compulsory sex scenes with the old folks?" I said. "Do I start with the accepted major premise: if they aren't fucking it isn't fiction? (Unless, of course, they're sucking, then it's okay too.)"

"Do you have to be as repulsive as you say they are?"

"No. That's why I won't discuss their novels with your old folks."

"They aren't all like that."

I said name one.

"Well, if you won't talk about any American, talk about Césare."

I said Césare was as bad as any of them. The only good thing about him was that he really *liked* women and *amore*. But the effect was about the same.

"Then tell them stories about him. He's a regular mine of stories. Tell them about his visit the other day, they'd love it. Make them laugh."

I said what if I didn't consider Césare's visit a laughing matter.

She sat up in bed so abruptly that she slopped her coffee. "Oh, what's the *matter* with you? Can't you laugh at yourself any more? Laugh at me, then. Laugh at Minnie. Laugh at Césare. Don't just be a carping old man. It doesn't matter what you say to them, it's the interest you take in them that counts."

I said what if I didn't take any interest in them. What if they scared the pants off me and gave me the glooms.

"Joe," she said in despair, "it isn't *you*. You've always been such a joker. And you're not unsympathetic. I know you're not. You're a . . . *marshmallow* about other people's troubles!"

She sounded so distracted that I quit playing my little game, which when you think of it is a little cruel. Even if I don't want to talk to her shut-ins, I don't have to rub it in. So I fell back on the prepared position of a legitimate excuse. "An aching marshmallow," I said. "If I go out in the wind the way my joints are now, you'll be taking care of me in bed."

"Have you been taking your indocin?"

"Popping them like peanuts. And that's another thing, those pills eat away your stomach wall. Two more days and I'll be back to my adolescent ulcers."

At that moment the "Today" show took a break to let a girl who "teaches college" tell about her headaches, and how she has found that there is something in Anacin, she doesn't know what it is, but it *works*. Ruth, who is dangerously susceptible to suggestion either overt or subliminal, said to me, "Maybe you ought to switch pain pills if indocin is so hard on you. Maybe Anacin *would* work. Or aspirin. Most people cure their arthritis with aspirin."

"Mama," I said, "you don't *cure* your arthritis with anything. You just chase it back from your borders, you set up a Roman wall to keep it off. That doesn't mean you've done it in. Off in the heather, back in the glens, it's sitting by a peat fire in its kilts, with its dirty knees showing and its teeth gleaming through its beard, telling itself that you mought of kilt it but you ain't whupped it. Then when your empire gets tired, and you have to pull back the legions to fight the Helvetians or somebody, here come the Picts and Scots sneaking down on your wall again with their black knives in their stocking legs. No switching around of the defenders is going to *cure* them. Did you ever hear of old Vortigern, who was a chief among the Romanized Britons? The legions kept the Picts and Scots off him for a good while, but they gave him plenty of bellyaches in the process. Then when the legions left, Vortigern called in Hengist and Horsa and a lot of Jutish raiders to take care of his problem. They were just as good at it as the legions, but they gave poor Vortigern even bigger bellyaches."

She sat staring. "What on earth is all that? All I did was suggest that some other pill might kill the pain just as well, and be easier on you."

"And all I did was demonstrate that one painkiller is as hard on you as another. Anything that's good for the joints is bad for the stomach. Ask Ben."

"Oh, Ben! He's an enthusiast like you. Sometimes I wonder if his medicine isn't as much witchcraft as science."

"But if he advertised on TV you'd believe him."

Oh, right between wind and water. She stayed irritated through a rerun of the news and through an interview with a Watergate defendant who forgave his persecutors and had faith in the American system. Finally she said, "Well, I don't suppose you should go out, if you feel that bad. But I wish you wouldn't pretend you don't care about those poor old people. You do it just to aggravate me. What if you were in a home like that, wouldn't you want to have things to do and people to talk to and ideas to talk about?"

I said I didn't ever intend to get into a home like that.

"Yes?" she said. "How are you going to avoid it?" But the implications of what she had opened up made her close the lid again. Fretfully she said, "What am I going to do, Joe? I can't read to them the whole two hours. I haven't dared tell them Edith isn't coming, they look forward to her so much. She was *so* good! She'd play them Chopin and Mozart for a half hour, and then play requests, anything from 'The Old Oaken Bucket' to *Hair* music. She'd even get them singing, they had a really good time."

Over her coffee cup she brooded at me, and I saw an idea dawn. "Hey, you know, the Pattersons haven't gone yet, or they wouldn't be going to Ben's tomorrow. I wonder if I couldn't call her and see if just this once more . . ."

"No," I said.

"What?"

"No, I wouldn't."

"Why not?"

"Because they aren't going away. That was an excuse. Ben told me when he and Edith were over the other day. Tom isn't going to make it. The reason she isn't playing for your shut-ins is that she's staying home to help him die."

I may have said it roughly, for I feel Tom Patterson's death sentence as something close and threatening. Not only does one watch—yet once more—the blotting out of a friend. One is reminded, without needing the reminder, that the line forms on the left. I jarred Ruth. If I am a marshmallow, she is a meringue. She has an affectionate and generous spirit, and she hurts for other people. Staring at me over the rim of her raised cup, she almost whispered, "Oh, why didn't you tell me! Why didn't she?"

"I didn't because Ben thought they want to keep it to themselves, and there wasn't a thing you could do. I suppose Edith didn't for the same reason."

Taking away a big globed tear from the corner of each eye, she brooded about it. "Yes. If that's what they want, they're entitled to it. Oh damn, I was *afraid* that was the way it was. But I should think their friends might . . . Shouldn't we, maybe . . . ? But what's Ben's dinner? Is that a . . . ?"

"Farewell? I don't think Tom's that close. He's got weeks,

maybe a month or two. I suppose Ben's just making a gesture of solidarity. Business as usual. Help them act as if nothing is changed."

"Ben's a nice fellow, he really is."

"Yes."

Her eyes came up, her questioning black eyebrows rose into her white bangs. "Is that why you've been so out of sorts? Thinking about Tom and not thinking you should tell me?"

"I almost wish it was," I said. "That would make me look good instead of just crabby. Maybe it was, some. But ever since Césare blew in on the big storm I've had sand in all my bearings. I don't suppose I was too thrilled to get a glimpse of us through Césare's eyes, either—off behind the garage in the long grass with four flat tires and half our parts gone. Also the mail we keep getting. One week Kenneth's institutionalized in Queens, as effectively dead as if they'd buried him. Next week Roy's dead in Savannah. Two days later we hear Dick's got Parkinson's disease in Princeton. Now Tom's moved into Death Row here. Even that ancient history we've been reading is a reminder of how old and helpless we're all getting. Doesn't it bother you to think of her buried down there in Bregninge, feeding her helpless harelip with a spoon? At our age, news is all bad. I don't *like* standing in line for the guillotine. I don't *like* being invited to my friends' executions."

Well before I finished that harangue, I was aware that it was definitely too rough. Ruth thinks she wants all this communion, and talking things out, but you can't tell her what you really feel. That isn't what she wants. She wants to be reassured. So I got up, hobbling like an old grandpappy, with my hand on my lumbago, and limped toward the bathroom door.

"Look," I said, pausing, "sometime I'll talk to your old folks, that's a promise. But not today. When I do, I'll come on like Rosie Bliven and help them down the golden steps, but today I've got to nurse my rheumatics so I'll be straightened out by tomorrow. I don't want a lecture from Ben on how the villagers of Vilcabamba, Ecuador, all live to be a hundred and thirty, and plow their fields with crooked sticks until they're ninety-eight. Also I don't want Tom Patterson feeling sorry for my lameness."

"All right," she said, appeased. "You'd better not even go down to your study. Take a Jacuzzi and wrap up warm and stay in bed all day."

"Yes, Ma."

She doesn't like that response, which smacks of irony and insubordination. Disgustedly she went into the other bathroom. Through the wall I heard her about her business, then the water running strongly in the tub. After five minutes she came in and said she had drawn me a hot tub and put the Jacuzzi in it. I caught myself in time, and didn't ask why she hadn't inquired whether I *wanted* a Jacuzzi. (My private opinion, diametrically opposed to hers, is that they do me no good.) She means well. Shut up, hold still, I want to take *care* of you.

I was still in the tub, working my stiff hands under the blast of the Jacuzzi's nozzle, when she poked in her head to tell me she was on her way. The sight of me in my bubble bath made her laugh. "You look like Nero, or Petronius, or somebody."

"No slave girls."

"Will you be all right? Can I do anything for you before I go?"

"You might hand me a razor blade out of the drawer there, so I can open my veins."

"Oh, Joe, don't *joke!*"

"One minute I'm not my old japery self, and the next I shouldn't joke."

"Your sense of humor is perverted." She looked at her watch. "Lord, I'll be late. You stay inside, now. I'll have to do some shopping afterwards, I won't be home till nearly one. Don't sit in the tub too long, twenty mintues is supposed to be enough."

"Yes, Ma."

She made a face and went. I sat on in my roaring mechanical massage parlor, a reluctant sybarite. It did actually feel good in the tub. The warmth was relaxing, the Jacuzzi drove and pummeled against whatever ailing part I exposed to it. The bathroom blind was up, and sunlight, broken by the wind-moved twigs of the plane tree outside, fluttered on the marble counter, and on the tub, and on me.

Plato's cave, with aqua-therapy. I was reminded of a remark of Willa Cather's, that you can't paint sunlight, you can only paint what it does with shadows on a wall. If you examine a life, as Socrates has been so tediously advising us to do for so many centuries, do you really examine the life, or do you examine the shadows it casts on other lives? Entity or relationships? Objective reality or the vanishing point of a multiple perspective exercise? Prism or the rainbows it refracts? And what if you're the wall? What if you never cast a shadow or rainbow of your own, but have only caught those cast by others?

I got into a sort of awkward yoga position so that the jet could play on my swollen big toe joints, and sitting that way I held up my arm and felt the muscle. A stringy, old-man's arm, but reassuringly hard. I do more regular physical labor than I did when I was younger. Still, an old man's arm, bony at elbow and wrist, and at its end an old man's hand with enlarged knuckles and raised veins. The chest and belly rising out of the bubbles were an old man's torso, too—too white, too hairy, without resilience.

What happens to young flesh to make it old? I pinched the skin on the back of my hand, and it stayed up like a ridge in putty, only slowly flattening out. Loss of elastin. But what's elastin? Why do we lose it? What chemical breakdown or slowdown occurs, what little manufacturing plant fails or goes on strike?

Inside the inelastic skin, within the still hard muscles, the joints go bad, grow knobs and spurs of calcium (removing it, according to my dentist, from my teeth and jawbone). The rough edges grate when they move together, and agitate the little nerves of pain.

But though we all deteriorate, we are given the privilege of deteriorating according to some poetic justice. We ourselves help establish the places and extent of our wearing out. My right shoulder and elbow are worse than my left because I was once a right-handed tennis player with a severe service and overhead. (Breaking my neck to beat Eigil Rødding when I was out of shape, I probably laid down an imperative that I will feel for life, even if I live to a Vilcabamba old age.) My right big toe is worse than my left because when I was ten years old, on an afternoon that I remember clearly, on the shore of Lake Calhoun in Minneapolis, I kicked Ole Sieverud in the backside and hurt myself worse than I hurt him. Disorder and early sorrow, and the consequences concentrated because I happened to be born right-handed and right-footed. If I had been born ambidextrous at both ends, my ills would be better distributed.

I ran my hand over the top of my head, slick and bumpy. For that I take not even partial responsibility. Baldness is inherited and sex-linked, they say. I was getting there by the time I was forty. How does *that* work? Somebody must have examined the process, down to exactly what happens in each hair follicle when the appointed gene flips the switch at the appointed time and turns off the lights in one more little chemical plant. If he had been set to it, could old Count Rødding, with his facility in remodeling nature, have bred baldness out? Probably, just the way he'd have bred furnishings into a terrier. A pity he didn't attempt it, for he and his son both bred for trophies, and a bald head mounted in the billiard room wouldn't be half so decorative as one with a senatorial mane. Suppose Karen Blixen's improvising had been true. If my mother had stayed in Bregninge and been subverted by the old count instead of coming to America and marrying an alcoholic skinhead on the C.M. and St. P., I might now be running my hand through hyacinthine locks instead of over a naked skull.

The chances we take, getting born so accidentally.

I turned the stopper handle and let the water start running out, and while the Jacuzzi roared on—it runs as long as the water level is above a certain mark—I put my distorted feet back into the jet. *Halex rigidus*, the X-ray man says, looking at my toe joints. Pretty soon *Homo rigidus*. Toes, ankles, knees, hips, fingers, wrists, elbows, shoulders. And bald head, eroded stomach wall, numb-white finger ends. I am a God damned museum exhibit of deteriorations.

The Jacuzzi, as the water dropped to the critical level, cut off, revived when my sloshing sent a wave against it, gave one suggestive ejaculation, and quit. That too. Hail and farewell.

I stood up in the tub and toweled off, looking out the window. Linnets and golden-crowned sparrows were chasing one another off the bird feeder. The morning was crystalline and inviting, but I could see from the way the trees and shrubs blew that the wind was from the north, which meant it was cold.

Dressed and sweatered, but in slippers, I wandered into the living room and dug out the *Britannica* and looked up rheumatoid arthritis. The unexamined disease is not worth having.

It turns out to be a disease characterized by destructive changes in the joints, its origin unknown but presumed to be either micro-organisms attacking the joints directly or the absorption of toxins of other micro-organisms in other sites such as mouth or intestines. Injury often appears to be a determining factor, and any condition tending to lower the general health may be a predisposing cause.

The acute or periarticular type, more common in women than in men, and making its onset between the ages of twenty and forty, appears not to concern me.

The chronic or osteoarthritic type, whose onset comes between the ages of forty and sixty, and whose causes seem to be injury, general ill-health, and exposure to cold and wet (chalk one up for Césare), has features that I recognize. Pyorrhea alveolaris or decayed or deficient teeth practically always present. (Yes.) Onset chronic and generally polyarticular. (Yes.) Pain variable and may be slight throughout. (Speak for yourself, John.) Swelling of joints nodular in shape and practically confined to the joint itself. (Don't know, have to look.) When the condition is polyarticular, usually a few large joints are affected, but none is immune. (That's the thing to remember, none is immune.) When monoarticular the hip or knee most likely to be affected. (No monoarticulate I. Since injury seems to be Fate in these matters, it's just as well I didn't knee Ole Sieverud instead of kicking him.) The formation of new bone occurs and may cause great limitation or even ankylosis; when this occurs in the spine the condition known as "pokerback" results. (Be patient—that's for later.) In the later stages the limitation of movement and muscular wasting may render the patient absolutely helpless but the condition is then often quiescent and painless. (God is kind.)

Now about treatment: Early diagnosis essential, etc. General health, etc. In the acute stage the joints should be given complete rest in a good position and oil of wintergreen applied. (What's a good position? What's oil of wintergreen?) In the chronic forms and as the acute stage passes off, the joints should not be kept completely at rest, massage and passive movement followed later by active movement up to a moderate amount of exercise being desirable to counteract muscular wasting and contractures. Spa treatment, radiant heat, hot air baths, and electric treatment sometimes effective. Adhesions may have to be broken down forcibly under an anesthetic.

Having no impulse to have any adhesions of mine broken down, with or without anesthetic, I resolved to accept counsel, submit to Ruth's management, and earn gold stars. She would come home to find me taking care of myself.

I found her infrared lamp in a closet and set it up so that as I sat reading with my feet on a hassock it would shine on my knees, ankles, and feet. The encyclopedia did not mention bourbon as a treatment for rheumatoid arthritis, either because the learned man who wrote the article did not deal in the obvious or because he wasn't that learned after all. The *Britannica* used to be a British publication, and perhaps did not know about bourbon, an American invention. It probably spelled whiskey without an *e*. When treatment is indicated, I say pile it on. So I got a tall drink and set it at my side outside the radiance of the lamp, and sat down to a spell of healing, a man safely and comfortably in out of the cold.

I had just about begun to enjoy looking after myself when the telephone rang.

It was Edith Patterson, calling for Tom as she always does. He has trouble making his unvoiced whisper heard over the wire. She wanted to know if I had a shredder for making compost.

Literally, I felt a thrill of pride for Tom. If you know the world is going to end tomorrow, plant a tree, that sort of thing. If he was going to garden, he wasn't giving up. But I couldn't help.

"Damn," I said. "I don't. I've been going to get one for the last two years. If Tom wants one right away, I think he can rent one. But if he'll wait a day till I can get around to buying one, he can break it in for me."

I had it wrong. "He doesn't want one," Edith said. "He's got one. He won't be using it for a while, and he thought a demon gardener like you might get some good out of it, with spring coming on. It grinds up everything, even good-sized twigs, and spits it out as the most perfect mulch. Could you use it?"

Her voice over the telephone is extremely soft and pleasant. She sounded like a friendly neighbor trying to give away surplus zucchini. But my initial thrill of pride had already chilled, and I was uncertain. Should I accept the shredder as a gift, and thus make it clear I knew why he was giving it away, or did I pretend it was a loan that he would eventually want back? I said, hearty and cautious, "I certainly could use it, but I wouldn't want to deprive Tom."

"It would just sit in the shed," Edith said.

"All right," I said. "I'll take it, and gladly, on condition Tom will call me the minute he needs it, or the day before he needs it, so I can load it up and bring it back."

"It doesn't need to be loaded. It's got its own little trailer. If you're going to be home, we'll drop it off."

"That's a lot of trouble. I can come for it as soon as Ruth gets back with the car."

"It's no trouble. We'll be coming right by."

She hung up, and I went back to the living room. The infrared lamp was shining on the hassock, where I had left it, and right in the middle of the cone of heat, practically smoking, was Catarrh. When I lifted him off it was like taking something out of the oven.

"You poor old bugger," I said. "Here, make yourself at home down here." I put my feet up onto the hassock and folded Catarrh down on the rug close to it. But warm as the rug was, he didn't like it. He sat up and eyed the hassock, and I could see in his mind, sluggish as an earthworm in adobe, the idea of jumping up on top of my feet. So I took him in my lap, and he settled down. He was bony, and his coat was dry and thin. Patting his scrawny shape, and thinking about Tom, I couldn't get out of my mind certain words like "relinquish" and "divest."

In about twenty minutes I heard the car door slam, and hobbled into the bedroom and got into my shoes and put on a windbreaker over my sweater. The wind outside was cutting. The grass flattened under it, the globulous eucalyptus trees around the water tank turned inside out in a gust. Edith and Tom were both out of their car, working at the trailer hitch. She was as usual imperturbable in her shades and a vicuña coat. Tom shocked me, he had grown so thin in the three or four weeks since I had last seen him. He was pale, too, and slow in his movements as if afraid he migh⁺ break something. And one odd touch. He was wearing an old baggy ꞈweeɗ jacket with leather patches on the elbows, but in its lapel buttonhole was the ribbon of the Legion of Honor. On the way to the scaffold, decorations will be worn.

He straightened up between the car and the fire-red shredder on its trailer. "H'morning . . . H'Joe." Having no vocal cords, he has to shape each word or short phrase separately and force it out on a hoarse blast of breath. "Where do you . . . h'want this . . . h'rig?"

"Let's unhitch it right there. The yard kid comes tomorrow, he can deal with it."

I saw Edith's eyes focused on Tom's hands, long, thin, and strengthless, trying to unscrew the lock knob on the hitch. "Here," I said, "let me get that."

He paid no attention. After a good minute, using both hands, he got the knob loosened, and together we lifted the trailer's tongue and pushed trailer and shredder back against the bank.

"I'm going to enjoy that machine," I said. "I've been wanting to try one."

"H'it's a . . . hell of a good . . . h'machine," Tom said. "H'like a . . . h'mechanized . . . h'mouth. But don't put your . . . h'foot in it."

We laughed, standing in the chilly wind. He had none of the look around the eyes, at once purified and overeager and desperately attentive, that I have seen around the eyes of some who have got the word. He is my age, maybe a little younger. With his bony face and his elegant lankiness and his short haircut, he belongs to that type, academics and professionals generally, ectomorphs, who never cease to look boyish no matter how old or sick they get. Mystery. If I felt an uneasy adolescent peeking from behind my old-age make-up, as if I were a sixteen-year-old playing Uncle Vanya in the high school play, what did a Tom Patterson feel, knowing the play was almost over? Was the boyishness simply appearance, physiology, bony structure, or did some unknown boy or young man still operate in the internationally famous architect behind the death mask and the ribbon of the Legion of Honor?

He stood in the wind regarding me mildly, a friendly and helpful neighbor. Behind him Edith's dark glasses were watching him, not me. He said, "H'Minnie says you had a . . . h'distinguished guest the . . . h'other day."

"Yeah. Césare Rulli. Right in the middle of the downpour."

"Is he fun?" Edith said. "His books are pretty saucy."

"Saucy is the word. Yeah, I suppose he's fun. If he hadn't just popped out at us we might have had you over to meet him. Just as well not, though. He sort of complicated crisis for poor Ruthie."

"That's what Minnie said. It must have been an Event." The eyes moved obscurely behind the dark glasses, and were on Tom again. "Is Ruth down at the home now?"

"Yes. Leading the lamentations at your absence."

"She doesn't need me. She's great, they love her."

"Her story is that they love *you*."

"I hope so. That's one of the things I'm most pleased to have done in my whole life. Well. We've got things to do. Ready, Tommy?"

"H'set."

"Oh, come in!" I said. "Have something to warm you up."

"Really, we've got to run. Give us a rain check?"

"I'll give you a season ticket. I guess we'll see you tomorrow at Ben's."

Tom was kinking himself into the car. Edith, opening the other door, turned her full face toward me, the lips still, the eyes hidden. They waved, smiling, from inside.

"Thanks for that machine," I said. "I'll be king of the compost heap."

Casually waving, they drove off as if that red machine did not mean any of what we all knew it meant, as if we were just parting after a drink or a game of badminton.

The shredder sat on its trailer. Temptation or obligation? I looked in the gas tank: full. I read the instructions that Tom had taped to the hopper. Nothing complicated. So I lifted the tongue and steered the trailer to the other edge of the drive and over the bank into the sunken area sheltered by woods, where I have a bed of herbs and things that will stand partial shade, and where I do my woodcutting.

On the second yank of the lanyard, she started. I threw into the hopper some leaves and twigs, and they flew out the blower as coarse dust. A little rain, a little time, the intervention of some sow bugs and earthworms, some enzymes and soil bacteria, and they would be back to the stuff out of which we are all made and to which we all return. God the Father, God the Son, and God the Compost Shredder.

Down there it was sheltered from the wind, and the sun had warmth in it. I got the wheelbarrow and some clippers and pruned the pyracantha bushes that deer had gnawed and broken, and threw the prunings into the shredder and watched them blow onto the heap. I got a little too interested in what I was doing, and the noise of the engine kept me from hearing the car on the hill. Ruth drove in and caught me before I could duck into the house: old Rheumatics himself, too achy to talk to the geriatric ward, out working in the yard without hat or gloves.

"*I* don't know!" she said, looking as if she might cry. "You com-plain about your joints and then you go and do exactly what you shouldn't. Sometimes I get *hopeless*."

"Why get upset?" I said. "What are we saving me for?"

"That's all right for you to say. *You* don't have to deal with yourself when you get achy and crabby. *I* have to."

"I'll come in if I get to hurting."

"Oh yes! Yes! You mean you'll stay out till you *start* hurting!"

"Well, the Jacuzzi made me feel a lot better," I said, not with-out cunning. "Then I took a good infrared treatment . . ."

"You did? Without anybody telling you?"

"All by myself. I was taking it when Tom and Edith came over with the shredder."

"Why did they bring that over here?"

"They're giving it to us."

"They're what? Oh." I could see comprehension darken in her eyes. Her scolding tapered off in a sound she could only have learned in Denmark, that half exclamation, half sigh on an indrawn breath that I remembered from kitchens of my youth where Norwegian and Danish and Swedish hired girls gathered for coffee and gossip. Standing by a Nandina bush whose new leaves were mixed red and green, whose berries were scarlet, and whose flowers were spread cones of white, she stared down at me. "Oh, Joe."

"Exactly. It sort of brings it home."

"Did they say anything?"

"No. Just they weren't going to be using it and thought I might. I sort of had the feeling I should try it out before tomor-row, so I could tell him."

"I suppose. Oh, that's sad. How did he look?"

"Bad. Waxy. Tottery."

"She?"

"Imperturbable, as usual."

"I wish I'd been here. Maybe I should call her."

"You'll see them tomorrow."

"That's right. Well, damn, I guess I'd better get us some lunch. Can you bring in the groceries?"

"Sure."

I was down below her, with one foot up on the low wall. With a heave ho, I jacked myself up to her level. You could have heard the adhesions crack clear over at LoPresti's. Ruth's startled eyes flew to mine. "My goodness, was that *you?*"

"In person," I said, hobbling.

"Are you hurt?"

"No, of course not."

But she continued to look scared, as if the sound of my snapping joints had suddenly revealed my mortal danger. Dead stick sounds. And she had been thinking about Tom. I could read her scared mind: Oh, my darling, what if it were *you!*

Getting old is like standing in a long, slow line. You wake up out of the shuffle and torpor only at those moments when the line moves you one step closer to the window.

That evening we were in our customary places in the bedroom, Ruth in bed, I in my chair, like a couple of Plantagenets on upholstered tombs. We were watching television, but she could not have been very attentive, because right across the grain of some upstairs-downstairs crisis she said, "I hate the thought of Ben's dinner tomorrow."

"I don't think you need to worry. Tom and Edith are completely on top of it."

"I hope so. Will it be big, you think?"

"I don't think we were ever at anything small at Ben's."

"Do me a favor?"

"Like what?"

"Like making a special effort to see Tom isn't left out? He has so much trouble talking, people might avoid him. It'd be awful if he got stuck off in some corner. Even if we aren't supposed to say so, this is his party."

"I'll keep an eye on him."

"You do the talking. Don't make him do it. Just be yourself."

"Strange prescription. Who else might I be?"

"You know what I mean. You can be very thoughtful when you try. Do you want to watch that? Why don't we turn it off."

I turned it off.

"Edith too," Ruth said. "Show her some attention. Make her laugh."

"The way I'm going to make your shut-ins laugh when I tell them about the contemporary novel."

"You're good at making people laugh."

She smiled and blinked, beguiling and encouraging me to be better than my opinion of myself. She looks upon me as a potential superstar who for numerous reasons has never got it all together, as they say on sports broadcasts, but will one day break out in a rash of base hits and runs driven in.

"I'll get her behind the pantry door," I said. "You'll hear lewd noises like the offstage cackling in *Who's Afraid of Virginia Woolf?* Which incidentally is about as realistic as the rest of modern literature's commentary on sex. Who *cackles* while he humps his hostess, for God's sake? Sex is the most fun you can have *without* laughing."

"All right, if you say so."

She lay there looking fond and friendly and, if the truth were told, very appetizing. "Just be your old funny self."

"Maybe my old funny self will get suppressed. You know how it is at Ben's. You tell yourself you and your woodwind friends are going to get together with the flutes tonight—haven't seen the flutes for ages—but when Ben's baton comes down, you come *in*. If he says dominoes, it'll be dominoes. If he says, 'Lets go out in the pasture and stir up the llamas,' we'll all become herdsmen of Andean cameloids. Remember last time, when I swore I was finally going to corner the Russian princess and satisfy our curiosity—what relation is she to Czar Nicholas, is she Romanoff or Golitsyn, did Rasputin dandle her on his knee, has she got hemophilia (don't tell me, I know she can't have), how did she escape being murdered with the rest of the royal family? Remember? I was determined. So Ben declares after dinner that we'll now play literary charades, and the only contact I have with the princess all evening is to sit at her feet and try to guess what book of Virginia Woolf's she's suggesting by coughing and sneezing and blowing her nose."

"You seem to have Virginia Woolf on the brain."

"As a matter of fact, it was a damn good charade."

"I suppose you have to tell me."

"A *Rheum of One's Own.*"

"You're cute. Why don't you get the infrared lamp and let it cook your poor joints while you read me some more diary?"

"You'd rather listen to that diary than watch *Upstairs Down-stairs?*"

"Oh, much!"

"You're going dead against the Nielsen ratings."

"I don't care. Will you?"

"Okay."

I got the lamp and set it up. No sooner had its red glow bloomed on the chair than old Catarrh, a heat-seeking missile if there ever was one, hopped off the bed and curled up where I wanted to sit down. I moved him enough to let me into the chair and then set him on my lap and set the notebook on him.

"This is nice," Ruth said. "Don't you love it in this bedroom? I do. It's so *comfy.* Especially when you'll read to me."

"'Comfy' is the word," I said. "Or scrumptious. Where do women get their vocabulary?"

But she was already sobered up from the six-year-old act. "It makes me feel guilty. I wonder what those two are saying to one another right now?"

"Those two?"

"Edith and Tom. Can they *talk* about it, do you think?"

"Wouldn't you want to talk about it, if it was happening to you? You'd have to talk about it. You don't think she's trying to kid him he'll get well, and pretend she doesn't know?"

"I don't suppose. Yes, I would want to talk about it, but I wonder if I could do it. Just to sit cold-bloodedly talking over the details. Ugh!"

"Well, we don't have to for a while."

"No. We're lucky, we really are."

"I always thought I was."

"See?" she said. "You can be really nice."

"Given provocation." Catarrh came struggling up and out from under the notebook, and I put the lid on and crammed him under again. I looked at Ruth to see if she was ready for me to begin, but she had a further remark to make.

"Does it seem strange to you?" she said. "Do you have the feeling it's a story about someone else, not us?"

"It is," I said. "It's a story about the countess. There are no stories about us—about me, at least. Everything that happens to me happens offstage, everything is reported by messenger. When I die, I'll have to read about it in the papers, because not even that will really have *happened* to me."

"What do you mean?" She was staring. As usual when she is baffled by something I say, she was ready to be hurt, as if there might be in it some hidden criticism of her.

"Nothing," I said. "I just don't exactly feel I'm the master of my fate and the captain of my soul. Are you ready?"

VVVVVVVVVVVVVVVVVVVVVVVVVVVVV

2

Havnegade 13, May 29:

"Bennyway," Ruth said this morning (she has these residual in-fantilisms, or Midwesternisms, or foreshortenings, or whatever they are, in her speech, another of her favorites is *jissec*), "benny-way, at least you're *feeling* better." That is her way of consoling herself for unslaked curiosity and the brevity of her castle experi-ence. We never did plan to stay more than the one night, but the way it worked out, we had to insist on getting out of there the first thing after breakfast, when our inclination was to hang around like a couple of village kids at a bathhouse knothole.

I felt sorry for the countess. She was sad about her grand-mother, and distressed that our holiday was spoiled, and unwilling to seem to hustle us away, but obviously very willing to see us remove ourselves from the area of family crisis. Manon developed a tic: she winked us out of the castle and into the Rover. Eigil we did not see, nor Miss Weibull. Nor the old countess, since she was dead. The little baron, rising to his duty as man of the house, came out with Manon and the countess and gravely shook our hands and wished us *farvel* and *god rejse*.

He also gave evidence of subversion. Just as I was sliding behind the wheel, so stiff I could hardly keep from groaning, he caught my eye with a little secret grin, and moved his hand to show me the *krone* between his thumb and finger. I nodded, he stretched his arm and snapped, and the coin tinkled on the step behind him, a miss. Manon, winking, turned to see what had made the noise. The little baron never blinked, never turned to see where his *krone* had fallen. There's a lot to be said for no-blesse oblige. He stood in line with the others and waved.

Nothing visible at the Sverdrup cottage as we drove by. I

slowed and pointed it out to Ruth, who gave me a queer little sympathetic grimace. We drove on by it: the deserted postcard.

So now for a week we have been speculating, and we know exactly what we knew before, and can draw only the same inferences from our information. We even have new questions. For instance, why has the countess stayed down at Ørebyslot for a full week? It doesn't take a week to bury an old lady, even allowing time for the clans to gather. She will have had to fraternize with Eigil, for it doesn't seem likely he would stay out of sight all this time just to accommodate his unfriendly sister. Have they made it up? Has the death of the old lady maybe given the countess an inheritance that will ease her situation?

I don't thrive in the presence of unknowns and variables. Extended guessing doesn't intrigue me as it does Ruth. I keep returning, when she gets to speculating, to the little we know. To wit:

Miss Weibull, a member of the (peasant) Sverdrup family, is pregnant. Count Eigil was seen (by me) emerging from the Sverdrup cottage, which is suspiciously well kept, more gussied up than any farm cottage is likely to be. Moreover, Miss Weibull lunched at the castle with the lady of the castle and her guests, a fact which embarrassed Manon and which the countess took as a deliberate affront, but which neither, obviously, could do anything about. The inference is that Eigil, in the old phrase, knocked up Miss Weibull, that he maintains her in the cottage as his mistress, and that at least on occasion, perhaps when he wants to insult his sister, he insists that she be taken into the family.

The countess abhors her brother. Karen Blixen says he is very able, but implies that he is skirt-crazy like his father, and suggests that the countess dislikes him because he *is* like her father. This in turn suggests that there was some sort of significant relationship between the countess and her father, that she is hostile to, or protective of, or shamed by, his memory. My single afternoon with Eigil persuaded me that, from his amateur archaeology to his scientific estate management to his topspin tennis, he is a man of parts. Also that he is a stiff competitor, as afflicted by *al-*

buer as any American or German, and could be tough on people (his sister, for instance?) who opposed or crossed him.

Nevertheless he can also be agreeable, and certainly he kept his bond and stayed away from the castle in order to give the countess her visit. So what is the cause of the sisterly detestation? Miss Weibull's interesting condition? Hardly. For one thing, that's only eight months old, at the most, and maybe four months visible, and the detestation has been there, by the countess' own word, for years. Eigil's insistence that Miss Weibull be brought into the castle might be a sound reason for his sister's dislike, but so far as I could see, that was a surprise to her, something new.

Right here there is an unrelated fact with potential significance: that Miss Weibull is no pullet run down casually in the castle yard by the castle rooster. She is a woman of approximately the countess' age. It seems probable that if indeed there is something between her and Eigil—and who could doubt it?—it must have started years ago, perhaps as many years as the countess has detested her brother.

And how about the effect I produced at the table by mentioning the name Sverdrup? Everybody there except Ruth and the little baron reacted as if to hydrogen sulphide. I may even have brought on the old lady's attack, though Ruth tries to assure me that nobody can take any blame for the strokes and heart attacks of a person nearly a hundred years old. Still, how do you read it? Here she comes out tottering, propped up by pride and will to do her matriarch's duty to her granddaughter and her granddaughter's friends, and *pow*, said friend utters the forbidden name, smoke rises, there is a stink of brimstone, beautiful ladies turn into snouted beasts, the plates slither with live eels, the family portraits reel on the walls, and the offending one saves himself only by laying his knife and fork crosswise. The matriarch holds herself together long enough to be helped out, and drops dead.

And what about the Doctor Faustus of genetics? They *hounded* him, Eigil says. For what? For hybridizing rhododendrons and breeding a select line of pointers?

"Well," Ruth said at breakfast this morning, "why do we go on gnawing on the same old bones? He was a prominent man—a *very* prominent man. Wouldn't there be some way of finding out about him? He must be in the Danish equivalent of Who's Who. Would you need to know more Danish than you do? I should think some librarian at the university could help you dig something up."

Which makes sense Maybe the embassy could help, too. It's time I checked in there anyway. Tomorrow. Since I've been feeling better (a spell of drier weather, or the effect of Eigil's tennis?) I feel more of an impulse to get out and around.

May 30:

Christ, wouldn't you a think I'm old enough to keep my fingers out of the Disposall? I'm not writing a book, or editing a newspaper, or conducting a criminal investigation. Nobody hired me as a private eye, I didn't have to get into this. But here I am just the same, and mainly what I seem to be doing is trying not to believe what I've found out.

There's no mistake in identification, that's sure. The girl at the humanities section of the university library was prompt, efficient, and imaginative. I sat at a table in the reference room and she piled things at my elbow a foot high: A history of Denmark. A history of science. The Danish equivalent of Who's Who. A picture book of Danish castles and manor houses. The roll of the nobility, equivalent to Burke's Peerage, what the English call the stud book. With my pencil and notebook I sat there for an hour, dictionary open, taking down facts.

Landgreve Aage Karl Rødding, 1874–1938, etc., etc., was the son of Greve Frederik Erik R., q.v., and Grevinde Charlotte Heddinge, daughter of Gr. Nis Heddinge, q.v. Married Anna Marie Krarup, a cousin, daughter of Baron Axel Krarup of Spøttrup, q.v. Children Eigil Johan, 1912–, and Hannah Astrid, 1914–. Since the 12th century the family seat of the Røddings has been at Ørebyslot, Lolland, q.v.

Which see. In the picture book on castles, Ørebyslot occupied six pages in romantic soft focus: the castle itself, its stepped gables and ivy lifting beyond the wrought-iron gates; views of the ballroom, the great hall, the dining room, one of the drawing rooms; views of the English park, complete with peacocks, and said to be superior to anything in Denmark except perhaps the park at Knuthenborg; a picture of a stag with a great rack of horns, another of a spotted fawn curled up among ferns; two views of the extensive botanical gardens developed by Landgreve Aage Rødding, famous throughout the world for his studies in genetics. The castle, park, and gardens, which during the early years of the twentieth century were the scene of brilliant social gatherings as well as the center of much important scientific work, have been closed to the public since Landgreve Rødding's death in 1938. The estate is presently owned by his son, Landgreve Eigil Rødding.

Nothing wrong with any of that, except that it made me wonder why the countess has never told us anything about her father. Obviously he was as distinguished as Eigil says he was. If I were halfway educated, I would have known his name the way I'd know the name of Pasteur and Madame Curie. He was obviously the sort of scientific national hero that Niels Bohr is now, the sort the Danes honor by giving him the Carlsberg Castle to live in. Along with King Canute, Hamlet, Søren Kierkegaard, Hans Christian Andersen, and Bohr, he is Denmark's contribution to the world mind. He came a little early to get into the nucleic acid and RNA and DNA and all that business that they're so excited about now, but he was into fruit flies very early, and he seems to have seen the possibilities of molecular biology when it was no bigger than a man's hand. Nevertheless, according to the history of science that gave him two full pages, it is as an extender and perfecter of Mendel, and as a contributor to the pragmatic sciences of hybridization and stock breeding, that he is best known.

In the 1920s, Ørebyslot was evidently a great laboratory where theoretical biology and experiments in breeding and hybridization went on simultaneously. A lot of the brilliance the countess remembers from her girlhood was a result of the double distinction of her father as a scientist and a great nobleman. Even the merely frivolous and sporting aspects of life at the castle, the royal hunts, the kennels, the cultivated wild coverts full of cultivated tame game, had that quality of double excellence.

But they hounded him. For what? Not a hint in my source books.

I got the reference librarian to bring me files of *Berlingske Tidende* from the beginning of 1938 up to September 23, when Rødding died, and started through them backward, beginning with the day after his death. His obituary was there all right. And right away a surprise. Rødding had shot himself, off in the woods of his estate at Ellebacken, near Helsingør. They hounded him to his death, then. But no indication in the newspaper story, so far as I could read it, about *why* he had shot himself—just the usual newspaper-story details. Body found by a farmer. Résumé of Count Rødding's career as a scientist. Details about the funeral and interment—funeral private, interment at Ellebacken rather than at the family seat of Ørebyslot. (No explanation of that, either.) List of survivors, only two: Greve Eigil Johan Rødding and Grevinde Hannah Astrid Wredel-Krarup. Astrid's mother, it appeared, was already dead.

There was not much point in the riffling through browning pages that I set out to do. Without an index I was simply lost, and since my Danish was lame and slow I wouldn't have found anything anyway unless the name Rødding had jumped out at me from a headline. After a half hour of it I left the library and went outside and took a cab over to the American Embassy on Østerbrogade.

Instead of going in to see Mr. Burchfield, the Public Affairs Officer who was said to be well informed about things Danish, I should have come straight home to Havnegade 13 and buried my nose in a book.

Rødding? he said. Oh sure. The biologist. The one who was caught sleeping with his daughter.

At first I thought he was joking. No, I didn't. But I wanted to, and I pretended to, for right at the cold center of my receptive processes was the obituary article I had just got through reading, with its note about survivors. Only two, Greve Eigil Johan and Grevinde Hannah Astrid. I managed to say, in effect, Oh, come on, this wasn't any Jukes or Kallikak, this was one of the greatest men in Denmark.

That was just the point. That was what made the scandal so juicy. There was no question about it, apparently. Somebody peached, some servant as Mr. Burchfield remembers, and Count Rødding never denied it. Must have been insane—had to be—but no other sign of it than this taste for his daughter. Somebody from Very High Up was supposed to have gone to him and told him he had to send the girl away, and he did, for a while. But some time later—six months, a year—it was discovered that he had brought her back.

He really *liked* her, says this PAO with a grin.

How did it end? He wasn't sure. The whole thing was hushed up, naturally, and what got into the scandal sheets was obviously jazzed up. But it is the PAO's impression that Rødding closed his castle, shut the place off to scientists and all the social business that used to go on there. Naturally the court no longer went there for its fall hunt. But not too long after the scandal got out, Rødding went up to some place he owned near Helsingør and shot himself. That sort of proved it. Nobody the PAO had ever talked to doubted that the gossip was true.

Maybe he killed himself because it *wasn't* true, I said. Maybe a man like that would be destroyed by that sort of gossip.

Well, maybe. The PAO had never really investigated—just heard talk. Still, it was noticeable that the Danes never played up Rødding as one of their big stars. The castle was apparently still closed to the public, everything just crashed to a stop.

Well, that too, I said. If you were the son of a man driven by gossip to kill himself, wouldn't *you* close the castle?

Then I realized I was getting too defensive about the Røddings, and drawing the curiosity of the PAO. I changed the subject and pretty soon said I was pleased to have met him, and would see him again probably, and shook his hand and got away.

Now tomorrow, according to the postcard we received yesterday, the countess will be back. She will have it on her mind to "explain us" what happened at lunch. (And just incidentally, could it have been this scandal in 1938 that interrupted her education and kept her from going to England to perfect her English? Did her father never get around to pushing her into that sea? Did he keep her at home for other reasons? Was it the scandal that led her to accept the harelipped cousin for a husband?)

Also, what kind of story will she cook up for us? Who wants to sit and listen to some fable about Miss Weibull? I can just imagine it. There she will sit, a Lorelei in sensible tweeds, a highly bred female who is subject to the giggles and who says she lives not in the head but below the belt and feels better than most people think. Was that naïveté and imperfect knowledge of the language, or an inadvertent self-revelation? How can I listen to her lie? I have liked her too well.

I don't want the truth, either, if what the PAO told me *is* the truth. Should I say to her, *Did* you sleep with your father? And was it some sort of drunken or insane rape you couldn't help or was it, as the PAO suggests, something that lasted for a long time —years, maybe? And do you hate your brother because he's vile, as you say, or because he knows too much? (On the other hand, Manon must know as much, and the old countess too. How come they don't despise you, or you them? What's that, female solidarity? But why didn't any of them rescue you when you were struggling to stay afloat after your husband left you?)

Shall we believe your story about being the wronged wife of a traitor, or was that a lie too? And did your husband leave you for another woman, or did he finally find himself unable to bear the long unyielding disgrace of being married to you? Shall we remember that evening at the opera house and ask ourselves if there was something besides hatred of treason on the minds behind the eyes that watched you?

It makes me sick. Ruth and I have spoken more than once about how much grace, stoicism, and humor she brings to the effort to make a life for herself without help from anyone. I have wondered if we might be her sponsors and help her emigrate to

America, where she could get out from under this cloud. I have had fantasies of her spending weekends in Yorktown Heights, or perhaps living permanently in the guest apartment I would fix up out of Curtis' room. Yes, Doctor, I have played with a daydream in which she fills with affection and loyalty a place left empty and sore by my failure with my son.

From the bed Ruth said, "Did you really think you . . ."
"What?" But I knew what she meant.
"Never mind. Go on."
"Wouldn't you rather have some Thurber or something, instead of listening to me tear a passion to tatters?"
"Of course not. Please."
"I guess I was pretty upset."
"Who wouldn't have been?"
"I get more upset, too. Are you ready?"
"Yes."

Incest. That's a rough word. I don't know whether it's a sin, a crime, a sickness, or a biological taboo. But I am aware of a puritan disgust, I react like Mrs. Bertelson. I ask myself if this is any worse than the mistakes, especially the sexual mistakes, that we all make. It was a sort of love affair, I suppose. She has strong feelings, and her father was the greatest man she knew. They *weren't* Jukeses or Kallikaks, they were superior products of selective breeding from a nearly pure strain, people of beauty and intelligence. What if they were father and daughter? Is there some species wisdom that forbids such matings? Is it the threat of doubled flaws and weaknesses in the children? Maybe that's all folklore. Anyway they certainly wouldn't have had any intention of having children, so why not? Love is love, I try to tell myself. She is a generous and affectionate woman, and her father was a great man.

I can't help it, I wish to God it wasn't true.

Ruth is down at Illums Bolighus, looking at Hans Wegner and Finn Juhl chairs, supported by a vision of refurnishing a couple of rooms at home. "At least let's get *that* out of this trip," she says, implying that so far we haven't got much. Bennyway I'm feeling better, I could tell her. Only I'm not.

The afternoon is drizzling, the cobbles of the quay shine with their pewterish gleam, the traffic pours across the Knippelsbro. The Skagen produce boat is back, moored to the end of the dead-end canal, and the poodle is running up and down the deck past his sign, *Hunden Bider*. I am getting sick of that view. I am about ready to go home, or go south to *das Land wo die Zitronen blumen*. I watch a car pass, spraying water across the cobbles, and reflect that we are as free as anybody on earth. Four weeks remain of my self-granted leave of absence. We could pack up tomorrow and go anywhere.

A blue Volkswagen pulls up at the edge of the quay. A man gets out, hunched into his raincoat and with his plastic-covered hat pulled down, and runs around to open the opposite door. An umbrella emerges, opening as it comes, with a woman under it. I would recognize that straight carriage in the biggest crowd. The man turns his face, and I recognize him too. The quisling. Pull back from the window, get into the bedroom in case she brings him in and thinks she should introduce him. I don't want to see her, much less him. How did *he* get into this?

We'd better leave, and fast. We don't belong in this Gothic romance. Complicated and incredible, the countess said when I blew up the luncheon with the forbidden name. I believe it. I suppose I should give thanks that it diverted me when I needed diversion, and send it back like the unintelligible and unpublishable manuscript it is. If we move out, the ex-husband can have his oriole's nest back, and there they'll be all snug, scandal shacked up with disgrace, everything solved.

That idea depresses me as much as anything in this whole depressing day.

June 1:

I must get it down, before I forget any of it, or start inventing.

She knocked about five. We had a warm reunion, on my part false, and a drink. We never did get any dinner, only a glass of milk and some King Christian IX cheese, with caraway seeds in it. She had come to keep her promise, as I had been sure she would, but first we went through the rituals, the questions, the condolences. When those ran down she faced us and fixed her mouth, leaned and set her glass on a table, straightened again and folded her hands in her lap. Her eyes slid over to me; she was obviously wondering why I was so stiff and ill at ease. She herself showed the effects of a bad week, but her eyes were clear and incredibly candid. Every time I caught her glance I wondered how she could do it. No pretense, no nervousness. To one who didn't know, she would have been utterly persuasive. "So, now," she said. "I promised to explain you all things."

"You don't have to explain anything to us," Ruth said. "We were just awkward strangers in the wrong place at the wrong time. We just made it more difficult. I'm sorry."

Considering that she has been devoured with curiosity all week, it was a generous thing to say. But the countess didn't take the offer. She sat with her hands in her lap, looking her age, as why shouldn't she?

"I am sorry too that you had to be there. For my grandmother, I am glad she could finally die. She was too proud to do anything but wait for her time. Others could shorten it, not she."

Her clear eyes came my way, and I couldn't meet them. She had no right to her look of cleansed and purified resignation.

"It is so fantastic you should have come here and found *me*," she said. "Karen knew—you remember, when she heard your mother was born in Bregninge? She is truly a witch. I can tame horses and cure warts, but she knows things." Helplessly, with a plausible and engaging confusion, she spread her hands. "Where shall I begin?"

Ruth looked at me. I had told her nothing of what I had heard at the embassy, and all I could think right then was what a goodly outside falsehood hath. When it was clear I wasn't going to say anything, Ruth said hesitantly, "You were . . . I guess it all started when Joe mentioned the people who brought his mother up."

"Yes." For a second or two she sat looking down at her quiet hands, folded in her lap. "Well, I must start far back, before I was born. My father. He was a very great scientist. We have never talked about him. Have you not heard of him? Aage Rødding? No?" When we shook our heads, she made a wry face. "That seems strange. I would have thought . . . But why should you? He was a very great scientist, but he made a terrible mistake. Not the way people said, not for any vulgar sordid reasons. To him it must have seemed perfectly logical. He was always as cool and . . . how do you say it? Objectionable?"

"Objective?" Ruth suggested.

"Objective, yes. Finding out the secrets of life was his obsession, and Øreby and the family were so to say his instruments. It wasn't that he pursued peasant girls, as Karen said. He and my mother were—I think—a loving pair."

"You've never mentioned your mother, either," Ruth said.

"She died," the countess said. "She killed herself. So did he. Both of them, because he made that mistake. But I wonder, I don't know, I think he never understood it as a mistake. He thought people didn't understand. He thought he might discover things that could be discovered in no other way. That was what Karen meant about Doctor Faustus."

"How old were you when this happened? When they died?"

"Oh, I don't know," the countess said. "Twenty-three? Twenty-four? I had been married about two yearss."

I made a mental note. He must have married her off, then, before the thing came out in the open. Perhaps, if he had sent her away and then brought her back again, as the PAO said, he tried to cover things over with that phony, arranged marriage. And they must have gone right on.

"Both of them," Ruth said sympathetically. "That was hard. That's terrible."

I couldn't keep still, though I had sworn I would. "Eigil says they hounded him," I said.

She twisted her head sharply to look at me full face. "Eigil? Have you talked to Eigil?"

186

"I spent the afternoon with him. We played tennis, and he showed me around."

"At Øreby?"

"Yes."

"He never mentioned it," she said, and stared at me as if I might be dangerous. From her point of view, and considering what she was trying to explain without giving the truth away, I undoubtedly was. "But then you know . . ."

"Nothing," I said. "Only that he's proud of your father, and defensive about him." I felt that my face was wearing an expression of bitterness and blame. I couldn't look at her, so quiet and resigned and acceptant and plausible, without thinking that if both her parents had committed suicide over this she had to have a pretty flexible conscience to go on living with herself.

The countess understood the feeling of my look, if not its meaning. The blood that came into her throat and temples might have been the emblem of any of a dozen emotions, but it looked to me like resentment. "If only he had not been quite so sympathetic," she said, and stiffened her back. That gesture is part of her inheritance and training, the same stiffness I had noted in the old lady, her grandmother, and in Manon, and even in the little baron when he muffled his coin-snap on the steps. When in doubt or trouble, when pushed into a corner, when caught in a lie, stiffen the back.

Her glance slid away, our little angry confrontation broke off. Abruptly businesslike, she said, "Well! Shall I tell you all things? I feel you are my good friends, I want you to know. Though I confess it was so nice for a while, knowing someone who did *not* know. The beginning is since many yearss, perhaps even before the beginning of this century. My father was interested in genetics, all kinds, but especially human, and that was hardest to study. He kept elaborate records of our family—genealogies, with all the cousin marriages and accounts of what every individual was like, how tall, their weight, their eye and hair color, who was mad or exceptional in any way, their fertility, everything he could find out. Infertility interested him very much, because in inbred families such as ours infertility becomes more and more common. I, for instance, am childless. So is Manon, who is another cousin. So is Karen. So are many of us."

"Your brother too," Ruth said.

"No," said the countess, with a flash of eyes. "Not my brother. I will get to him. My father corresponded with people all over the world—anthropologists who had studied primitive tribes, also the Mormons in Utah. He wanted to know about the effects of inbreeding and the effects of polygamy. Many Danes were converted to Mormonism and went to the United States in the bad times after the Bismarck war. As I understand it, polygamy was forbidden by the time my father began inquiring, but there were many who remembered it or had lived with it, and the Mormon Church kept records as good as my father's own. He could study families in great detail through several generations. He thought of polygamy among human beings as like ordinary stock breeding, you know—one bull to a flock of females. He had herd books and stud books on all his animals, and those were the models for what he tried to do with people. That is only part of it, of course. All things related to genetics fascinated him. Among our own family what he had most to observe was inbreeding, those cousin marriages."

Her voice was unanimated and toneless, her eyes had none of the brilliance they had when she was talking happily, or laughing at some joke. They were dully clear, earnest, and sad. It was hard to think of her as lying, or at least hiding part of what she pretended to tell.

"Also he knew of certain illegitimacies," she said. "From times to times men of our family had got peasant girls in trouble—there really *was* something like the *droit de seigneur*, and Rødding blood is in the veins of many Lolland families. These families my father kept records on. He was trying to trace certain traits, dominant or recessive. It seems he wanted very much to know what the kind of breeding called in-and-in breeding would produce in humans— what it had produced in ours, really, and if what had happened would correspond to what happens in animals. I don't think he expected his results to shake the world. I think he was testing Mendel with human subjects, and I think he was worried about the increasing barrenness in our family. Maybe he expected that our line would run so thin that an outbred line would have to replace it—we would have to go outside the aristocracy if we wanted heirs. I say only what I have thought, not what I know for certain. I think he wanted to take a human line that he knew well —ours—and breed it to another, not closely related strain, as a cattle breeder would breed out from an inbred line."

She looked at us, each in turn, rather grimly. She wanted no ambiguity. "He used himself," she said. "That way there could be no objections, he thought. He would make this quiet, controlled experiment and keep very close records. He chose one of the Sverdrup girls, Helga. Her family had always been close to the castle, as gamekeepers and bailiffs, the women as maids. At least twice, girls of the family had been made pregnant by Røddings. They were peasants, but they were all strong, handsome, prolific people, and though they were cousins of a kind, their line had not been bred thin. Somehow my father bought Helga Sverdrup, or made her believe she would be serving science."

"*Min moders veninde?*" I said.

She is so responsive that even in her humiliation, even while protecting herself, she had to smile. "Yes."

"You think Karen Blixen was right about why my mother emigrated?"

"I think my father must have paid her passage. How could she, a poor girl of sixteen? I think she was in the way. He would have had to be careful. Some time later Helga Sverdrup's parents also emigrated, with their other children. This is all before I am being born."

By that time, possibilities were beginning to pop up in my mind like mushrooms, and not all poisonous, either. "What happened?" I said. "Did they have children? Who's Miss Weibull?"

"My half sister," the countess said. "My father's daughter by Helga Sverdrup."

It was like putting a quarter in the slot machine and seeing the wheels spin and stop with the inevitability and rightness of the last judgment: bar-bar-bar. I sat there feeling all my congealed puritan disgust and poisoned confidence pour out of me in a jackpot of relief. Ruth was saying incredulously, "Your *half sister?*"

"Where is Helga Sverdrup now?" I said.

"Dead. She died when I was a child. Margaret Weibull and I are within a few months of the same age."

"Did she grow up in the castle? Did you know she was your sister?"

"Oh no. I knew her, she was around, she and her mother had some sort of privileged position—servants, but higher than servants. I used to think it queer that my mother was always looking after them, like some half-embarrassing poor relations. But we didn't play together. My father would not have permitted it."

So much for the democracy of science.

"I found out about her only later," the countess said. "My mother told me—the week before she took pills. She wanted me to know. She said that if I had no children, and Eigil had none, these people would inherit Øreby. It was like—breeding your own barbarians. Fortunately she was wrong. At every death, now, the state takes so much that there will be nothing for them, and only their contribution to science will last."

A spitting instant of spite, not her natural expression, unbecoming in her if you wanted to look at it that way. But she was going right on.

"There were also boys. Three, all older than Margaret Weibull. They were kept around for a while, tested and examined by my father, educated somewhat, and then sent away as apprentices. I think he helped them with money, but he did not want them around after they stopped being children."

"They could have blackmailed him, if they knew."

"I'm sure. Fortunately they didn't know."

"Why wasn't Miss Weibull sent away like the boys?"

"Ah! That is the whole thing! She is amazingly discreet—no, she is sly. She had to be to do what she did. My father had her educated, she was sent to France for a time."

At the request of Somebody Very High Up? And then brought back? "I don't understand his genetic experiment," I said. "If he was trying to study these things through several generations, wouldn't he have kept the boys around, and tried to steer their marriages?"

"He had Margaret Weibull."

"What?" Ruth said. "I don't understand either."

"Tell me," I said. "When I walked past the Sverdrup cottage there was a girl there, young, quite pretty. I thought she looked a little like Miss Weibull. Who's she?"

"Margaret Weibull's daughter. In the stud book"—her eyes flashed up—"my niece. There are two older children, boys, and another girl, younger, perhaps nine or ten."

"And who's the father of Miss Weibull's children?"

"The boys are my father's."

"What did you say?" Ruth said. "Oh, my goodness!"

"Your father had two sons by his own illegitimate daughter," I said.

In a squeezed voice she said, "It was to continue his . . . experiment."

"And where are they?"

"Odense, working as furniture makers."

"You don't have any contact with them?"

"No."

"Does Eigil?"

"I don't know. Perhaps."

The straightness of her back had unstiffened by degrees. She tightened herself into erectness so forlornly that I said, "This is too painful for you."

"No. I want you to know all things."

"Well . . . all right. The two boys are your father's. Whose are the girls?"

"My brother's. *Her* brother's."

I may have whistled. Ruth was reduced to flabbergasted silence.

"It is hard for you to understand," the countess said. "It is hard for me. Do you see, Eigil worshiped our father. Anything he did

191

was right. I don't know, when the scandal came out, whether it was then he decided to . . . take over the experiment, take our father's part and carry the results another generation or two? Does it sound, in a way, logical? Or whether, even before the exposure . . . it sounds incredible, his own son, his own daughter . . . whether he may have encouraged Eigil to carry it on."

"Well," I said, "I guess I don't understand the state of mind. I never thought of incest as that cold-blooded. Or does Eigil like Miss Weibull?"

"I don't know. I honestly don't know."

"Poor Manon!" said Ruth. "She knows all this?"

"Of course. My father kept all that separate. I suppose only my mother knew. But Eigil, because of what happened to our father, must be an upside-down puritan about it. All the family must accept, everybody must co-operate. I'm surprised he doesn't make Manon prepare the chamber when he intends to sleep with that woman."

"She's going to have a child very shortly. That's Eigil's, I suppose."

"Yes."

"Does she live in the castle?"

"Yes. I didn't know, or I would not have gone, and taken you."

"Tell me something else. When I first saw Eigil, he was coming out of the Sverdrup cottage, but you say Miss Weibull doesn't live there. What would he have been doing there, just looking after a piece of the estate, or something else?"

She was steady as a rock, but her mouth twisted as she spoke, until she was all but snarling. "Can't you guess? My brother and my half sister now have a daughter of breeding age, the one you saw. To the in-and-in breeders, the mating of half brother and half sister is the best combination of all. What shouldn't we be able to expect when a child of that mating is bred back to her father? There is the nine-year-old, too. In no more than seven years, she will be ready. And if this one who is about to be born should be a girl, or if the one who is now sixteen should have a daughter, then there will be still others. When they will be ready, Eigil will be no more than about sixty. There will be many, many scientific results, as well as many heirs to choose among when the legitimate line runs out."

She spat it out like a mouthful of acid. Eight feet apart on our gilded Empire chairs, we sat in an embarrassed triangle. All at once Ruth jumped from her chair and threw her arms around the countess, crying, "Oh, Astrid, what a bitter, *bitter* life!"

I stopped. Propped in bed, wincing, solemn, shaking her head, Ruth said, "*Wasn't* that a terrible story to have to tell! She really did have a bitter life, and it can't have improved much. Do you suppose, while she's living in that house her brother gives her, this still goes on? Is that what she and Manon have to talk about when they see each other?"

I shrugged and closed the notebook. Sitting there with that closed episode in my hands—closed, petrified, written down and put away and carefully disremembered—I had a fatalistic sense of how delusory are the options that seem to open during the course of a life. In an instant, the opportunities that open like the eyelids of someone rousing from coma can close again, and be closed forever. Even if the eyes stay open after death, you can look into them and see not a glimmer of what for an instant was revealed. Close them, weight them with pennies.

"That poor woman," Ruth said, comfortably and yet cautiously too, with a sidelong look at me as she reached to adjust her heating pad. I shut off the heat lamp and left Catarrh cooling in my lap. "Is it late?" Ruth said. "Even if it is, let's finish it tonight. Is there much more?"

"There isn't any more. That's it."

Now she sat up. "What do you mean, there isn't any more? It can't end *there!*"

"It does, though."

"But . . ."

I opened the notebook to the last scribbled page and held it up for her to see. "Nothing but some jottings—some flight times, some telephone numbers, something in Danish—*Den Hvide Flip,* what's that mean? The White Collar? A store, I guess. And that's all."

She was sitting straight up, really distracted. "But that's such an *anticlimax!* You *must* have gone on with it. Are you sure there isn't another notebook somewhere?"

"Only the three. This one's got half its pages left. We went home pretty soon after this."

"Oh no," Ruth said. "What's the date of that last entry? June? June first? We stayed nearly another month. I remember, we got home just a day or two before the Fourth of July. There was *lots* more. We took her to Roskilde to see her friend in that nunnery for unmarried noblewomen, and there was that performance of *Hamlet* at Kronborg Castle, and we spent a weekend at Ellebacken, right toward the end. There was a whole flurry of things, we were with her all the time."

"I guess I stopped writing when we'd found out all her secrets."

"But you've left out everything we were reading for!"

"So?" I shook the notebook by its rings to show her there was nothing more in it.

Quite a long silence while she watched me from the bed. Finally she said, "Of course, I see, you wouldn't have put that down."

"Put what down?"

"What we were finally going to talk out."

"What if there wasn't anything to *put* down?"

"Wasn't there?"

"Meaning you think there was."

"Meaning nothing. Oh, Joe, we're too old just to clam up and get mad! I was never sure, that's all. Up to the time when she told us about her father, I thought it was just friendly. Nice. Then afterward I didn't know. You got more and more interested in her. You're not very good at hiding things. You *were* interested in her."

"Sure I was interested in her. So were you."

"Not the way you were. How could I be? I couldn't help seeing. All those last few weeks, when we were together all the time.

194

That night up at Ellebacken, Midsummer Night, after we'd stayed up late to watch the fires, I woke up about three in the morning and you were gone. I went to her room, and so was she."

"I couldn't sleep. I went for a walk."

"With her."

"No, by myself. And ran into her."

There are times when, if you look into the eyes of another person, and there is an emotional charge going between you, even the steadiest look seems to break up into pulses and quivers, as if innumerable tiny lines of force were dispersing in all directions from the focused beam. We looked at each other that way, and she waited, not believing me.

"She hadn't been able to sleep either," I said. "We took a walk along the edge of the beechwoods, and when we came to the lake we got into an old rowboat and rowed out to the island where her father is buried. She showed me his grave. Then we walked back to the cottage."

"And that's all?"

What happened to me then is incredible. This is 1974, the age of infidelity, when casual coupling and wife swapping and therapeutic prostitution are accepted forms of violence as normal as mugging and murder, when practices that in my youth would have outraged a two-dollar whore are apparently standard in every middle-class bedroom and are explicated, with diagrams, in manuals sold in college bookstores, and celebrated, with whinnyings and slobberings, in every novel you pick up. These days people hesitate for a marriage license no longer than dogs in a vacant lot, and marriage vows, those quaint anachronisms, are about as binding as blue laws from the Code of Hammurabi. These are times when Count Rødding's little experiments in human genetics would strike people as repulsive only because they unduly enlarged the population just when inbreeding was bringing it under control. Moreover, I am almost seventy, all passion spent, nearly as bald as a cue ball, rheumatic and irritable and unsatisfied with myself, a comic Pantaloon. And guilty of nothing but being tempted—guilty of it once, twenty years ago, and never since.

Whatever Ruth has had to forgive in me, it hasn't been women. So what do I do? What, that is, does the insecure adolescent in me do? He stands up so suddenly that old Catarrh is dumped onto the rug. In the phrase that is as old-fashioned as the guilts and emotions that shake his hands and roughen his voice and blur his eyes, he goes all to pieces.

I found myself in the bedroom door, really shaking. I could hardly talk. "No," I managed to say. "That isn't all. I kissed her. Once. If that's what you've been wanting to talk out, now we've done it!"

In the hall I clawed a coat off a hanger. As I opened the door the night air was cold in my face. The night was still and misty, the moon was nearly straight overhead, with a pearly ring around it. I walked up and down the drive gritting my teeth, with tears in my eyes—Marcus Aurelius Allston, the spectator bird, having the feathers beaten off him in a game from which he had thought he was protected by the grandfather clause. That other night, Midsummer Night twenty years before, filled his mind as moonlight filled the hilltop where he walked.

3

I shut the door softly on the interior darkness and the close smell of mold and disuse. It was lighter outside than in. It had not been actually dark all night long. The dusk was gray and faintly luminous, swimming with things half seen and things illusory. I reached out and touched the whitewashed wall, raised my head to look at the crisscross of half timbering disappearing under the shadow of the thatch, looked down and moved my feet and saw the dark crushed tracks I left in the grass. But at a little distance there was no such certainty; everything was marbled and deceptive. The celebrated light nights of Denmark are for hallucination and witchcraft, not for plain seeing.

Where the drive turned in, the cypresses were black, distinct in shape but blurred in outline. While I stared at them trying to focus them into clarity they melted into the gray of the beechwoods beyond the road. From horizon to zenith the sky was almost too pale for stars. Off in the west a humpbacked moon lay stranded, colorless as a jellyfish. The air, utterly still, carried a fragrance of wood smoke mixed with the sweetness of mown grass that rose from the lawn.

Walking softly, I went around the cottage to the grassy terrace from which we had watched the celebration at midnight. The big fire that had leaped from the beach below had burned down to a red core, and off on the Swedish coast opposite, north and south of the overtaken lights of Hälsingborg, other coals glowed dully. Not a sound. No cheep of a wakeful bird, no stir in the ivy or thatch, no slightest sigh of moving air. The yelling of the pagan rites of midnight, when hundreds of Danes and Swedes drunk on beer and summer and love had thrown their witch effigies onto the flames and sent the malignant spirits howling back to their home in the Harz, might never have been. Successful exorcism. The countess had made us listen, where we sat on blankets on the grass. She said you could hear the rushing in the air.

"Aren't you afraid?" I said. "You claim to be a witch."

"Yes, I am afraid," she said, "but not of burning. I am not witch enough. They do not burn you for curing warts."

In the dusk I could not read her expression, but it seemed to me there was something like self-contempt in her voice, and it troubled me.

Now, two hours later, I stood in the wet grass, sleepless, restless, obscurely distressed, caught between a day that would not properly die and one that was not ready to be born. The whole world, and I with it, hung at the very peak of summer, holding its breath before starting down. I shivered, more with the sense of something ending than with chill. It was a time for departures. Our own was only a week away, and I didn't want to go. Ruth did. Now that I was feeling better, she said, there was no reason to stay. But I understood, and was resentful. More than once, as she went about making the arrangements and reservations, I had wanted to shout at her, Don't *push* me!

I was full of cobwebs, sad with the late hour, depressed. I needed to walk it off. So I went soft-footed around the cottage again, and out across the lawn to the gate between the cypresses. There I stopped to look back at the cottage on its dark lawn—medieval and picturesque, historical and false, survival not only of the ancient northern village culture but of a time when Astrid Rødding was a rich titled girl who could afford to play peasant, and whose father indulged her with a crofter's house to play in.

While I was looking, the door opened quickly and closed again, and she stood on the doorstone.

At that distance she was only a shape. It was her way of moving that told me who it was. From under the cypresses I watched her, and it seemed to me that a hundred feet away she might hear the beating of my heart. I thought she bent her head, listening as I had listened. I thought she looked up at the sky. Then she was coming toward me across the grass.

To prevent her running into me in the dusk and being fright-
ened, I stepped out into the open and said, "*God morgen.*"

"Oh! Who is it?"

She stopped, and true to my nature when my emotions are involved, I played the horse's ass. The buried adolescent in me, as
uncertain as the dusk I stood in. I dropped my voice to sepulchral
depths and said, "*Jeg er en hekse. Jeg har mistet min vej. Kan De
siger mig vejen til Harz?*"

"Mr. Allston, is it you?"

"Who else?" I said, already disgusted with myself. My heart
was still pounding. She wore a kerchief on her smooth head, and a
sweater like a shawl around her shoulders. She looked like an illus-
tration from a folk tale, some shawled human creature caught east
of the sun and west of the moon.

"You startled me," she said with a laugh.

"I'm sorry."

She moved close. I could smell the faintly musty smell of her
sweater, stored a long time without airing in the unused cottage.
"Couldn't you sleep either?"

"No."

"It is never a good night for sleeping, Midsummer Night.
Things are abroad."

"Like us."

"Yes, like us. Where were you going?"

"I don't know. Just for a walk."

"Is Ruth asleep?"

"Yes. She doesn't lie awake the way some people do."

A pause. Her face lifted to look at me, a shadow face with only
the faint flash of eyes. "There is a path around the lake," she said.
"That is where I was going."

"May I come along?"

"I would like that, if . . ."

I knew she was thinking of Ruth. So was I.

Across the road she darted her flashlight ahead until it found a
path between the beechwoods and a field where hay had been

piled on racks to dry. "Do you need the light?" she said. "Can you see? Shall I leave it on?"

"Let's do without it."

The shapes of hay, vaguely luminescent, enlarged by the diffused shadows thrown by the moon, watched us as we passed between them and the woods. "It's like a field of schmoos," I said. Then I had to explain what schmoos were. She said they belonged in Scandinavian folklore along with trolls and dwarves and other shapeless shapes of mist and darkness. Her mood was somber, she walked beside me withdrawn into herself.

When she stumbled, I took her by the arm above the elbow.

Touch. Her arm was both firm and soft. Having taken hold of it, I did not let go. I couldn't have felt that contact more if her arm had been the handle of a funhouse shock machine. In one tingling flash she was less tall, more feminine, more accessible. I remembered the time when she had shed her tweed uniform and frolicked like a suddenly physical Valkyrie in the sound. The things that had maintained formality between us—my poor-boy's sense of her title and caste, the awkwardness of her family history, the defensive playfulness, the too bright smile—were all forgotten. Walking her down that dark path was like dancing, the sort of dancing that was orthodox when I was young, the kind the modern young have deprived themselves of, the kind that authorizes, to music, a physical contact otherwise taboo. It was as if she had taken down her hair. Without a word spoken we groped along the dark edge of the woods, as different from the two people who had just paused as ozone is different from oxygen.

After a little distance she said, "Do you remember the day when you turned your car and drove us back through the young beechwood, the day we went to Karen Blixen?"

"Yes."

"I think it was that day when I began to know you."

I had her by the arm, I felt the blood pulsing in her elbow.

The path curved away from the woods along a fence, where it was lighter, and then back again through the woods along what seemed to be a cart road. "This was once all my father's, and then mine," she said. "They took it away, all but my little cottage, when Erik was tried."

"You told us. It's too bad."

Ahead, the darkness of overhanging trees lightened as if we were coming to a clearing. There was a mossy smell. The countess stopped, holding me back, and shot her flashlight ahead and down. It gleamed off dark water, a tarn straight out of Poe. When she shut off the light again, the water still lay there, darkly burnished, reflecting no stars. It graded so gradually off from the land that I might have walked right into it. We stood listening. Not a sound.

"It's like death," the countess said. "Or resignation, hopeless resignation.. Do you know that poem of Goethe's that we were all made to memorize? *Über allen Gipfeln?*"

"Yes. Say it."

"Perhaps I can't remember after all." She hesitated, and her face turned toward me, still and almost featureless in the twilight, with its glint of eyes. She laughed as if embarrassed. "If I had not seen you go through the beechwoods a second time, I would not dare speak poetry to you in such a place. You are not to laugh."

"I won't laugh."

She cleared her throat like a child reciting. "*Hør Du, nu.*"

"You *Du* me."

"Yes," she said. "Yes, I do. If I didn't I could not speak this sad poem to you. It is a poem made all of whispers."

She said it in whispers.

> *Über allen Gipfeln*
> *Ist Ruh.*
> *In allen Wipfeln*
> *Spürest Du*
> *Kaum einen Hauch.*
> *Die Vögelein schweigen im Walde.*
> *Warte nur, balde*
> *Ruhest Du auch.*

I felt her shiver. "I do not like Midsummer Night," she said. "For many people it is a time of celebration and happiness, the freedom of summer. For me it is always sad. It makes me feel that I am dead but have not yet left the body, and do not want to leave, but cling to it whimpering and crying. Tonight is the worst. Do you know why I could not sleep?"

"Why?" I was still holding her by the arm.

"Because you are soon leaving. The only dear friends I have had for many years."

"I'm glad you don't want us to go."

"How could I? I was dead, and you taught me what it would be to be alive again. I understand why you must go, but it makes me very sad."

"Must we go?" I said. "Why must we?"

"Because you have obligations," she said promptly. "You have work to do."

"What obligations? What work? I could give all that up tomorrow."

She started moving again down the grassy track along the shore. "You are not the kind who shirks things," she said, as if she knew. Her left hand came over and pulled at my fingers around her arm until I let go. I must have been gripping her painfully hard.

We passed out from under the trees crowding close to the shore, and there was more light, a wider sky. The obscure became the faintly visible. Dry rushes crackled underfoot, and the low edge of the sky was scratched with bending lines of tules. The path ended at a narrow dock that jutted out into the water. As I followed her out onto the old felty planks, the colorless moon reappeared doubled, pale in the sky, pale in the black water. At the end of the dock a rowboat sat absolutely motionless on its shadow.

For the first time since she had come out her cottage door I saw her eyes clearly, the glint of the moon in them as she stooped to fumble for the boat's painter, tied to the dock post. She squatted there, looking up at me. "Can you row, or shall I?"

"I'll row. Where are we going?"

"I want to pay a little visit. Will you mind coming?"

"Of course not. But visit who, at this hour?"

She didn't reply. Pulling on the rope, I felt that the boat was half full of water. It took some straining to haul it onto the dock and tip it. The wooden knockings, the dark sound of pouring, went back into the stillness as if into blotting paper.

When I had the boat back in the water I stood to help the countess down, hoping to re-establish the tingle of touching flesh, but she used my arm as impersonally as she would have used a groom's.

She shot the flashlight beam past me, moved it around to get her bearings, and then gave me directions from the stern, steering by some dark landmark. I was clumsy at the oars, which seemed to have been whittled out of tree limbs. The boat was water-logged, the left oar kept slipping out of its worn notch so that we lurched in zigzags where the adolescent in me would have liked to skim that old hulk across the pond like a skipping stone. Concentrating, I held the lame oar to its job, carefully dipping it into the moon's reflection, carefully pulling, carefully swinging it back over its skitter of pale drops until it bit again into the moon.

"We are close," the countess said. "Slowly, it is hard to see exactly." The light shot past me, probed a moment, and went out. "A little on the right oar," she said. "Now pull, both, hard!"

The prow grounded in mud. Before I could ship the oars or stand up, she had squeezed tippily past me and jumped ashore. The boat surged another two feet up the bank as she hauled on the painter. I stepped ashore into mud to my shoe tops and followed her up a brambly bank onto the level.

Her light darted ahead across a clearing overgrown with high grass and vines. "Come." Her hand groped and found mine. Touch again: her hand was cold and smooth. In the middle of the clearing she stopped, holding the light at her feet. Quickly she crouched and brushed the grass away from a square stone as she might have brushed hair back from a face. I read the inscription: *Landgreve Aage Rødding, 1874–1938.*

"This is where he is buried," the countess said. "This is where he came to shoot himself."

"Was that before or after your mother?"

"After."

"Was he insane, you think?"

"Perhaps. Not at the end."

"You've had hard things to bear."

"Ah!" As if my sympathy bothered her, she tried to pull her hand away from mine. I held on, and after a tug or two she let it lie quiet.

"And still have," I said. "What are you going to do? How will you live? Will you have to rent the apartment again?"

"I will hate it, after you, but I have no other thing to do. My designs pay me too little."

I asked the question that had not been far out of my mind since the day her quisling delivered her at the door after her stay at Ørebyslot. "What about your husband?"

"I don't know."

"You don't know? It's none of my business, but surely you're not going to take him back."

"I don't think so. No, of course not, I will not. And yet, you know, he is so miserable, an outcast."

"Doesn't he deserve to be?"

"Deserving your punishment does not make you less miserable."

"But think what it would do to you!"

Her face, which she had turned away, turned back. "I said you were not one to shirk," she said. "Would you tell *me* to shirk?"

"But, my God, you don't owe him any duty! You don't owe anybody any duty except yourself. They've all lost any claim on you, your husband and all the rest of them. Why haven't any of them helped you during all the years you've been in trouble?"

I could feel her resistance, or reluctance, in her fingers. There I stood holding her cold hand, running my thumb over the smooth knuckles as if I had rights in her skin, and yet feeling how remote she was, lost in some medieval curse or spell, hypnotized by duty or obedience or noblesse oblige or whatever it was. I smelled the faint mildewed odor of her sweater, and it made me angry that she should have to wear such things, worn out, left over.

All at once I couldn't stand any more. I couldn't stand to see her go back into the moldy cellar of her life, I couldn't stand to have her at once so warm and so cold, so sympathetic and so without initiative or hope. I dropped her hand, I took her by both shoulders, I brought her face close to mine. Her eyes had no more light in them than her pale skin.

"Listen!" I said. "*Listen!* You don't deserve any more punishment. You've paid your debt, ten times over. You can't stay here, scratching out just enough for yoghurt and cheese. You can't go on sharing the only things you have left with strangers. You shouldn't *have* to take in lodgers! You can't let it all settle back on you, it'll smother you. You can't let that man work on you. He made his bed, let him lie in it. You're coming with us, you understand that? I can make a job for you, or find you one somewhere else if you'd rather. There aren't ten people in New York with your capacity in German, French, English, the Scandinavian languages, art, the whole business. You don't have to grind out wallpaper designs for Illums. You can be an illustrator, or a translator, or an agent, or anything you want. You can't stay here and mold. You're too special."

Utterly unresponsive, she hung in my hands. I turned her so that the moon, almost blurred out in the ground mist, would fall on her face and in her eyes. Her face was pale and sad, her eyes without brightness, her body without elasticity or response, without even resistance.

"Do you think I have not dreamed of such a thing?" she said. "It is not so easy as it was for your mother, even. It must be very wonderful to have the freedom of the poor."

"You think you're not poor enough?"

"Not free enough."

"Why not? I'll pay your fare. I'll get you a work permit. We'll be your sponsors. You can live with us."

She twisted and then faced me again, ten inches away. "You say 'we,'" she said. "You say 'us.' Have you talked about this with Ruth?"

"I don't have to. She's very fond of you, she hates as much as I do to see you trapped here."

"I think she is fond of me," the countess said. "As for me, I love her, she is generous and warm. She is my dear friend, and she is your wife, and she wants to get you away from here and away from me, and she is right."

"Astrid . . ."

"You have said my name, finally. I wondered if you ever would."

"Astrid, Astrid, Astrid," I said. "I'll say it ten thousand times a day, in penance or prayer or praise or however you want it. But you can't stay here. I can't go away and *leave* you here!"

"Oh, my dear Joseph," she said. She put up her face, and I kissed it. Her hands came up around my neck. For a second or two we were molded, fused, vulcanized together. Then she was pushing at my chest, wanting away.

I didn't try to hold her. I couldn't look at her. I turned and looked instead at the spread of still water. My eyes were hot. Blinking, grinding my teeth, I concentrated on the lake, the dim rushes, the dreary almost-light. Day had sneaked up on us. I could see the tangled grass, the running blackberry vines. If anything had been watching our ridiculous, scalding, hopeless embrace in that suicide's clearing, it had withdrawn into the woods.

Without looking back, giving her the same chance I needed myself, I went down to the boat and pulled it around until I had it pointed out. Then I did look back. She stood where I had left her. I think she had been watching me all the time I had my back to her. In the imperceptibly lightening grayness of dawn she looked as forlorn as a beggar woman.

"We should go," I said.

"Yes."

I stooped and pulled the stern of the boat farther up on the shelving mud so that she could get in without sinking in the slime. As I turned again, I caught her just straightening from the curtsy she had dropped toward her father's gravestone.

I said nothing. She came down to the water and I helped her in and rowed her across to the dock, which reached toward us out of the rushes like charcoal lines in a Japanese drawing. Walking back to the cottage, we hardly spoke. In the shadow under the cypresses, gray now instead of black, and filled with a sad visibility, we looked at one another. We did not touch.

"You first," she said.

I went across the drenched grass to the door. There I stopped. Obscure under the dark spiral trees, she watched me. I opened the door to go in. At the last second, as the door was closing, I saw her put her hands to her head and bend over from the waist in a wild, abandoned movement as purely physical as if she were vomiting.

She straightened, and I closed the door.

4

From our front walk to where the drive turns down the hill is two hundred feet. Thirteen round trips make just about a mile. Many times, especially in winter when it is too muddy to walk across country, Ruth and I have carried the carcass up and down that thirteen-lap course before going to bed. It is rather like walking the deck of a ship, for the hilltop is level and high and exposed to the stars. It is one of those places where the condition of being human is inescapably sad. The lights along the dark hills are scattered and without confidence, conurbia down in the valley is only a glow on the sky. The hazed moonlight is deceptive, there are somber pools of shadow under the oaks. From up on that chilly platform you can look back down your life and see it like a Kafka road dwindling out across the Siberian waste. You can raise your head and look into the infinite spaces whose eternal silence terrified Pascal.

My absurd tears were dry after a lap or two, but I did not feel like going back in. I didn't know what I would say to Ruth, or how I would act. The performance I had just put on had left me alarmed about my own unacknowledged possibilities. If the truth were told, and I suppose it had better be, I wanted to be alone for a while with that possibility I had renounced, or been made to renounce, twenty years before and carried around with me like a cyst ever since.

What was it? Did I feel cheated? Did I look back and feel that I had given up my chance for what they call fulfillment? Did I count the mountain peaks of my life and find every one a knoll? Was I that fellow whose mother loved him, but she died; whose son had been a tragedy to both his parents and himself; whose wife up to the age of twenty had been a nice girl and since the age of twenty a nice woman? Whose profession was something he did not choose, but fell into, and which he practiced with intelligence but without joy? Had I gone through my adult life glancing desperately sidelong in hope of diversion, rescue, transfiguration?

That is the way the modern temper would read me. Babbitt, the man who in all his life never did one thing he really wanted to. One of those Blake was scornful of, who controlled their passions because their passions are feeble enough to be controlled. One of those Genteel Tradition characters whose whole pale ethos is subsumed in an act of renunciation. One who would grasp the handle but not the blade. Milquetoast. *Homo castratus.*

I could imagine how the Danish adventures of Joseph Allston would be written up by Césare Rulli, or by any of the machismo brigade, or by the Pleasure Principle seminar, or by any of those romantics, male and female, who live by the twitch, whose emotional shutter speed is set to catch the moment of orgasm, whose vision of the highest reach of human conduct is expressed by the consenting adult.

Well, the hell with it, I do not choose to be a consenting adult, not just to be in fashion. I have no impulse to join those the Buddha describes, those who strain always after fulfillment and in fulfillment strive to feel desire. It has seemed to me that my commitments are often more important than my impulses or my pleasures, and that even when my pleasures or desires are the principal issue, there are choices to be made between better and worse, bad and better, good and good.

Then why cry over it, twenty years later? Because in every choice there is a component, maybe a big component, of pain.

I would hate to have a recording of that conversation I held with myself, lurching up and down the moonlit drive. It would sound like the lecture of a scared graduate assistant, taking over the philosophy class in the professor's absence. The walking did me more good than the thinking, even though my toe joints had me wincing, and my hips felt as if I had jumped off a ten-foot wall.

There are two big live oaks along that two-hundred-foot stretch, one in the corner above the turn and the other where the drive widens into the parking area. Between them is open meadow in which, last fall, I sowed two hundred daffodils by throwing the bulbs broadcast and digging them in where they fell. Every time I turned at the top of the hill and started back toward the house, I was looking across them toward the moon. There was not enough light for them to show yellow; their bowing heads gleamed palest silver-gilt above the pale grass. When I came back, moving out of the shadow of the oak, individual blossoms grew luminous, like big exhausted fireflies.

I kept on walking, lap after lap, leaving my shadow behind me as I turned at one end, finding it still with me when I turned at the other. My feet hurt me so that I hobbled, on my head fell dew as insubstantial and chilly as moonlight. I must have been on at least my fortieth lap when, turning at the far end, I heard heels on the asphalt back by the house, and saw Ruth's shadow coming toward me as if through silvery, settling dust.

When we were fifty feet apart, she stopped. I came on. "Hi, darling," I said, as casually as I could.

We met at the edge of the live oak's shadow. In a voice that had difficulty being loud enough, she said, "You'll get all cold."

"I've got a sweater and jacket on."

"But your head!"

"I haven't got arthritis in my head. At least I don't think so."

A jet coming in from Hawaii winked over the ridge beyond Woodside. Down on the county road some hot shot in a sports car *vroom*-ed his engine through three gears and howled off into the muffling canyon. Ruth said, "I thought maybe I'd better . . . I didn't know where you were."

"Just walking. Want to?"

I thought there was gratitude in the way she took my arm. We walked in to the edge of the patio and turned and came out again. Orion was coming to meet us, then he was entangled in the oak, then as we came into the open again he was free. The daffodils in the meadow were touched with pale nocturnal gold.

"I'm sorry," Ruth said.

"I'm the one to be sorry."

"I brought it on. I was determined to force it out of you. I don't know why."

"You wanted the pebble out of the shoe."

"I suppose." We walked twenty steps in silence. "No, I know why I did it," she said. "Why I could never quite forget it. It was my vanity. My goodness, after all this time! I could see it happening, there at the end, and I knew I couldn't compete with her."

"You compete all right."

"No. She was remarkable. I'm not. If you hadn't fallen at least a little bit in love with her I'd have thought there was something wrong with you." She laughed, a little breathy puff of sound. "Then when I saw you were doing it I couldn't stand it."

Another twenty steps. "I always thought you must hold a grudge against me for insisting we come home. I was sort of surprised you came."

"You shouldn't have been surprised."

We turned at the hilltop. This way, Orion walked with us. "No," she said. "I should have known you wouldn't shirk your obligations."

She made me mad. "It was not obligations that made me come! I simply made a choice, and it wasn't all that difficult, either."

Still another of those spells of silence, broken only by the sound of our steps. The St. Bernard that lives on the lane beyond LoPresti's barked at something in the voice of a lion, and a chorus of yapping and woofing broke out from all around the hills. "Wasn't it?" Ruth said, almost as if she wished it had been. "Then why, in there . . . a little while ago . . . ?"

The same question I had asked myself. I gave her the same answer. "I don't mean it was easy. I mean there just was never any real choice. There was no question. I don't deny I was smitten. I wanted to do something for her. I hated leaving her behind. I would have liked her company the rest of my life. In other circumstances, if you hadn't existed, I'd certainly have tried to marry her, and I think she might have had me. But those circumstances didn't exist, and I never really fought you about coming home. I left all that behind, and eventually I forgot her. There have been stretches of two or three years when I haven't thought of her, not once, and if her postcard hadn't sent me looking for that diary, I probably wouldn't have thought of her yet. That's kind of sad, I'm sorry about that. But I'll tell you something else. If I'd played the game the way people seem to expect, and jumped into the Baltic, all for love and the world well lost, and cut myself off from you and what you and I have had together, I couldn't have forgotten you that way. I'd have regretted you the rest of my life."

She hugged my arm. I put it around her. We took another turn up the drive.

"For a long time after that, I hated myself," she said. "I should have had more pride. I shouldn't have tried to hang onto you if you wanted to go. I should have been thinking about you, not myself. But I just couldn't. I decided that even if I was only your obligation I'd rather be your obligation than your ex-wife."

"There was never any danger of your being either."

"I'm very lucky."

"We're both lucky. And she was terribly unlucky. God distributes with an uneven hand."

It seemed a good idea to kiss her, there in the open moonlight between the oaks, in sight of the ghostly daffodils. She crowded against me and kissed me like a passionate girl. "Oh, Joe," she said, "don't be unhappy! Don't be depressed! We *are* lucky. Think if one of us were alone. Think if we were like Tom and Edith."

"That's for later."

"Don't say such things."

Off in the hills one of the dogs that had been barking erratically ever since the St. Bernard had roared now left off barking and began to howl. *En hund hyler i natten. Absit omen.* Under the heavy sweater she wore I felt Ruth shiver.

"You're cold, we'd better go in."

"I'll walk longer if you need to."

"I've walked about five miles as it is."

"You scared me in there."

"I kind of scared myself."

"But isn't it better to have it all talked out, and over?"

"Marvelous. Like after a sauna, all wrapped up in towels."

In a gesture of half-embarrassed playfulness she reached up and rubbed her hand around on my sterile skull. "Joe, your head is *freezing!* You really must come in. Come along and I'll fix you a nightcap to warm your head. Would you like a hot toddy? Or a brandy?"

One of the nice things about getting something talked out is that it brings on a spell of pampering.

We walked back toward the house, and through the dark upwelling of juniper that borders the walk, and under the three birch trees, their trunks slim and white and their twigs, against the light-filled sky, lacy with the first tiny formings of leaves. The entrance was damp, and sweet with the smell of daphne. Two young people with quite a lot the matter with us, we stood for a moment, breathing it in.

The truest vision of life I know is that bird in the Venerable Bede that flutters from the dark into a lighted hall, and after a while flutters out again into the dark. But Ruth is right. It is something—it can be everything—to have found a fellow bird with whom you can sit among the rafters while the drinking and boasting and reciting and fighting go on below; a fellow bird whom you can look after and find bugs and seeds for; one who will patch your bruises and straighten your ruffled feathers and mourn over your hurts when you accidentally fly into something you can't handle.

"I wonder how it is on the other side of the house?" Ruth said. "Remember that night when we came home from a party, a night like this, moonlight, with a ground mist, and when we walked out on the terrace there was a lunar rainbow arched clear across the valley?"

"I remember."

"It was just such a night as this. The moon was about in the same position. Do you suppose there's a lunar rainbow out there now?"

"They're pretty rare. I never saw but that one in my life."

"Let's go look."

"There won't be one."

"How can you be sure? The conditions ought to be just right. Let's go look, at least."

So, arm in arm, we went and looked. Of course there wasn't one.